MURDER ON THE MISSISSIPPI

FRANK DODGE MYSTERY #4

DEAN KLINKENBERG

Travel Passages

CONTENTS

For my parents, Buster and Marilyn Robin Klinkenberg, for their unwavering, unconditional love and for the occasional kick in the pants (metaphorically speaking) when I needed it.

Chapter 1

I held on tight as water shot up and over me, splashing my face as our sleek boat ripped through the Mississippi's current like a chainsaw through pine, turning sharply to blow past driftwood and sandbars.

"You sure know how to pick your vacation days," Brian Jefferson said.

I sighed. "Thanks for ruining my fantasy," I said, then opened my eyes and turned to him. "And I'm not on vacation."

Fine. I wasn't racing upriver; I was standing calmly on the deck of a clumsy but dignified replica of a classic Mississippi River steamboat, the *River Voyager*. And we weren't on a heart-stopping ride, either; we were plodding our way through the murky waters of the Mississippi. My face was wet all right, but that was from a breeze blowing rain into me. It had been raining since we boarded at the wharf in the Port of New Orleans.

"I know, I know." Jefferson shook his head. "You got some big assignment to write for another fancy magazine."

"To write a feature for *Luxe Liners*." I shrugged. "I don't know if that counts as a 'fancy' magazine."

"If *Luxe* is in the title, then yeah, it's fancy."

"I'm not complaining." Ruby nudged Jefferson, then looked at me. "I'm grateful. I've never been on a river cruise, and I don't care if it rains the whole time. This boat is so elegant! I feel like I could be traveling with Mark Twain."

"But you got stuck traveling with Frank instead?" Jefferson said.

"There are worse people to travel with," she responded as she glanced at Jefferson, then to me. She smiled. "I never get bored when I'm around you two."

"And there are worse places to be," I added. I didn't care about the rain. Or the pace of our progress. I felt excited to be back on assignment. And to get this particular one. "This boat is special. One of the biggest to cruise American rivers. Space for nearly four hundred passengers and a hundred and fifty crew. From stem to stern, she's four hundred and twenty feet long. And we have five decks to explore."

"Why do we assume boats are female?" Jefferson asked.

"Because they're strong, reliable, and beautiful?" was Ruby's quick come-back.

"It's an old tradition," I added. "But what Ruby said."

Jefferson looked at me, then Ruby. "Thanks for clearing that up."

We stood in the Bow Bar, on deck two. I sipped black coffee as we mostly sheltered from the rain. As soon as my feet had hit the gangway earlier that afternoon, I started outlining the article in my head. I'd booked an eight-day trip—courtesy of *Luxe Liners*—and got to bring along a guest—Ruby Beck, my eighty-six-year-old friend from small-town Iowa—also thanks to the magazine. Ruby stood next to me—barely five feet tall—a blue-gray jacket that matched the color of her hair protecting her from the rain. When I told Brian Jefferson—my best friend and a damn fine homicide cop in St. Louis—about the assignment, he liked the idea of eating and drinking for a week on a cruise, so he booked his own room. He was standing next to Ruby but a step behind us, to make sure he didn't get his new leather jacket wet,

I assumed. Or the dark gray beret on his head, a hat I'd never seen him wear before.

We had boarded in New Orleans, quickly unpacked, then headed right to the Bow Bar to look at the river. Then the rain started. Maybe it wouldn't last. The weather experts had predicted occasional storms for the rest of the day, followed by a gradual clearing through the next morning. But it was May along the southern Mississippi, and anything was possible. Storms could blow in with little notice, or a midsummer-style heat wave could blanket the river. We'd had a cold winter and cool spring in St. Louis, so I was pulling for the latter.

As we looked out at the rain falling on the river, Kenny LeJeune, the boat's first mate, entered the bar. He was about six feet tall, with fine ash-blond hair drifting to gray. His face was rugged with high cheekbones but well-balanced, a face I figured rarely left him standing alone at a bar. "I remember you," I said as he walked toward me. "You showed us how not to drown if we fall into the river."

He smiled. "As long as you do what I showed ya, y'all will be fine." He spoke with an accent that I placed in central or southern Louisiana, probably in Cajun country, given his name. "We take our safety drills seriously, of course. And not just because we're required to." He reached out to shake my hand. "Glad to have ya on board, Mr. Dodge. If ya need help with anything for your article, I'm your best bet. Track me down, and I'll do what I can to get ya what ya need."

"Like some time with the captain?"

"Already arranged. You'll be having dinner with him tonight." He looked over at Ruby and Jefferson. "Along with your companions, of course. Enjoy your cruise." He nodded and left.

"I don't think I'll ever forget those instructions," Ruby said. "Like I needed to be reminded that we're floating on a big river in a boat that could sink—"

"—or catch fire," Jefferson added.

"Dangers that used to be a lot more common with steamboat travel," I said. "But not anymore."

"What do we do now?" Jefferson asked. "'We've got some time to kill before dinner.'"

"With the captain," I added as I raised my eyebrows. "Let's walk around. I'd like to get a feel for what's where."

Before we'd left the bar, I heard someone calling my name. "Frank Dodge?" I turned around to see a squat gray-haired man carrying a clipboard walking toward me. "I'm Barry Riggs. The hotel manager."

"Oh, hi." We'd chatted only via email to that point. "Nice to meet you in person."

"Same." He looked at my companions, then said, "I don't want to keep you from your friends. Just wanted to introduce myself in person." He reached out to shake my hand. I obliged. "We're excited to have you on board to write a feature article about your experiences on our boat. If there's anything you need—anything at all"—he smiled and waved his hands in front of him—"please don't hesitate to find me. We'll do everything we can to show you the kind of cruising experience we offer." Jefferson raised an eyebrow.

"Thanks, Barry," I said. "I'm looking forward to the next eight days. I appreciate your help." Barry nodded, then left.

"Looks like you're gonna have the whole crew kissing your ass on this trip," Jefferson said.

I didn't mind the idea. I considered it payback of sorts, after all the crap I'd been through getting started as a writer.

Jefferson, Ruby, and I left the Bow Bar and walked into the library/lounge (which also served as a game room), a dark space with a low ceiling layered with the scent of perfume and moss. The leather armchairs looked inviting. Stories about the Mississippi from past and present filled bookcases, and portraits of river captains lined the walls. I snapped a few pictures with my phone as Jefferson and Ruby browsed books and game titles.

We left the library/lounge and walked past the purser's office and gift shop. "The Eads Bar is back that way," I said as I pointed past the stairs toward the stern of the boat. "But let's go on up another level to deck three. There's an open-air lounge sprawling across the bow I'd like to see." They nodded.

"We aren't going out there, are we?" Ruby asked after we had climbed the stairs. "I didn't bring an umbrella."

"Nah. Let's just peek through the windows." White Adirondack chairs scattered across the deck, with wire mesh tables next to many of them. "I found my spot," Jefferson said. He looked up at the sky. "If it ever stops raining."

Backtracking to the staircase, we continued our ascent of the boat, up to deck four. The Mark Twain Room—the office for the boat's river historian—sat at the bow and faced upriver. The doors were locked, but I peeked inside and saw tables covered with maps, more shelves filled with river-themed books, and an old anchor in a corner.

On the other side of the stairs we'd come up, a hallway with a secured door blocked our path. "Officers' quarters?" I asked. Jefferson and Ruby shrugged, and we walked on.

We detoured along an outside corridor and maneuvered around the deck chairs that sat outside most of the cabin doors. "Don't drop by unannounced," Jefferson said as we passed his cabin, then he patted my back. Up the stairs again, we walked the perimeter of the cabins on deck five—passing the stateroom Ruby and I shared near the bow, a small suite with twin beds—then picking up our pace as a light wind pushed rain in our faces.

After climbing one more set of stairs—"Good thing they have elevators on this boat," Ruby said after catching her breath—we stepped out into the open on the hurricane deck, essentially the boat's roof. The pilothouse occupied a prominent spot at the bow, and a small room with a lot of windows housed four treadmills not far behind it. We covered our heads with our jackets and raced toward the stern, past more Adirondack chairs and under the roof that covered the bar of the Paddlewheel Pub.

Even in the rain, we could hear the boat's large red paddlewheel steadily churning water, keeping the boat moving against the Mississippi's current with a rhythmic *thump-thump-thump*. The half-moon-shaped bar, dry under its metal canopy, wrapped from one side to the other, with a bored-looking bartender trying to look busy by running a cloth back and forth over it. A piano sat tucked in the far corner under the roof, but no one was playing it. I felt a gentle damp breeze blow around me; other than the roof, nothing protected the pub from the elements.

Jefferson stepped up and ordered his usual—Beam and Coke—but I wasn't in the mood for alcohol yet. I got iced teas for me and Ruby. The sweetness of the first sip startled me. "Damn it," I said. "I forgot where we are. Should've asked for unsweetened tea."

"I don't mind," Ruby said as she sipped through the straw. "I like it sweet."

"Aren't you going to ask how much you're paying for that drink?" I asked Jefferson. "Drinks cost extra on this cruise, you know."

"Nope." He sipped from the glass, closed his eyes, and muttered his approval. "I'm just gonna enjoy myself on this trip. Not gonna sweat what it's costing me to have a few drinks every day."

We walked toward the back rail on the port side for a closer look at the wheel propelling us forward. We paused next to a group of three Black women, nodded hello, and eased into small talk with them.

"I'm Michelle Green," said the woman closest to Jefferson. She wore a striking black, strapless dress. Her skin was radiant and smooth. Thick braids of deep black hair cascaded down her back. She reached out and shook his hand, then shook hands with Ruby and me as we said our names. "These are my sisters, Yolanda and Angela." Yolanda's face was soft and warm. She wore her hair long, well below her shoulders, with just a hint of gray popping out here and there. Her black dress hugged her body, accenting her generous curves. Angela wore a dress just as elegant as Yolanda's but red. Her face was warm too, her black eyes radiated confidence. While Yolanda's hair flowed down her back, Angela had opted for a short bob cut that draped symmetrically over her face. All three of the sisters had perfectly trimmed eyebrows and had applied makeup to accentuate their natural features without going overboard.

Michelle faced me directly. "What brings you on this cruise?"

"I'm working," I said. "I'm writing an article about this boat for a cruise magazine."

"And I'm a freeloader," Ruby said, then laughed. "I get to be his companion."

Michelle turned to Jefferson. "And what about you?"

"I needed a vacation. Badly. And this seemed like as good an option as any."

"What did you need a vacation from, badly?"

"I'm a police detective in St. Louis. Homicide Division."

Michelle crossed her arms, checked out Jefferson from head to toe, then glanced back at me. "So, you're here to make some money." I nodded. She then smiled at Ruby. "You're here for fun." Then back toward Jefferson. "And you're here to forget." He nodded slightly. "How nice," she scoffed. "Well, I'm here to find my father's killers," she said, keeping her eyes focused on Jefferson. My jaw sagged. "Four white men murdered him and dumped his body in this river, the Mississippi." She turned to the water and pointed, then turned back around. "His killers are on this boat now. And I'm here to make them pay."

CHAPTER 2

"The police found my father's body buried in mud on Davis Island, washed ashore near the old plantation where Jefferson Davis enslaved my ancestors," Michelle continued. She crossed her arms. "He'd been missing for months. We had assumed the worst." Yolanda and Angela exchanged glances, then looked out at the river as Michelle talked. "Still," she continued, "when they actually found his body, pulled his bruised and broken corpse from the mud . . . it was devastating. Mama said his body was so badly deformed that she barely recognized him." Her hands were shaking. "It hurt more than I ever imagined. I was just eight years old, but I still remember every detail—the phone ringing, my mama crying, my aunts coming over to look after us kids, the adults whispering back and forth." She wiped tears from her eyes. "The whole feeling that the world, our world . . . my world, had just been crushed."

"I'm so sorry," Jefferson said as he reached out toward Michelle's shoulder. She took a step back, and he let his arm drop.

"Don't be sorry. I'm not." She crossed her arms. "I got over feeling sorry a long time ago. They killed him in 1974. Some say I should be over it by now." She cast a subtle glance toward her sisters. "But I'm still mad as hell"—her eyes narrowed—"and I won't rest until I hold those men accountable."

Michelle was on a mission, but she certainly didn't look the part.

"They got away with it?" Jefferson asked as he took a half step backward.

"So far." She glared at Jefferson. "So far. But their luck's about to run out. I've been dogging them for forty years. And now I'm so close." Her arms fell to the side, and her jaw clenched.

"How do you know they're here?" Jefferson asked. "On this boat?"

Michelle scanned the area around us. "I got a tip. Four men killed our father, two of them brothers. The brothers are supposed to be on this boat."

"But not the other two?"

"One of 'em is dead." She scanned the boat. "The other tipped me off."

Jefferson raised his eyebrows. "Ratted out his co-conspirators, huh?"

"Yes. He called me. Blocked the number so I couldn't call him back. And it was a quick call, but he said he wanted to do something to make amends. Even if it wasn't much. He told me the brothers would be on this boat."

"Then you know who they are?" I asked.

"No." She looked away. "They changed their names a long time ago. He wouldn't tell me their new identities. Said he wasn't ready to go that far, so I'd have to figure that out on my own. Then he hung up."

Jefferson fixed his gaze on Michelle, nodding slightly. "Do you have anything to go on? To narrow your search?"

"Sure. They're white, male, and between sixty and seventy years old."

Jefferson grimaced. "That's still gotta be a lot of people."

"I get that." She took a step toward Jefferson and pointed at his chest. "But I'm going to flush them out and deliver the justice that should have been served forty years ago!"

"Michelle, honey." Yolanda rested a hand on Michelle's shoulder. "We need to get moving. It's time for dinner. We can't exact justice if we're hungry, right?" she asked quietly, her smile looking forced.

Michelle shook her head and dropped her arms. "Fine. Let's go eat. Then we get to work." She turned to Jefferson. "Nice meeting y'all." She looked each of us over, then said, "Enjoy your vacations."

"Thank you for sharing your story, Michelle," Jefferson said. He reached out to shake her hand. She grabbed it lightly, then quickly let go. "I'll be around. I hope we get more time to talk. Enjoy your dinner."

Michelle walked away slowly and smiled ever so slightly. She kept her eyes on Jefferson until her back was nearly facing him.

"Oh, my!" Ruby exhaled after they were gone.

"'Oh, my!' indeed," I echoed. "We should get moving, too. We have a date with the captain for dinner tonight, remember?"

"I remember," Ruby said.

We raced back to our rooms to change clothes, then walked down to the dining room. Ruby wore a cream-colored pantsuit, with a string of pearls around her neck. Jefferson, following a few steps behind Ruby and me, was dressed in the suit he wore to work most days, a respectable dark gray jacket and slacks a touch frayed around the edges. He looked distracted, deep in thought. As we descended the stairs, I loosened my tie, then tightened it again, hoping the knot would look a little less askew. As we passed a floor-to-ceiling mirror in the staircase, I glanced at myself. Columbo. I look like fucking Columbo in a fedora.

When we got to deck one, I said, "Let's take a quick detour. I'd like a peek inside the auditorium." They nodded OK.

We slipped around the staircase and went in. Rows of cushy chairs upholstered in red velvet faced a small stage. We couldn't see much of the stage itself, as it was hidden behind a tall curtain covered with the *River Voyager* logo done up in Victorian Gothic script layered on top of a colorful *Harper's Weekly*–style image of the boat.

I jotted down a few notes. "That'll do for now," I said.

When we reached the dining room, a dozen people had lined up at the entrance. We saw Michelle, Yolanda, and Angela being led to a table. While we were waiting, I studied the room. It was a beauty, although after hearing Michelle's story, I didn't feel right taking pleasure from looking at it.

I'd heard that the design had been inspired by the grand hall of the nineteenth-century steamer *Princess*. Four times a day, the crew of the *Princess*, mostly enslaved Blacks, transformed what was basically a long, narrow parlor into a dining room suitable for the boat's first-class passengers. No one had to work that hard on the *River Voyager*, however. This room was for dining only. And it was a stunner. Ornamental brackets painted gold along the edges spanned the ceiling, with multi-globed chandeliers hanging between them. White wainscoting covered the lower part of the walls, while just above it wallpaper ran to the ceiling. Clusters of round tables covered with white tablecloths filled the hall, each table surrounded by eight high-back chairs upholstered in red with ample cushioning. Along the outside walls, small square tables with two chairs offered more intimacy for couples or space to breathe for the shy.

As we waited for our table, the aroma of grilled steak drifted toward us. "That's not gonna make me hungry," I joked. Ruby smiled. Jefferson didn't respond, his gaze fixed on the sisters as they sat down.

When it was our turn, the hostess escorted us to a table near the back where two people had already been seated. After we sat down and said who we were, they introduced themselves as Bucky and Mathilda Jones, newlyweds from Nashville—although given their apparent ages, I guessed it was a second marriage (or a third or a fourth . . .). Bucky's face was narrow and practically gaunt, but he had a strong jawline. He was so thin, two of him could have fit into his chair. Mathilda leaned forward to say hello. Her dark brown hair hung neatly down to her shoulders. Black liner traced her eyebrows. Composed. That's what I thought of her. Composed.

"I'm retired. Used to sell cars," Bucky volunteered. "I taught kindergarten," Mathilda said. "This is our first river cruise together," Bucky said. "But not my first cruise," Mathilda added as she placed a hand over her chest.

"That must be him, the captain," Ruby said. We turned toward the entrance to the dining room, and Mathilda said a slow, "I'd say so."

My eyes drifted from the well-appointed man in the uniform to the person he was walking with. I saw a familiar face, an all-too-familiar and not at all welcome one—Helen Kraft. She looked at me over the top of her tortoiseshell-rimmed glasses and winked.

Chapter 3

Everyone stood up as he approached. "I'm Captain William Smith." He made the rounds, a quick handshake with Bucky and Mathilda before turning to me. He had wavy, thick gray hair matched with a neatly trimmed gray beard that, from a distance, looked like it wrapped around and connected with his eyebrows.

"Dodge. Frank Dodge," I said as my turn came.

"Mr. Dodge. Welcome aboard." He gripped my hand like his life depended on it, his intense blue eyes fixed on me. "Let me know if there's anything I can do to help with your article. I'm sure you'll find everything runs smoothly on this boat." He let go.

"I appreciate the offer." I slipped my right arm behind my back and gently shook out the discomfort. "I'd love to see the pilothouse if that's OK."

"Of course. We've got a group touring tomorrow morning." He spoke slowly and with an accent, but my knowledge of dialectical variations in the South wasn't good enough to pin it down. "You can join them." He scanned the dining room, then looked back at me. "Be there by nine."

"Perfect. And maybe the engine room at some point, too?"

He stepped away from me. "Of course," he said after a pause, then regarded the other diners at his table. "Please sit." He forced a smile. "Enjoy the meal."

We took our seats. Helen sat on the captain's left, between him and Bucky. She flipped her hair back after she sat down, and I rolled my eyes. I hadn't seen her since Dubuque, hadn't heard much about her in the nine months since then, in fact. What had she been up to? I was in no hurry to find out. I still couldn't believe she was entirely blameless for the mess that played out back then, the fire that ultimately took three lives. Her hands had some dirt on them, I was sure. But I had more important things that needed my attention, such as choosing an entrée.

The captain had arranged for us all to get the same appetizer, but we still had to choose soup or salad and the main course. I thought a Caesar salad sounded about right, and I jumped at the chance to try quail.

"What the f—" Jefferson caught himself before finishing that thought. "Quail? Really? You're gonna eat some tiny bird when you could have short ribs instead?"

"I've never had quail. Seems like a good time to try it out." I unrolled my napkin and placed it in my lap. "Maybe you should, too."

"No. Hell, no." He slid a knife closer to his plate, within easy reach. "I'll stick to the ribs and let them stick to me."

Ruby chose scallops, which were new to her. Fresh sea scallops weren't a regular menu item in her native northeast Iowa.

"Everything looks amazing," Helen said as she reviewed the menu. "I'll take the cobb salad, please."

The server took our menus, nodded at the captain solemnly, then turned and walked away.

Bucky, dressed in a white dress shirt with a light blue trim and a faded blue tie, leaned forward to thank the captain for the dinner invite. Helen leaned back in her chair, watching the captain as he talked with the rest of us.

"You are welcome, Mr. Jones. We like to do something a little extra special for our newlyweds." The captain looked away as he spoke to Jones, his eyes scanning the dining room again.

"So, what does it take to become a captain of a boat like this?" I asked. Bucky sat back in his chair and looked at Mathilda. He had a hard time looking away from her.

Captain Smith's eyes opened wide, and his tall forehead crinkled. "It's a long road, of course. It helps to have a steady hand and demeanor. Can't be easily riled." He took a sip of water. "I worked my way up from nothing. Started on the river as a deckhand as a young man. One of the tow companies I worked for was having trouble finding enough pilots, so they gave me a chance to learn. Not sure what they saw in me, but I was grateful for the opportunity."

Now that I had a closer look at him, I noticed how those affecting blue eyes were sunk deep in their sockets. "How different is piloting a boat like this versus a tow?" I asked.

"Well, for one thing, piles of processed corn never complain." We all laughed. He didn't. "Each boat has its own challenges, but the river will, of course, always keep life interesting. You never know what she's going to throw at you from day to day."

Before he could say anything more, a couple of servers had returned with small white plates covered with golden round crab cakes. They put a plate in front of each of us.

"Please, go ahead and eat," the captain said. He leaned back in his chair.

I wasn't about to argue. I cut off a bite of crab cake, cracking through the perfectly fried, crisp but not oily exterior, revealing big lumps of crab meat inside. I dipped the bite in the tangy rémoulade sauce on the side, then enjoyed the explosion of rich flavors in my mouth. Ruby had carefully cut a small piece and was chewing it slowly.

"Frank," Helen said.

"Helen," I replied. She ignored my tone.

"I'm sure you must know this—forgive me if you do—but this is Captain Smith's final cruise, at least as an employee. He's retiring."

"Yes. I heard about that," I answered, keeping my eyes on the crab cake in front of me.

"American River Cruises, the company that owns this boat, hired me to follow him around on his last cruise and write about it. I'm so honored"—she rested a hand on her chest, then turned to look at the captain—"and I don't know what I did to deserve the honor."

I nearly gagged on her canned modesty. "I don't know, either," I mumbled.

"What was that, Frank?"

I quickly picked up my napkin and wiped my face. "What a treat that must be for you!" I said loudly.

"And what brings you on this cruise, Frank?" She looked at Ruby and Jefferson. "Taking a little vacation with your friends?"

"If only. This is a working trip for me. I'm writing a feature for *Luxe Liners*." How had she not heard me talking about that with the captain? Was she fucking with me? "Maybe you're familiar with it?"

"Can't say that I've heard of it, but good for you." She smiled, or maybe it was a smirk. Either way, I didn't like it. The servers returned, and the empty plates disappeared, replaced immediately by salads. My Caesar was every bit as good as I had hoped. The dressing was so fresh I could practically taste the sea water that the anchovies had been swimming in.

Bucky was less interested in his salad than in talking with the captain, so after a couple of quick bites, he leaned forward again and asked about the captain's retirement plans.

"I own a small hunting camp in Mississippi, on the river. I'm hoping to spend a lot of time there." He looked down at his plate and forked some lettuce and a slice of tomato. "Looking forward to the quiet."

Bucky kept the captain chatting during the salad course. Then the entrées arrived, and everyone's attention shifted back to the food. Jefferson got his wish: thick chunks of beef rib floating on garlic mashed potatoes. Ruby's scallops, lightly browned, rested on a throne of braised thick-cut fennel and artichokes, all of it surrounded by a moat of golden polenta. I looked down at a deboned quail sliced in half and wrapped with slices of bacon, with drizzles of a balsamic painting circles on the plate around it. A pile of greens and a pudding-like corn casserole filled out the plate.

"Perfect," Jefferson said as he dug a fork into the closest chunk. Ruby took a bite of a scallop, chewed, then nodded her head slightly as she mumbled, "Goodness." The quail was marvelous: moist, slightly gamey, rich. I could have made room for another.

The entrées temporarily slowed the pace of the conversation, but soon Helen broke the silence. "What exactly is a hunting camp, Captain?" She set her knife and fork down next to her plate. "It sounds so rustic."

He chuckled. "The name's kinda deceiving." He wiped his mouth clean with a napkin. "It's just an old tradition in the South. It's an escape, a private retreat—my private retreat." He rolled his shoulders back once. "I own it. My property has a small cabin with all the modern amenities—indoor plumbing, running water, electricity—all the important stuff. It's also elevated on piers," he said as he rubbed his chin, "because the river can get pretty high down there, and I'd rather not have to wash out the muck every year." He looked away from Helen and observed the servers as they took our plates away.

"Do you actually hunt," Helen asked, "or is that a misnomer, too?"

He chuckled again. "Sure, we hunt. Sometimes. We fish. Sometimes." He looked back at Helen. "Other times we sit on the deck—screened off from the bugs, of course—to enjoy a beer and conversation." He wiped his mouth with a napkin. "Mostly it's about taking it easy."

"Sounds lovely," she said without breaking her gaze.

No one had any appetite for dessert. I, for one, had had my fill of Helen's saccharine sweetness during dinner. "It's been a pleasure meeting y'all," the captain said. He moved the napkin from his lap to the table, slid his chair back, and stood up. "Please, take your time. No need to rush off from the table, but I need to check in with my crew. Enjoy the rest of the cruise." He gave us a low bow, then walked away from the table.

"Well, that was delightful," Helen said. "Please excuse me." As she got up, the rest of us followed. On the way to the exit, Helen came over to me. "Our paths cross again, Frank." She flipped her hair back. "Maybe we can help each other out?" She raised an eyebrow.

"I'm not sure what I have to offer you, Helen. Let's just stay out of each other's way—you know, like professionals—and get our jobs done, like professionals." I turned my back to her and walked away.

CHAPTER 4

"Let's check out the show," I said. Ruby gave an enthusiastic nod. "Sure," Jefferson said, his eyes focused on his phone.

"Didn't you use to take your kids' phones away if they texted while walking?"

"I'm not texting. Or walking." He looked up at me. "Yet."

He slid the phone into his shirt pocket and glared at me. Then we walked the short distance to the auditorium for the eight o'clock musical revue. The show was due to start in a few minutes, so the room was nearly full. We settled into three seats near the back.

"What were you looking at so intently?" I asked Jefferson. "Did you get Michelle's number already?

"Mind your business."

"Leave him be," Ruby told me. "Let's just enjoy the show."

On cue, the curtain rose, the lights darkened, and the crowd chatter dropped to a murmur. When the floodlights lit up the stage, two men and two women in nineteenth-century outfits sprinted onto the stage. One of the men ran directly to the piano on stage, sat down, and launched into a catchy ragtime tune. I recognized the man and the song right away. It was Deion Boyd, and he was playing "Felicity Rag," the tune he had played for me four years before, when we met at a museum called Ragtime Renaissance Hall in St. Louis. Just before we hooked up. Before I ghosted him.

I liked him. A lot. But he was in a relationship back then, one that allowed extracurricular activities but with two rules: don't stay overnight and just one hookup per person. He was finishing up a dual degree in music and history. The museum had hired him as an intern. He showed me around, we connected, and, well, we hooked up later. He wanted to stay in touch and texted me a few times. More than a few times. I ignored them. All of them.

Jefferson leaned over to me. "Hey, that guy at the piano looks familiar. Should I know him?"

"Probably," I whispered. "You walked in on me dancing with him at Ragtime Renaissance Hall about four years ago."

"When you say 'dancing,' do you mean dancing, or is it a metaphor for something else?"

I elbowed him. "Dancing. Literally dancing."

"Oh, yeah. I remember." He got quiet for a minute. "You called me in to help find a Scott Joplin musical score that had gone missing?"

"No. You just took over the investigation."

Jefferson smiled. "Hmm." He got quiet again. "Didn't you end up sleeping with him, too?"

Ruby shifted in her chair, then leaned toward me. "Will you two please be quiet?"

"Of course," I said to Ruby. "Yes," I whispered to Jefferson.

Deion was nearly a head taller than the other performers, and he'd let his hair grow out on the sides. For forty-five minutes he and the other performers ran through ragtime standards. Deion played enthusiastically as the others danced and sang. In between some songs, one performer would give a quick lesson on the history of ragtime, one particular song, or music on riverboats. It was a fun show, and it sure looked like the four performers enjoyed doing it. They lined up on stage for the curtain call, then disappeared backstage. When the lights came up, Jefferson turned to us and said, "See you in a bit. Gonna try to catch up with Michelle and her sisters." He got up and hurried out of the auditorium.

Ruby was tired after that, so I walked her to our room. "I'm not quite tired yet," I told her. "I'm gonna head to a bar for a nightcap."

"Of course. As we agreed when you invited me along, don't slow yourself down on my account. I'll see you in the morning." We hugged, and I left.

I went down to the Bow Bar, but it wasn't very busy. I thought about staying to cheer up the glum bartender, but instead I climbed on up to the Paddlewheel Pub. A passenger on the *River Voyager* was never far from a drink. And I needed to explore all the possibilities.

As it turned out, the Paddlewheel Pub wasn't much busier, but I liked being close enough to hear the whooshing sound of water spun around by the boat's paddlewheel. As I walked toward the middle of the bar, I recognized one guy sitting on a stool. It was Bucky, who we'd had dinner with earlier that evening. He was alone, without a tie, and hunched over a drink. I looked at him closely. He carried a wiry torso on a short frame, his skin tanned to just a summer or two short of leathery. His hair—what remained of it—looked needle-thin and light brown. I sat next to him.

"Mathilda turn in already?" I asked.

He looked up. "Oh, hi. It's Frank, right?"

"That's me."

He leaned back and swiveled his chair in my direction. "Yeah. Mathilda wore herself out today. Thought I'd come up here for a nightcap."

"Congratulations on your wedding."

The bartender came over. "What'll it be?" He was tall with a skeletal frame, an older guy, older than I would have expected from someone working a service job in the resort business. I asked for a beer.

"Thanks," Bucky said. "It's a fresh start for both of us."

"Not your first marriage, I assume?"

He chuckled. "Nah. Third." He tilted his head toward me. "Wasn't a very good husband the first two times," he mumbled. "Or father, for that matter."

"So, the third time's the charm."

"Yes. Feels like it." He curled his lips into a smile and nodded. "Like a fresh start."

"How'd you meet?"

"I sold her a car." He laughed. "I sell cars for a living." He shrugged. "Used to anyway. Retired recently. She'd come into our dealership looking for something reliable but cheap."

"Who isn't looking for that?"

"Tell me." He straightened up in his chair. "Well, we just hit it off. I found a good car for her, then I asked her out. She didn't say yes right away. Maybe she'd heard too many stories about car salesmen." He shook his head and frowned. "Can't say I blame her." He spun his glass back and forth slowly. "But I wouldn't give up." He lifted his head. "And it sure looks like it's worked out fine now." He smiled.

"A river cruise is a nice way to celebrate."

"Sure is. It's something I've wanted to do for a while. Expensive, though." He scrunched up his face. "But worth every penny for a honeymoon."

"What's your impression so far?"

"Just love it." He folded his arms over his chest. "This boat"—he looked from side to side—"is like a piece of art, ain't it? Love the food. And it sure was fun to sit at the table with . . ."—he seemed to lose his train of thought—"the captain."

"That was a treat." As we chatted, he made direct eye contact only once. When he did, his green eyes looked pale and tired. Still, he seemed genuinely happy at that moment, more so than I might have expected from someone marking a third marriage. "I don't think I would have had a chance to sit at his table if I weren't writing a story about the boat."

"You a journalist?"

"Not exactly. A writer, generally, but mostly I write about travel." I scanned the bar. "I'm working on a profile of this boat for a national magazine."

"I see. I suppose that's all right." He leaned toward me. "Make a good living doing that?" he asked softly.

"Define 'good.'"

"Kinda like selling cars, huh?" We laughed.

"What's retirement like?"

"Still trying to figure that one out. I've got more time to spend with family. That's nice." He nodded. "But I miss going to work, having something to do. You know, feeling useful."

"It's a big change. That's why I don't ever plan on retiring. As long as I can write, I'll have something to do."

"Maybe I should learn to write." He grimaced and looked down. "I've got some stories to tell, that's for sure."

"Go for it! No reason you couldn't."

"Except I'm not very good at it. At writing." He smiled. His phone lit up, and he picked it up. "Shoot. I gotta run. Need to get back to the cabin and see how Mathilda's doing."

"Nice chatting with you, Bucky." He nodded at me, dropped a twenty-dollar bill on the bar, and left.

I texted Jefferson to invite him up for a drink.

> Busy

> Catch up with you in the morning

I gave up and called it a night.

When I woke up the next morning around seven, Ruby was already awake and showered. She was sitting in bed reading.

"Morning," I said, then stretched.

"A delightful one at that. I haven't slept that well in years. How about you?"

"Slept about as good as any other night." I flipped the covers off me and sat on the side of the bed. "I'm going to wash up. Breakfast after that?"

"Yes. I'm ready whenever you are."

As we walked toward the dining room, we heard an announcement over the PA system: "Bucky Jones, please come to the purser's office." On deck two we passed Mathilda Jones huddled with a couple of crew members. She was crying.

"Oh, dear," Ruby said. "I hope they're OK."

I felt a chaotic energy in the air that I didn't think I was making up. Crew scrambled from place to place, their faces grim. When we reached the dining room, I asked our server if something had happened.

"A man's gone missing," she whispered. She leaned in close to us. "He may have gone overboard."

Chapter 5

Word quickly spread among the passengers that someone had gone missing. At breakfast we could hear people whispering to one another, sharing prayers for divine intervention and theories about what had happened. One couple near me assumed he had been murdered, that someone had must have shoved him off the boat. Probably his new wife, out to take his money, they speculated. Or, someone else said, maybe he'd jumped in the river on his own, committed suicide. He could have had cancer or maybe felt guilty for having an affair.

"These people didn't even know him," Ruby said. She'd overheard the same conversations. "They have no business gossiping about what happened." She waved a fork at me. "They should keep their crazy ideas to themselves." She looked at me, and I nodded.

After we ordered breakfast, I excused myself, leaving Ruby alone for a few minutes to track down the security chief, who was huddled with a police officer and a couple of uniformed Coast Guard personnel. "Excuse me," I interrupted. They turned to look at me. "I think I was one of the last people who saw Bucky Jones."

The security chief invited me into his office. "Bo Hopkins," he said, then shook my hand. If his handshake was any indication, he was strong enough to withstand a category-five hurricane. He pointed to a chair across from his desk. "Please." We both sat down.

"He was sitting at the bar in the Paddlewheel Pub when I showed up last night," I said. "I congratulated him on his marriage, and we just made small talk from there." Chief Hopkins asked a lot of questions I didn't have an answer for. "I'd only just met him," I kept repeating.

"Where did he go after he left the bar?"

"He got a text message, then he excused himself. Said he was going back to his cabin."

"When Mrs. Jones woke up this morning, she was alone in bed. She called his cell phone, but it rang from the table next to their bed." Chief Hopkins explained that she had walked down to the dining room and around a couple of decks, asking if anyone had seen her husband, growing more and more panicked. She eventually worked her way to the purser's office, where she reported him missing. That was where Ruby and I had seen her. "No one saw Mr. Jones after he left the bar." He leaned closer to me. "Who sent the text message to him?"

"Don't know. I couldn't see his phone."

"There were no recent text messages on the phone we found in their stateroom."

That confused me. "I was sitting next to him. His phone vibrated like he'd gotten a text message. He looked down at it like he was reading a text, then he told me he had to go. That's all I know."

Chief Hopkins eventually got the point, but even the thick-rimmed glasses over his eyes couldn't hide his frustration. I gave him my phone number in case he had more questions I could answer with "I'd only just met him."

The crew had searched the boat but had turned up nothing. The cruel truth, the most likely scenario, was that he had gone overboard, but no one had found any sign of how or where that might have happened. He'd just vanished. By the time Mathilda had reported Bucky missing, we'd been docked at our first stop, at the Camellia Crossing plantation, for a couple of hours. There was a small chance that Bucky had snuck off the boat after we'd docked, but the boat's security cameras didn't show anyone entering or leaving in those two hours. The captain called the Coast Guard to report him missing. They started their search downriver of the plantation. Good luck.

We were cruising Cancer Alley, after all, the busy industrial corridor between New Orleans and Baton Rouge, a part of the Mississippi so thoroughly reshaped and confined between earthen walls that it barely resembles its old self. In those hundred miles, Ol' Man River had been thoroughly refined, confined, and contained. The river ran fast and deep through there, as if it couldn't wait to get away from itself.

Giant container ships destined for the open ocean floated next to barges filled with feed corn. Chemical plants looking like Tinkertoys lined much of the riverfront, processing goods from the underbelly of the American economy: plastics, nitrogen, sulfur, gasoline—industries that were too toxic for the rest of the country but welcomed by the political class of Louisiana. Factories that discharged noxious sludge into the Mississippi. The industries loomed over small communities where poor folks lived in decrepit shotgun homes adjacent to the sinking concrete tombs of their ancestors. If Bucky had gone in the river here, he had died in a roiling, spoiled, toiling mess, a part of the Mississippi that swallows bodies, tosses them around in its corrupted waters, and refuses to give them back.

By the time I returned to the dining room, Jefferson was just wandering in. "I wondered if we'd see you today," I said. "How was your night?"

"Good." He sat down and took a sip from my water glass. "Did you order already?"

"Yeah. A while back."

He looked over the menu. "I'll tell you about my night in a minute. After I figure out what I'm in the mood for." We watched as he scanned the menu. "Got it." He got the server's attention, then ordered steak and eggs with orange juice.

"I assume you heard a passenger went missing overnight?" I asked.

"Yeah. The guy from the captain's table last night—the newlywed, right?"

"That's right." Ruby said. "And people around us are already making horrible assumptions about what happened."

"Welcome to my world," Jefferson said. As a homicide detective, every case he worked on brought out conspiracies and unfounded assumptions. "What do we actually know about what happened?"

"Not much," I said. "I had a short chat with him last night at the Paddlewheel Pub. He disappeared sometime after that."

The server returned with Jefferson's orange juice. He drank a third of it right away, set the glass back down, then wiped his mouth. "You were the last person to see him?"

"Seems so." I leaned back in my chair, and Jefferson stared at me. "But he must have gone back to his cabin for at least a few minutes. His wife found his phone on the table next to their bed. He'd had his phone with him when we talked at the bar."

"But no other signs of him on the boat?"

"None."

"They won't find him if he went in the river, I suppose."

"Unlikely."

"Talk about spoiling a honeymoon. How's his wife doing?"

"Not sure. We saw her crying near the purser's office on our way down here, but I haven't heard anything about her. Maybe she's already off the boat."

"Damn. What a tragedy."

"Let's talk about something else. Tell us about your night."

"I will"—he took another sip of orange juice—"but first you gotta promise me to stay out of this, this disappearance. You're here to work on that article." He pointed at me as he talked. "And I'm on vacation." He leaned back and put his hands behind his head.

"Of course. I'll get my article done."

"*This time*, you mean?" I recognized that annoying voice but turned around anyway. Helen Kraft was hovering over my shoulder.

"Yes. This time." I turned back to face Jefferson. "As long as no one tries to steal my work again," I mumbled.

"'A man can fail many times,'" she quoted, "'but he isn't a failure until he begins to blame someone else.'"

"When did you become an expert in John Burroughs?" I frowned and picked up my coffee cup. "Besides, it isn't blaming others when it's true. It's called accountability."

"Tell yourself whatever you need to, Frank." She flicked her bangs to the side. "But, as you may recall, we aren't even working on similar articles this time." Her voice dropped off then. "And I've got my hands full this time trying to write about the captain."

I turned back around to look at her. "How so?"

Her face turned light red. "I . . . I just haven't found the story yet." She twisted and untwisted strands of her hair. "He's had a long career on the river, but it's . . ."—she bent over toward me—"it's just so boring. He's told me so much about the boats he's worked on. So many details. My eyes glaze over. But that's about all he talks about."

"Maybe you just need to keep building trust, get him loosened up." I couldn't believe I was giving her advice.

"Perhaps so." She forced a smile. "Anyway, enjoy your breakfast. Don't let me intrude any longer." As she walked away, our server showed up with breakfast.

"You were about to tell us about your evening last night," I said to Jefferson.

"Right. I got to spend some time with Michelle."

"I thought you might . . ."

"Now, don't go getting all excited. We talked. That's all." Our server came back and refilled our coffee cups. "I wanted to find out more about what happened to her father."

"Did you?"

He forked a piece of sausage, then paused before raising it to his mouth. "Yeah. I did." He crushed an egg yolk with the sausage, smeared it until it was completely yellow, then ate it.

Chapter 6

"Her father was killed in July 1974, not long after the Vicksburg boycott," Jefferson said.

"What was the Vicksburg boycott?" I asked.

"Wasn't that in 1972?" Ruby asked. "I think Black residents of Vicksburg boycotted white businesses for months, right?"

"That's right, Ruby. I'm not surprised more people don't know about it." He leaned forward and rested an elbow on the table. "It was after the big, high-profile civil rights fights of the sixties. Blacks in Vicksburg were still trying to break free from white supremacist rule. Early in 1972 a middle-aged white guy raped a seven-year-old Black girl." He scowled. "Did you hear me right? I said he raped a child. Well, a judge convicted that man of quote-un-quote 'contributing to the delinquency of a minor' and nothing else." He waggled his fingers to show the quote marks. "The S.O.B. got fined fifty bucks."

"What bullshit," I said.

"But typical. This time, though, the Black community fought back. They organized a boycott of white-owned businesses in town. The community organized fleets of cars to take Black folks to places like Jackson, Tallulah, or Port Gibson, where they could do their shopping. They demanded greater Black representation in city government, including among—especially among—police and firefighters, and they wanted the offending judge kicked off the court." He paused, then nodded subtly. "The boycott lasted for weeks, and while they didn't get everything they wanted, it did turn the tide."

Jefferson sipped some coffee. "Isaac Green, Michelle's father, had lived through that time. He was running a small five-and-dime, a neighborhood department store, in Vicksburg. A group of white gangsters ran an extortion scheme in Vicksburg at the time. They convinced Black business owners to pay them a small fee, and they would in turn use their influence to keep the cops from harassing them. Of course, a share of the money they collected went into the sheriff's pockets, too.

"Green wouldn't have it. He refused to pay the fee. They kept coming back and demanding money, though, warning him that the cops would come in any day and shut him down. Rather than give in, though, Green collected evidence about the extortion scheme. Good evidence. Damning evidence." Jefferson's eyes opened wide.

"The gangsters found out that he was about to take his evidence to a bunch of newspapers, including one in Jackson that was Black-owned. But before he had a chance to meet with any reporters, he disappeared."

"How awful," Ruby said.

"A few weeks later, they found his body on Davis Island," Jefferson said.

"Davis Island," I said. "Just a little downriver from Vicksburg. As Michelle said, the land where Confederate President Jefferson Davis owned his plantation and dozens of human beings."

"Right," Jefferson said. "The men had taken Green into the woods, where they beat him to death. Then they dumped his body in the Mississippi River."

"Terrible," Ruby said.

"He was thirty-one years old, and he left behind a wife and three girls. Michelle was eight, Yolanda six, and Angela just three. Michelle remembers the day they got the call his body had been found. Remembers like it just happened."

"Yeah, I remember her saying so."

"Right. When we met her. Well, her sisters, not so much. They were too young." He sat up straight.

"What happened to the killers?" I asked.

"Nothing. Not a damn thing."

"What a surprise," I said.

"No one was ever charged for the murders, but everyone knew who the killers were: four young white men from Vicksburg."

"And Michelle knows their names?"

"Yeah. Let me check my notes." He pulled out a piece of loose paper. "Brothers Ray and Lester Bell, Lonnie Sims, and Otis Morris. Michelle swore to herself that she would track down the killers and hold them accountable. It took a few years, well into her career as a college professor in New Orleans, before she made much progress. For a long time, Black folks in town were afraid to say anything. They worried they'd be next. And white folks sure weren't going to turn on one of their own." He slipped the note back into his shirt pocket. "But times change. People change. Even in Vicksburg. Most of the fear dissipated, so older Black folks who remembered that time told her the names of the four men they were sure had done it. A newly elected Black sheriff helped her confirm that they were responsible."

"But knowing their names didn't turn out to be enough," I said.

"No. It wasn't that simple. Or going to be that easy." He crossed his arms. "Green's murder sparked outrage. There were marches in the street and threats of another boycott. That first boycott had hit the pocketbooks of white merchants hard, so they weren't exactly eager to go through another one. The sheriff had to come out and say publicly they were looking for the killers and would hold them to account." He leaned forward and set an elbow on the table. "Privately, though, he already knew who they were. And he told them to get out of town. Which they did. And that's when they changed their names."

"Shit," I said.

"Yeah, shit. It took a while to figure out that they had new identities. She couldn't find any record of them after the murder—nowhere. She got desperate enough that she hired a private detective to look for them, and he searched all around the South. But even he struck out. Never turned up a hint they still existed. The detective, who could be very persuasive according to Michelle, went back to the sheriff, who disclosed to him that he'd heard a rumor the killers had changed their names when they left town. The sheriff insisted he wasn't entirely sure if that story was true. And if it was, he had no idea what names they went by after they fled."

"So, Michelle was back where she started," Ruby said.

"Not quite," Jefferson said. "She knew their real names, so she put together a list of all of their relatives." He smiled. "Like I said, she's persistent and creative. She found a few relatives who still lived in Vicksburg, so she shadowed some of them."

"She had time to run her own stakeouts?" I asked.

"She made time," Jefferson said. "It cost her a marriage, but she made time. She'd leave New Orleans on weekends and during semester breaks. Sometimes she graded papers while sitting in her car staking out someone's home." He shook his head. "And it worked eventually. For one of the men anyway: Otis Morris. He came to Vicksburg to visit his sister one evening when Michelle was watching her house. When he left, she followed him back to his motel." He raised his eyebrows. "Then she got out of the car and confronted him in the parking lot. Said she knew he'd killed her father."

"Wow." And I thought I took chances. "That was bold. And risky."

"Yeah. Just a little. I scolded her for doing it by herself, but she was afraid he'd leave again. She didn't want to take that chance. And then she reminded me she doesn't need advice from me or anyone else." He chuckled. "She's a pistol." He cleared his throat. "Anyway, he—Morris—freaked out. He started running toward his room, but she caught up and cornered him. Then he surprised her." Jefferson leaned forward again. "He apologized."

"He what?" I asked.

"He said he was sorry. But he swore he hadn't done anything to hurt her father, that he was just a dumb kid doing what he was told to do so he could make a few extra bucks. When the leader of their gang, Ray Bell, wanted to kill her father—to make an example of him so no one else would fight back—he didn't want to go along. So he said. But they had threatened him, too. So, he helped kidnap Green, then went with them into the woods. He played watchman as the others beat him, although he told Michelle that Ray Bell did most of the beating.

"After the murder, the four of them all did as the sheriff advised and left town. Ray Bell told them to change their names and start over somewhere new, so Otis went to Atlanta and became Michael Johnson. He called his family every now and again, but he couldn't stay away completely. He'd slip back into town every couple of years to see his sister. Michelle spotted him on one of those visits."

"Amazing. I don't think I would have had the tenacity to do what she did. Did he give up the other men's names?"

Jefferson shook his head. "No. He pleaded ignorance. Said that just before they fled, they pledged not only never to share their new identities but also never to speak to each other again."

"I can't imagine Michelle would have been satisfied by what he said, though," Ruby said. "She must have kept hounding him."

"You're right. She's doesn't give up easily." Jefferson frowned. "But she didn't have much choice. About a week later, he turned up dead."

"Shit," I said. "Someone confronts one of the killers in person, then he turns up dead. Hard to believe that was a coincidence."

"Exactly. He was silenced. Had to be. Someone else was afraid of getting found out." He rubbed the back of his neck. "Which almost certainly means he was lying about not knowing the aliases of the other killers."

"And now she's been told that two of the killers are on this boat." I did some quick math. "So, four men killed her father. One is dead, and the two brothers are on this boat, right?"

"Right."

"That means Lonnie Sims has to be the one who tipped her off about the brothers, right?"

"That's right."

"So, he felt a need to repent for his role in the murder, but apparently not fully." Jefferson looked confused, but I went on. "He told Michelle the brothers would be on this boat, but he wouldn't divulge their names."

"Right," Jefferson said.

I scratched the back of my head. "Brian—"

"Go on."

"Bucky Jones—the guy who just disappeared—was probably . . . Well, I'd say he was about the right age to be one of the killers, right?"

Jefferson tilted his head and looked at me. "I suppose so. What are you suggesting, Frank?"

I fidgeted in my seat. "All Michelle has to go on is that she's looking for a couple of white guys in their sixties. Then a white guy in his sixties disappears. Have you considered the possibility he could be one of the brothers?" I hesitated. "And that maybe she had something to do with his disappearance?"

Jefferson grinned. "Nah, Frank. I haven't considered that. Not the last part. Because it's not possible."

"What makes you so sure?"

He cleared his throat. "'Cause I was with her. All night."

"And you said nothing happened . . ."

"And I wasn't lying, either. We talked. That's all. We talked until we fell asleep."

"Fine. So, she didn't have anything to do with Bucky's disappearance." I tilted my head. "But the guy we knew as Bucky could still be one of the men she's looking for."

"Yeah." He nodded slowly. "That's true."

We were quiet for a moment, then I said, "I guess this means you're already helping her find two men, the brothers Ray and Lester Bell."

"Absolutely I am."

"What happened to being on vacation?"

"This *is* vacation for me, Frank. You know that." He reached over and patted me on the shoulder. "Nothing I love more than helping someone hand out some justice."

"Especially when that someone is attractive and single."

"It doesn't hurt."

"What is it about you and Michelles?" I asked.

"Are you suggesting I should stay away from her because she shares a name with my ex?"

"Not at all, buddy. Just noting the coincidence. So, what's next?"

"I'm going to do what I can to find these two men on the boat, the brothers who killed Isaac Green. You're going to write your article. And Ruby is going to enjoy the vacation of her life."

Chapter 7

I picked up my phone to check the time. "Ruby and I need to get going. We tour the pilothouse in fifteen minutes."

"Have fun," Jefferson said. He stood up and slid his chair from the table.

"Will we see you for lunch?" I asked.

He shrugged his shoulders. "Maybe. Text me." He turned to leave the dining room.

"He's a man on a mission," Ruby said, watching as he walked away.

"I think you're right." I worried that his vacation was turning into work, but he seemed energized. Part of me hoped he would take some time to relax and not lose himself in a new chase—in a new woman—but who was I kidding? He wasn't much for sitting around and reading. And Michelle and her mission were too good to pass up. "Ready?" I asked Ruby.

"Ready."

The pilothouse rose from the forward section of the hurricane deck. We joined a group of six others and stepped into the living-room-size compartment, all of us led in by John Mathews, the boat's river historian.

The room was square, with tall windows all the way around. A U-shaped control center wrapped around the front of the room, the metallic surface broken up with gears, buttons, and levers, many of them hard to read because sunlight was reflecting off them. A monitor displaying digital river maps sat in one corner of the control center, and another monitor occupied the opposite corner. We were docked at Camellia Crossing, so the pilot on duty stood in a corner, nodding occasionally and smiling politely as he listened to Mathews describing what we were looking at.

Mathews pointed at one corner of the control center. "Over there, you'll see a VHF radio. It gets a lot of use. Tow crews talk frequently, because every time one passes another, they have to carefully plan who's going to be where. Tows don't randomly choose a side to pass on, they have to coordinate it. And the downriver tow always has the right of way." He glanced at the pilot and nodded slightly "After all, barges floating with the current can't easily slow down, much less stop on a dime."

Mathews explained that the *River Voyager* carried two pilots who rotated on and off duty every six hours. The captain was also a licensed pilot and would sometimes take a shift guiding the boat, but most of his time went to administrative tasks. In a pinch, the first mate could also pilot the boat. "But if you'd ever seen him driving a car, you wouldn't in good conscience put him behind the wheel of this boat."

Everyone laughed, some nervously, then Mathews's shoulders stiffened suddenly. The pilot, who had been leaning casually against the wall, stood up straight. I turned to the door and saw Captain Smith walk in. He tipped his cap and said hello.

"Anything you'd like to say to the group before we leave the pilothouse, Captain?" Mathews asked.

"I just want to thank you again for choosing to cruise with the *River Voyager*." I didn't feel much sincerity as he spoke. Maybe he'd done a few too many pilothouse tours. "If you have questions about the boat—how we operate it, for example—you can ask Mr. Mathews. He may be the only person who knows more about this boat than me." He gave a sideways glance to the pilot, then back to Mathews.

"Thank you, Captain," Mathews said. He then turned back to us. "OK. That's the end of the tour. If you have any questions, you can find me in the Mark Twain Room on deck four."

On the way out, I sidled up to Mathews. "Am I mistaken, or did I sense a change in atmosphere when the captain walked in?"

Matthews replied without looking at me. "Captain Smith is a throwback, Mr. Dodge." *Does everyone on this boat know who I am?* "He's an old chain-of-command, don't-give-'em-an-inch type of leader. Nothing more than that." He picked up his pace to get ahead of me, then disappeared down the stairs.

After we'd stepped onto the open deck and into the bright sun, I said to Ruby, "We've got some time to kill yet. Up for a tour of Camellia Crossing?"

"Oh, yes. I've been looking forward to it. I've never toured a plantation before."

"I think we'll have to walk there, though. It's a short hike over the levee, then down their famous oak-lined drive to the house. That OK?"

"Yes. That'll be fine." She gently nudged me in the side. "Just don't walk too fast."

We exited the boat down the gangway, then walked up the levee. When we reached the top, we stopped to take in the view of the antebellum plantation mansion and its environs, and we wiped sweat off our foreheads. "Oh, my," Ruby said. "So beautiful. That house looks just like I imagined a plantation home would look. And those trees line up perfectly . . . the way they stretch down the road."

"Those are live oaks. Native to Louisiana. And each one is a couple hundred years old." I held out my arm. "Shall we walk between them?"

She smiled. "Let's do it."

She wrapped an arm under mine. We plodded down the slope of the levee's back side, crossed a narrow highway, then continued down the drive under the canopy of live oaks and into their welcome shade. Ruby didn't say much as we walked, her attention occupied with looking from side to side until we reached the plantation house. It was a big one. Three stories tall and painted light yellow. White Corinthian columns framed the house, one placed every ten feet or so. A double staircase curved from the second floor down to the ground, each half mirroring the other. A porch stretched around the second floor, providing shade for the patio space underneath it. We stopped in front of the house to take it in.

"It's a beautiful sight," Ruby said, "but who really needs that much house? When we looked at it from the levee, I was really impressed." She paused and scanned the building. "Now that we're in front of it, I feel like it's a lot of showing off."

I nodded. "You are an observant one, Ruby. Both of your comments are spot on. The house was supposed to impress people passing by, but the owners also meant to overwhelm people when they got close, to show off just how rich they were."

She shook her head. "I've never understood why people need to do that. It's one thing to build a beautiful house. We have some of those in Friesburg. But it's another to . . . to flaunt it." She frowned.

We picked up a brochure, joined a tour, and went inside. The guide, a woman in her seventies dressed in a blue hoop skirt, described the house's complicated ownership history. One owner had lost it in a poker game on a riverboat. The next was better at spending money than making it. All the owners, though, grew sugarcane. As we walked from room to room, our guide turned her attention to the architectural details and furnishings, mixing in a story here and there about the eccentricities of a previous owner—such as the man who always insisted on having a gold-colored napkin in his lap when he drank his whiskey.

By the time we were on the second floor, Ruby was clearly losing interest. I could tell she wasn't listening to the guide's stories as attentively. She seemed restless. "Frank," she whispered to me, "would you be offended if we left the tour now?"

"Not at all. Is something wrong?"

"I could use a rest." She looked pale. "I'd like to sit down for a few minutes. And I've heard enough."

We excused ourselves from the tour and exited through the back of the house, where we found a bench on the patio. We sat where we had a partial view of a garden filled with the namesake camellias.

"You OK?" I asked.

"Tired, like I said." She placed her hand on mine. "Just need a few minutes off my feet."

"That's fine. We have plenty of time." I looked around. "What did you think of the tour?"

"It's a beautiful house, of course. And you know how much I love antiques." She paused. "But this place feels, I don't know . . . cursed." She looked at the gardens, then back to the mansion. "These people, the plantation owners, they made their money from slavery, right?"

"Yeah. They did."

"But we heard so little about them—the people who were slaves—during the tour."

"No. She did mention slaves a few times, but she didn't tell us anything about who they were or the lives they lived."

"Exactly. Aren't their stories worth hearing, too?"

"Maybe people don't want to be reminded of that . . . unpleasantness when they're touring these beautiful homes. We like to keep our history simple. And neat. Avoid thinking too deeply about why things were the way they were."

"Maybe some people. I'm not one of them." She sat quietly for a minute. "Is there someplace here where we might learn more about the people who were slaves?"

"Yeah, sure." I pulled the brochure out of my back pocket and opened it to the map of the grounds. "We'll need to walk a little again, though." I pointed to a walking path. "Just down that way there's a collection of old slave cabins. You up for a little more walking?"

"Yes. Give me just another minute, and I'll be ready."

We took our time walking the gravel path to the six slave cabins. As we entered the first one, Ruby stopped in the doorway and looked around the space. Before she took another step, she whispered something, then did the sign of the cross.

The cabin was dark and dank. A small frame bed covered with a straw mattress occupied one corner of the room, near a rocking chair and a small table. Most of the rest of the cabin had displays about the living conditions of the enslaved people at Camellia Crossing. Ruby carefully read each one and studied the photographs, then did the same in the other five cabins. Occasionally she'd look at me and shake her head, but she didn't say a word.

"Enough?" I asked after we left the last one.

"Yes." We walked back to the boat in silence.

CHAPTER 8

"I'm going back to lie down in our cabin," Ruby said after we were back on board. "Just need a little rest." She patted me on the arm, then turned and headed toward the elevator.

"Well, if it isn't Mr. Frank Dodge," I heard a familiar voice say.

I turned around and smiled. "Hey, Deion. You were really terrific last night. Loved that ragtime show."

"So, we're just going to pretend that everything is fine between us?"

"Can we?"

He crossed his arms. "I sent you at least a dozen text messages. Even called you a couple of times. You didn't bother to answer. None of them. I haven't heard from you in what—four years? Why should I talk to you at all now?"

"Yeah. I'm sorry about that." I grimaced. "We'd just had a good time, a very good time." I winced. And hated how that sounded. "I didn't want to spoil that memory?"

"What?" His head tilted to the side, and he put a hand under his chin. "You thought we might fight after we'd slept together? Or maybe you thought I'd get all clingy and wouldn't leave you be?"

"No. No. I didn't think any of that." I rubbed my forehead. "It's just that, in my experience, the longer you get to know someone, the more complicated it all gets. And you had a boyfriend. I didn't want to make your life more difficult."

"We hung out, got to be friends. Or so I thought."

"We did."

"We felt a mutual attraction, so we spent an evening together. A fun, beautiful evening. Or so I thought."

"I did, too."

"At least we agree on something. So why did you disappear on me after that? Didn't think you were that kind of person." His arms dropped to the side, and his face softened. "I left your place feeling happy. Joyful, practically." He stepped closer to me. "We connected. That meant something to me. Then just a couple of days later, after not getting any responses from you, I felt . . . confused. Sad. Had I done something wrong?"

I didn't like feeling defensive. I closed my eyes for a few seconds, then opened them again. "It had nothing to do with you." I waved a hand in front of me. "I know everyone says that, but, in this case, it's absolutely true." He raised his eyebrows. "That was a rough time in my life." I debated how much to tell him about my late partner, Greg Williams, but decided to save that for another time. "Meeting you was . . . it was a rare bright spot for me in an otherwise dark period. I wanted to hang on to that moment—our evening together—for as long as I could." I caught his gaze. "You're right. I was a jerk for ignoring your texts. I'm sorry. Very, very sorry."

He tapped a foot a few times as he stared at me. "Are you in a better place now?"

"I am. Much." I nodded. "Look, I don't expect you to forgive me, but I can hope, right? I'd love to hit Reset and get back to being friends." I held out a hand.

His eyes narrowed, then he shook his head from side to side. "Frank Dodge. You are something. Now I remember why I liked you." He stared at me for another minute. "Apology accepted." He reached out to shake my hand. I grabbed it and pulled him in for a hug. "But don't push your luck," he whispered into my ear.

We let go and took a step back from each other. "You really killed it on the piano last night." I said.

He pulled back, and his head dropped down. "Thank you."

"I mean it. Your great-great-grandfather, Tom Turpin, would have been proud."

"Stop." He pushed me gently. "What are you doing on this cruise? Vacation?"

"No. Work. I got an assignment to write a feature about this cruise for a magazine."

"Congrats! I guess you *are* in a better place." He crossed his arms and nodded. "Are you with us for the whole cruise?"

"I am." I smiled. "What are you up to now?"

"Just on my way to rehearse. We're rolling out a new show later in the cruise. Still needs work."

"Can we meet for a drink sometime?"

"Sure. But coffee would be best. We're not allowed to drink alcohol when we're working on the boat."

"That seems puritanical."

"Yeah, but them's the rules." He smiled. "Gotta run." He took a step away from me, then stopped. "I'm easy to find around here. Come find me when you're ready for coffee." He left, and I watched as he disappeared around a corner.

On my way to the Bow Bar, Barry Riggs, the hotel manager, zipped past me, then turned around and came back. "How's it going, Mr. Dodge? Need anything?"

"Not yet. Just back from the plantation tour."

"How'd it go?"

"Meh." I fluttered a hand.

"Wonderful!" he said. "Got to run." He turned his back to me, then scurried away.

The Bow Bar wasn't busy. Most of the passengers were probably still on the bus touring a carefully curated past. I filled up a plate with salad and fruit from the buffet, then sat at a table near the bar. The mood felt subdued. I watched the bartender drying glasses, trying to look busy. The people near me spoke softly and poked at their food. News of Bucky's disappearance had taken the joy out of the cruise, at least for now.

I made a few notes about the lunch buffet as I finished eating, then went to the bar. Maybe I could get a couple of quotes for my article. "That was a nice mix of food on the buffet," I said. "Is it like that every day?"

"Pretty much." She was tall, with auburn hair and a slight, sharp nose. "People have their favorites, so we make sure we bring those out every day. The meat sometimes changes, but you'll always find a salad about like what we have today and similar sides."

"Well, I enjoyed it." I sat on a barstool. "How long have you worked on the *River Voyager*?"

"You're the journalist, right? The guy writing a piece about this cruise?"

She surprised me. They prepared the crew well. "Yeah. Guilty as charged." I smiled.

"Off and on, about a year." She picked up a rag and wiped down the bar.

"Good place to work?"

She lifted her eyes to check me out. "It's fine." She looked down again at the bar. "I like the people I meet. Co-workers are good." She shrugged. "There are worse places to be."

"Have you worked other industry jobs?"

"Sure. I've been bartending about ten years. Worked a few seasons at resorts in the Caribbean. That was OK. I may go back, but this is better."

"How so?"

She stopped wiping the counter and stood up straight. "Honestly, the customers here are more laid back. Less . . . I don't know . . ."

"Entitled?"

She laughed. "Yeah. I suppose you could say that. Just don't quote me saying that." She rinsed the bar rag in the sink below the bar. "We get a lot of repeat customers, too. That's nice. I can get to know people a little."

"Got any advice for people to get the most from a cruise like this?"

"Yeah. Don't overthink it." She laughed. "Some people try to get the best bargain out of everything. It's not worth the effort. These cruises aren't cheap. If you can afford to book one, give yourself the freedom to buy whatever else you want while you're on board. Want a margarita instead of a beer? Then get a margarita. Don't fret it. Have fun." She leaned forward slightly. "And tip your bartenders well."

"Good advice." I made a few notes, then slid my notebook into a pocket. "This is just out of curiosity, totally off the record." I rested an elbow on the bar. "Any news on the disappearance of that passenger?"

"No." She looked from side to side. "I don't expect much, either."

"Why's that?"

"If he went overboard—which it looks like he did—it could be weeks or months before his body turns up. The captain feels horrible for the family—obviously—but he reminded the crew that we can't sit around and wait for news. We have a business to run—he was emphatic about that. Even in difficult times like now. I heard the Coast Guard is searching for the guy. It's out of our hands."

"Has anything like this ever happened before?"

"Ha. Not when I've been around." Another passenger set a glass on the bar. The bartender moved it to the sink below and washed it. "One of the old-timers, a guy in the engine room, told me about one other time a passenger disappeared. Years ago. Somewhere around Memphis, I think? His body washed up weeks later near Greenville. He'd either slipped and fallen into the river or he'd jumped in on purpose. I don't remember the details exactly."

"And the cruise wasn't canceled?"

"No." She pulled the glass out of the sink and dried it. "The show must go on."

"What's his name, this engineer? Maybe I can talk to him."

"Ted Stevens. He's the assistant engineer. I'm sure you can find him if you just ask around."

"Thanks. What a way to start a cruise!" I stood up. "For the sake of the guy's new wife, I hope they find him soon." I pushed the barstool back in place. "Thanks for the chat." I dropped a ten-dollar bill on the bar and walked away.

The article I was writing about the cruise was going to pay well, and I appreciated that, but it was a bore to work on. But writing about someone falling off a boat and disappearing into the river?—now, that sounded more like my style.

CHAPTER 9

It was just past three on the second day of the cruise, and I was already running late. I wanted to catch the day's lecture, so I picked up my pace as I walked to the auditorium. The lecture was already underway. At the podium, the boat's river historian, John Mathews, spoke with the zeal of a mannequin, and a used one at that, given his cheap suit and cockeyed bow tie. He was talking about the inner workings of a plantation house.

"The staff," he said, "kept the house humming behind the scenes." *Not staff. Slaves. Why couldn't he just say slaves? Or, as historians might say today, enslaved workers or enslaved cooks?* He described the kitchen first, and after his first descriptions of the type of wood used in kitchen cabinets, I nearly turned around and walked out, but I saw Ruby sitting a few rows from the back. I walked over and sat next to her.

"Good rest?" I asked softly.

"Yes." She kept her eyes on the speaker. "He's worse than the plantation house tour we took earlier today," she whispered.

I nodded. "Don't have to stay."

"I know." She paused. "But what else am I going to do right now?" She shrugged. "I'll stick it out, but don't feel obligated to stay on my behalf."

"Thanks. There is someone I hoped to track down today." I turned back to look at the river historian, who was going over the standard kitchen appliances of the day. *Ugh.* "I'll see you at dinner, if not before. Six?"

"Yes. That'll be fine."

Ted Stevens worked in the engine room, which I knew I could get to from the Eads Bar, at the stern end of deck two. A public staircase led down to a viewing area, where passengers could get a look at the machinery that moves the boat's paddlewheel. As I descended the stairs, the smell of industrial oil and cleaners climbed up. At the bottom of the stairs, only a low gate stopped me from walking right into the heart of the engine room.

"Any chance Ted Stevens is around today?" I asked a passing mechanic.

"Nah." He was carrying a small piece of something shiny and running a cloth over it again and again. He paused rubbing it long enough to look at me. "Works nights." He took the baseball cap off his head, revealing a tight crew cut of prickly gray hair. He ran the back of his hand across his forehead. "What you want him for?"

"I understand he's worked on riverboats a long time. I'm writing an article about this cruise, and I was told he might have some colorful stories about the ups and downs of river life." I handed him my business card. "When would be a good time to catch up with him?"

He looked at my card, which now had a fresh thumbprint on the front. "I'll have to run it past the captain." He looked back up at me. "Don't see no harm, I guess. I assume the captain already knows about you?"

"Yes, sir. I enjoyed dinner with him last night." I smiled slightly. "What's your name?"

"I'm Chuck, Chuck McDowell." He put his cap back on. "I run this here engine room—chief engineer and all."

"Nice to meet you, Mr. McDowell." I looked at his greasy hands. "I'd shake your hand, but it looks like they are currently occupied."

"And a mess." He resumed rubbing the piece of metal again. "I'll check with the captain and get back to you."

"Thanks." He turned away from me and shuffled toward the middle of the engine room.

I had some time to kill, so I returned to the bar and jotted down a few questions about the engine room that I thought might add flavor to my article. Then I took my time walking up to deck four, hoping to formally introduce myself to the river historian. I assumed he'd be done with his lecture by then. I was right. I found him sitting in his office, the Mark Twain Room, talking with a couple about steamboat engines. When they left, I introduced myself.

"Yes. I remember you," he said. "I know why you're here." I raised an eyebrow. "Sorry. Just that you're a reporter here to write an article about us." His voice was rough, like gravel, and he was about my height. And his bow tie was still askew. He looked tired. Not sleep-deprived, just tired.

"For a minute I thought I was in trouble."

"I'm not the one you'd have to deal with if that were the case." He leaned back against a wall. "What can I do for you?"

"Thought I'd stop by and see what riches you have hiding in this room."

He laughed. "If you consider maps and books full of folktales to be treasures, then, yes—we're pretty rich in here."

As he gave me a tour of the room, I asked, "How often do you lecture during a cruise?"

"At least once every day. Sometimes just to tell our passengers what to expect from their day trips."

I wondered if all of his lectures were as bad as the one he'd just given in the auditorium on the slave economy. "I heard part of the lecture you gave today."

"That right?" He crossed his arms.

"Seems like you left out some important details."

"Such as?"

"Such as the folks who toiled on plantations weren't 'staff.' They were slaves."

"I opened with that fact, Mr. Dodge. Maybe you missed it." He leaned back against a table. "Besides, people on these cruises—they don't want to have to think too hard. And they sure don't want to feel bad. Or guilty. So, I respect that. They're adults." He stood up. "They know how to find out more if they want to." He pulled a pack of cigarettes out of his slacks. "Anything else I can do for you, Mr. Dodge?"

"That'll do. For now."

"You're welcome to stick around and sift through the materials in here if you'd like. I'll be back in ten."

"No thanks. I need to run. Got a few other introductions to make." He nodded, then closed the door behind us.

I'd been so busy that I hadn't noticed how beautiful the weather was. The rain had drifted away, and the air had warmed to the low eighties. I went back to my stateroom, which I had to myself. Maybe Ruby was enjoying the sun somewhere, too. I changed into a bathing suit and grabbed a towel. I had some time to relax on an Adirondack chair on deck three and maybe get some quotes about the cruise from other passengers.

Out on the open deck, a light breeze blew. It felt refreshing and slowly carried away the residue of engine oil lining my nostrils. Most of the deck chairs were occupied, but I found one on the port side near the back, out of the sun.

I nodded to my neighbors, four older white women who didn't seem they were into sunbathing. The jumpsuits and shawls were a giveaway.

"It's a bit chilly in this spot, isn't it?" I said.

"Yes, but I don't mind," one of the women said. "I rather enjoy days like this, before the heat really settles in."

I introduced myself and told them I was writing an article about the cruise. They were lifelong friends—Taylor, Laura Lee, Sandra, and Donna—who had grown up in Memphis but no longer lived in the same city. This was the first time the four of them had been together in a decade.

"Why did you pick a river cruise for your reunion?" I asked.

"We wanted a way to spend quality time together," Laura Lee said, then pulled the green shawl back up around her shoulders. "We didn't want to be so busy that we wouldn't have time to talk to one another."

"We haven't all been together in ten years," Sandra said. "Talking and catching up was our first priority. That's why a river cruise seemed perfect for us." She fiddled with her glasses, cat-eye-shaped lenses in a black frame with small crystals studded around the top. "We have activities to keep us from getting bored, but plenty of time to sit and chat."

"When you grew up in Memphis, did you do much on the Mississippi?"

"Not at all." Sandra snickered. "We lived way east of the river, around . . . Do you know Memphis?"

"Sure. Relatively well."

"In Germantown," Sandra said. "We weren't anywhere near the river."

"What did you think of the Mississippi when you were growing up?"

"Not much," Laura Lee said. "We were told it was dirty and dangerous, that only . . . We were told that people from our part of town didn't go to the river."

"So only Black folks hung out near the river?" I asked.

"Well, that's not quite what I was saying. . . . But, yes, that was the implication, I suppose." She tugged lightly on her shawl again.

"Now that you've had a little time on the river, what do you think?"

Taylor jumped in. "This part of the river isn't exactly . . . scenic, is it?" She lowered her sunglasses—they looked expensive, maybe Ray-Bans—and scanned the area around us. "This is very . . . developed. Industrial. The plantation houses are beautiful, of course, but the river itself—well, she's not much of a looker down here."

"You're right, of course." I looked to my left over the railing. "The refinery over there"—I pointed—"isn't going to wow anyone with its charms. But I'll have to check back with y'all once we get upriver of Baton Rouge."

"Yes, please do."

"I'd hate to leave you with a negative impression, Mr. Dodge," Taylor said. She covered her eyes with the sunglasses. "The food has been fantastic. Just top-notch. And the bartenders sure know how to mix a good cocktail." They all nodded. "It's just that—"

A commotion up front interrupted our conversation. A few sunbathers got up and walked to the rails and looked down. "Is that her?" I heard one of them ask.

I walked over, too, and watched as Mathilda Jones, Bucky's widow, walked down the gangplank. A young porter walked behind her, carrying her bags. Mathilda wore a black hat and sunglasses but still covered her face with her hands as she left the boat. The captain walked on one side of her—looking ahead, not at her—and a cop on the other, comforting her with an arm around her waist.

CHAPTER 10

I thanked the four women for talking with me and left them to chat with one another. I went back to my stateroom for a quick change of clothes, then down to the library/lounge, where I settled into a well-padded wing chair and pulled out my notebook. I'd been making good progress collecting the raw material for my article about the boat. I felt organized—efficient, even. I spent a few minutes figuring out what I might still be missing until I was interrupted by the sound of the PA system clicking on.

"This is Captain Smith. May I please have your attention for a moment?" He paused. "I know many of you are already aware that one of our passengers went missing overnight. After a top-to-bottom search of the boat, we have been unable to locate him. We believe, unfortunately, that we lost him to the river." He got quiet again. "We are all devastated by this tragic turn of events. The chaplain will keep her office open until ten this evening for anyone who would like to talk. You'll find her office on deck two near the purser's office.

"The Coast Guard has asked us to remain docked at Camellia Crossing just a little longer, so they can finish interviewing a few more crew members. If anyone on board has information that may help the investigation, please visit the purser.

"I anticipate we'll be underway again about two hours later than our scheduled departure time. We will still dock in St. Francisville by tomorrow morning, with no interruption to the day's planned activities." He cleared his throat. "Thank you for your patience during this difficult time. Our hearts and prayers go out to the family of the missing passenger."

I looked around. The other passengers in the library/lounge turned to one another. They looked concerned, but almost relieved. The captain's brief acknowledgment about the tragedy seemed to calm folks and shift their energy from speculating about what happened to feeling empathy for the family. At least for now. I felt confident that those same folks would soon go back to baselessly speculating about Bucky's death.

I texted Ruby and Jefferson about dinner. We agreed to meet at six. I threw together a quick outline of my story, which helped me see a few places it could use a little more depth. I wanted to talk to someone in Engineering, and I still needed to experience what the remaining port excursions offered. A few more quotes from the captain wouldn't hurt, either. Overall, though, I felt good about the article.

I moved forward to the Bow Bar and sipped on a beer as I watched the river. The view was better than when we'd boarded, the sky clear this time. The sun shone brightly, but the dense, silt-laden water swallowed light rather than reflecting it. The boat was tied up to secure pilings (river pilots call them deadmen) on the river side of a tall levee, a serpentine earthen wall that runs for hundreds of miles from Missouri to Louisiana. Not far ahead of us, the river bent to the right, and I could see a row of chemical processing plants lining the opposite shore. Bleak. That's one word many people might use to describe the view, including the four polite women I'd chatted with earlier. But as I glanced just upriver from where we'd tied up, I saw an egret prowling the shallow waters along the edge of the levee. Next to that, a couple of willow trees had found just enough ground to put down roots. I smiled and finished my beer. Nature finds a way.

As it turned out, we had extra company for dinner. Jefferson had invited Michelle, Yolanda, and Angela to join us. They each wore fine dresses and heels. I felt like a bum for what I wore to dinner: jeans and a gray button-down shirt I'd bought at JC Penney (on clearance).

"Hello again, Mr. Dodge." Yolanda said.

"Frank. Please call me Frank."

"Mr. Frank, then." She smiled. Yolanda had a bright, inviting face: *Talk to me; I'm a good listener.* "Enjoying your cruise . . . Frank?"

"I'd enjoy it more if I didn't have to work, but—" I caught myself. I didn't want to sound ungrateful. "Actually, yeah. I'm lucky. I get to experience all that this cruise offers, and someone else is paying for it. So yeah. I'm enjoying it." It didn't seem appropriate to ask her the same exact question. "How's the experience been for you so far?"

She gave Michelle a little side eye. "I'm doing my best to make the most of it." She unfolded a napkin and placed it on her lap. "The food has been really good, y'all. I look forward to each meal."

Angela said, "I'm loving the food, too."

"Are you making any progress with your search?" I asked Michelle.

"Some," she said softly. She looked over at Jefferson.

"We have more on our hands than we anticipated," Jefferson said.

"*I* have more on *my* hands—" Michelle corrected.

"Sorry. I can get a little carried away. Right, Frank?"

"That's an understatement."

He glared at me. "Anyway, this boat has almost four hundred people on board. Even after we . . ." He cleared his throat. "Even if Michelle limited our search to white guys in their sixties, she still ended up with a lot more people to check out than she expected." He glanced at her. "We've got a list of what? thirty? forty guys?"

"So far." She crossed her arms and sat back.

"How did you narrow the field to those thirty or forty?"

Jefferson looked at Michelle. She nodded at him. "I wish we could say we had a systematic process. We've basically been wandering around the boat a lot and looking at people. Subtly, of course. Not trying to attract attention."

"And then what? You walk up to them and say, 'Hi. What's your name? Where were you in 1974?'"

Jefferson frowned. "You aren't far off, actually. We've tried striking up conversations with a few of these guys, but, damn, that takes a lot of time." He rubbed the back of his neck and looked around the dining room. "At this pace, we'll never be able to check out thirty or forty people in the time we have."

Michelle sat up straight. "We need to figure out a way to speed this up. To zero in on better suspects." She focused on me. "Which is why I'm very interested in what you told Brian about the man who just disappeared. Or went overboard."

"He was in the right age bracket," I said. "Have you found any other reason to suspect he might be one of the men you're looking for?"

"Yeah. He disappeared into the river. No one ever just falls off these boats. Never." She slowly articulated each syllable of *NEV-ER*. "I asked around."

I didn't say anything about the story the bartender had told me. I hadn't had time to get any more details about it anyway.

"When someone dies while I'm around," she said, "I get a little suspicious."

"We've done some digging into his life, into Bucky Jones's life," Jefferson said, then raised an eyebrow. "It raised more questions than it answered."

I'd shared a meal and drinks with Bucky. I wasn't convinced he was the killing type. "What'd you learn about him?" I watched as Jefferson pulled out a notebook. "You're getting serious, I see."

"Told you I would, Frank." He flipped through a few pages. "Bucky Jones. We did some searches on the Internet and found the car dealership he worked for. Used to work for. He retired. Lived in Nashville for a while, but we're not sure how long. Mathilda is his second wife."

Our server arrived, ready to take our orders. "You all go ahead," Michelle said. "I need another minute to look over the menu." We took our turns ordering—surf and turf was a popular choice at our table.

"Second?" I asked after the server left.

"Second what?" Jefferson looked at me, confused.

"Second wife?"

"That's right," Jefferson said. "First wife divorced him."

"Hmm." At the Paddlewheel Pub, Bucky had told me Mathilda was his third wife.

"The thing is . . ." Jefferson looked down again at his notes. "Bucky just shows up in Nashville in the late 1970s. He could have just moved there, but I . . . we haven't found any paper trail tying him to Nashville earlier."

"We haven't, in fact," Michelle added, "found Bucky Jones *anywhere* before then. Nowhere. It's like Bucky Jones didn't exist before 1975. Like he just materialized out of thin air."

Chapter 11

"Nothing at all?" I asked. "Absolutely no trace of him before 1975?"

"That's right," Jefferson said.

"Well, where exactly have you checked?"

"There's nothing for him in Nashville before 1978. We found him in Macon, Georgia, before that. He was there in 1975, also selling cars, but we didn't find any record of him there before then."

"No birth certificate? No driver's license before 1975?"

"Not so far."

"Right age. Mysterious background." I leaned back and folded my arms over my chest.

"I can see the wheels spinning," Jefferson said, a smile taking over his face. Then the smile flipped into a frown. "Too bad you've got work to do, Mr. 'I'm not on vacation.'"

"As a matter of fact, I was just going over my notes." I smiled. "I'm in great shape. Already got my outline done. Just need to check out some excursions as we move upriver."

"Is that right?" He smirked. "Sounds like a story I've heard before."

"I appreciate your interest in my father's murder," Michelle said. "But you're forgetting one important detail." She looked at Jefferson, then over to me.

"What's that?" I asked.

"That it was *my* father who died, and it's *me* who's been tracking the killers for years. This is *my* work, not yours."

I grimaced. "Sorry," I said. "I get a little carried away, too, sometimes." I sat up straight. "If there's anything I can do to help, I'd like to."

Michelle looked back to Jefferson.

"What?" He said. "You knew what you were getting into when you let a homicide cop get involved."

"And I'll tell you again what I told you at the start. I don't need your help." She pointed at him as she pronounced each word clearly. "I've been doing this on my own for years and don't need anyone's help." She sat back in her chair and crossed her arms. "Not even from a homicide cop," she said, practically spitting the words out.

"Michelle," Yolanda said as she reached over to put her hand on top of Michelle's.

"Don't Michelle me," she snapped and pulled her hand away. "I don't have time to deal with any of this. Papa's killers are on this boat. This is the best chance I've . . . we've"—she swept a hand around in a circle in front of herself, Yolanda, and Angela—"ever had to find them. We've got our hands full trying to find them, I admit, but as long as this boat is cruising, I'm going to do everything I can to find those men. Everything." She glanced at me and Jefferson. "And I won't be distracted by a couple of overgrown children who think this is just another fun puzzle to solve." She got up and left.

"Oh, dear," Yolanda said. I thought I saw her roll her eyes before she got up and followed Michelle out of the dining room.

"Sorry," Angela said. "This thing—finding Dad's killers—is really important to her. As you can tell."

"No need to apologize," I said. "I overstepped. Please let her know I won't do it again. I'm happy to help if she thinks I have something to offer. Otherwise, I'll stick to writing articles about cruises."

"Like hell you will," Jefferson mumbled.

"I heard that," I mumbled back.

Our food arrived just as Michelle and Yolanda came back to the table. As we ate, we went back to safe, getting-to-know-you small talk. Angela talked about her work as a senior manager at FedEx in Memphis. She was so different from her sisters. Michelle seemed driven by—obsessed with?—exacting justice for her father's murder. Each time I'd been in her presence, she was pissed off. Yolanda was the peacekeeper—calm but lacking the confidence of her sisters.

Angela struck me as smart, ambitious, and focused. She carried a confidence I suspected ran deep. She hadn't moved too far from home.

"No opportunities for me in Vicksburg," she said. "After I got an MBA from Ole Miss, I got hired with FedEx. I've been working my way up the corporate ladder since." I pictured her as a demanding boss, but fair, probably. "Do you know Memphis very well, Frank?" she asked me. "I assume, since you write about the Mississippi, that must have at least visited a couple of times."

"More than a couple," I said. "I've been making it my personal mission to sample ribs at every barbecue establishment in the city."

"And how's that going?"

"One weekend I managed to eat ribs at three different places." I cringed. "That was a bad idea." I winced. "Felt wiped out the next day."

"I bet." She grinned. "What have you figured out so far? Have any favorites?"

"I do." I nodded slightly. "First, I love the style, the dry rubs. But not every place executes it equally well. There's a place in Midtown I really love—Smoke & Mirrors. They had the perfect balance of great flavor with tender, moist meat."

"I know that place." She nodded. "Haven't been in a long while. Maybe I should give it a try again."

"You absolutely should." I sat back in my chair. "What about you? What're your favorites?"

"I don't eat barbecue as often as I used to—it's a little heavy for me—but when we do get some, I prefer Jim's in Germantown. It's close to where we live, and the ribs are consistently good, just like you described."

"And what are some of your favorite places to eat in New Orleans, Michelle? There's no shortage of good food there."

"Unlike my sisters"—Michelle looked at her nails—"food's not a big deal to me. I eat to survive. That's all. I don't much care what it is."

"I'm with your sisters," Jefferson said. "A good meal—well, nothing's more satisfying."

"Nothing?" Michelle asked. She looked at Jefferson and raised her eyebrows. "Really? You can't think of one thing better?"

Jefferson laughed nervously, then cleared his throat. "At least I get to eat every day."

"More doesn't equal better."

"I agree with Brian," Yolanda said.

"You would," Michelle said. "And it shows." She cast Yolanda some side eye.

Ruby gasped. Yolanda leaned toward Michelle, then glanced over at Angela, who was shaking her head from side to side. "Not worth it" I saw her mouth silently. Yolanda shifted back to the middle of her chair. "I may be bigger than you, but at least I'm loving my life."

"Yeah, well, maybe you should love it a little less."

"Maybe you should treat your sisters with more respect," Ruby inter-jected. Her face had turned red.

"I don't need some little old white lady telling me how to behave with *my* family," Michelle snapped back, then looked away.

"I may be little and old," Ruby said, glaring at Michelle, "but I know when someone needs to be told they're acting like a fool." Yolanda smiled, then quickly slid a hand over her mouth.

"OK, OK." Jefferson said, then he sighed. "So much for the small talk." He pushed back from the table. "I was hoping to make a few more phone calls before bed tonight, especially since this boat isn't going anywhere just yet. I'll catch up with y'all later." He looked at me. "Maybe in the bar?"

"A good bet. Text me when you're ready for a Beam and Coke."

Jefferson stood up and nodded subtly at the sisters and Ruby. "Ladies. Thank you for the interesting dinner." Then he walked out.

Yolanda and Angela got up right after him and left without saying a word.

"I guess we're all done here," I said to Michelle.

"Guess so." She stood up, glared at Ruby, then turned away.

"One quick thing," I said before she got far from me. "When I talked to Bucky Jones at the bar last night, before he disappeared, he told me that Mathilda was his third wife."

"So?"

"Well, Brian said that you and he found only two marriages for Bucky. I wonder . . ."

She turned around to face me. "Yes?"

"Well, given all the work that you've done tracking the men who killed your father, did any of them get married in Vicksburg? Before they changed their names? Before they murdered your father?"

I saw a brief flash of recognition in her eyes, then they narrowed. "That's very interesting, Mr. Dodge." She paused. "Frank." She tapped her cheek with a finger. "I'll have to check my notes again, but yes, I think I did find a marriage for one of them." She turned around, then back to me. "Thanks for the tip." Then she scurried out of the dining room.

Chapter 12

Ruby and I got up and slid our chairs under the table. "You've never had a problem with shyness, have you?" I asked.

She smiled. "I won't sit by quietly and let someone be treated badly like that."

"Yeah. That shocked me. I'd say there's some tension between the three of them." We started toward the exit. "Up for a show?"

"Of course!" She held on to my arm. "Especially something light. No more drama tonight, please."

The auditorium was nearly full, so we sat near the back. Not long after we'd sat, we felt a slight tremble. "I think we're underway again," I whispered to her.

The lights went down and the curtain up for forty-five minutes of river-themed tunes. Seven performers danced onto the stage while singing the first verse of Johnny Cash's "Big River." Deion was in the middle of the group.

I leaned over to Ruby. "See the guy in the middle, the one who played piano last night?"

"Yes."

"He's from St. Louis. We met a few years ago."

"When you say 'met,' do you mean you dated him?" she asked softly.

I chuckled. "'Dated' overstates it. We hooked . . . we spent a night together."

She glanced at me. "You can tell me more later. Let's watch the show for now." She turned back to look at the stage. "But he is quite handsome."

The cast performed some songs chorus-line style, then for other numbers scampered around the stage to strategically positioned instruments. When Deion sang an extended solo for "A Change Is Gonna Come," I closed my eyes and let his voice swirl around me. The cast medlied their way through classic river songs, lingering over "Ol' Man River" and going out with a rousing rendition of "Proud Mary." I still don't get how a guy from Southern California—Creedence Clearwater Revival's John Fogerty—could write a song that captured the spirit of the people along the Mississippi River.

Throughout the set, Deion shone like a diamond in a pot of gold. I relaxed in my seat and enjoyed every word he sang, every note he played on the piano. He even picked up a banjo at one point to play a lesser known song, "Mississippi River Dance," originally recorded by an Italian-born musician who performed under the name George McAnthony. The tune might have inspired the audience to get up and do-si-do if they'd had better mobility.

"That was fun!" Ruby said as we walked out after the show. "They were so good. I'd go to that show again."

"Me, too." The shows on tour boats can be cheesy and nostalgic, often attempting to re-create a past that never existed to cater to the delicate sensibilities of the typical passengers on a river cruise. That wasn't the case with what we had just seen. They picked pleasant songs, and the performers sang them well. Very well. "What do you want to do now?" I asked Ruby.

"I believe I'm done for the night." She took hold of my arm as we walked out of the auditorium. "I hope that's OK with you."

"Not a problem. Not at all." After we exited, we bumped into a crowd of people waiting for an elevator. "You OK with taking the stairs?" I asked.

"That's fine." We turned to go up the staircase, and her grip on my arm firmed up.

When we reached deck five, we stopped to catch our breath. "That Deion, your friend, was superb," she said. "I'm no expert, but he could have a very good career as a singer and performer."

"Yeah. He really could." I felt myself blush, then just felt embarrassed.

"You're still fond of him, aren't you?"

"It's that obvious?"

"To me? Yes."

"You've always been a tough one to fool, Ruby."

She stopped in front of the door to our room. "You don't have to try with me. To fool me. You know that, right?"

"I know. Old habits, though."

She hugged me. "Go have some fun tonight. You can tell me all about it in the morning."

"Thanks." She went in, and I made a beeline for the Paddlewheel Pub.

I found an empty barstool and texted Jefferson I was there. He responded with a thumbs-up and,

I ordered an IPA from the bartender, the same woman I'd chatted with earlier in the day in the Bow Bar. "Long day?" I asked.

"Filling in for the regular guy. He's not feeling well." She set down the glass she'd been drying with a towel. "Any luck talking with that engineer I mentioned?"

"Working on it." I scanned social media while I waited for Jefferson, trying to ignore the second-rate piano player begging for attention. Deion would play circles around him.

"What's up, Frank?" Jefferson said as he slid onto the barstool next to me.

"Just seeing what friends are up to back home."

"You have friends? Other than me?" He leaned toward me and softly poked me with an elbow. "Beam and Coke," he said as the bartender came back to us.

"That was quite a scene at dinner tonight," I said. I loved that I could be direct with Jefferson. We don't feel the need to dance delicately around the bush.

"Just a little uncomfortable, huh?" The bartender set the drink in front of him. "I'd already sensed some bad blood between the sisters, but I hadn't seen it blow up like that."

"What's it about? Normal sibling jealousies?"

"Sure. That's probably part of it." He sipped from the glass. "But I think there's more."

"Go on." I pivoted toward him.

"I'm just guessing here"—he looked around the bar, then lowered his voice—"but I think some of it goes back to their father's murder."

"How so?"

"Again . . . I don't know for sure. I just have a feeling about this." He lowered his head and leaned toward me. "Michelle has spent a lot of time and energy trying to track down the men who killed their father. It's basically been her mission in life."

"I noticed."

"I don't think Yolanda and Angela share the same passion for it. Angela, especially . . . Well, she's the youngest. Barely remembers anything about her dad. What she does know has mostly come from what Michelle and Yolanda have told her. Michelle, mostly."

"Are you saying they wish she'd drop the whole thing?"

"I don't know if I'd go that far. But I'm sure they think she's spent too much of her life on this. She's smart, you know. Real smart. Earned a PhD in criminology. Teaches at Tulane in New Orleans."

"Impressive. Takes a lot of smarts and patience to get a PhD. And Tulane's an excellent school." I nodded slowly, and my eyes opened wide. "But her sisters needled her about her personal life."

"Yeah. She got married once, but they divorced just a couple of years later. No kids."

"Maybe her sisters think she's given up too much in trying to find the killers?"

"Yeah. That's possible." He sipped again. "There's more, too, of course. I think Michelle resents them—sometimes—for not being as passionate about it as her. For not being willing to go the extra mile to find those men."

"To fulfill the mission with her. And give up as much as she has?"

"I think so." He leaned back on the barstool. "I think so. And I wish she wasn't so resentful."

"What do you mean?"

"Look. They're all good people. I like all three of them."

"But especially Michelle."

"Stop." He elbowed me again, this time with a little more force. "I just think family is important. You've got to stick together. And that's mostly what they've had for a long time. Just one another."

"Obviously their father died when they were children. But what about their mother? She could still be around."

"Nah. She died from cancer when Michelle was eighteen. Michelle basically looked after her sisters until they were old enough to look after themselves. And she managed to do so while taking college classes herself."

"Damn. Does Michelle even know how to live a 'normal' life?" I put air quotes around the word *normal*.

"Ain't nothing ever been normal about her life, Frank. Nothing."

"Hmm." I paused for a moment. "And what do you think . . . ? I mean, this is total speculation. But how do you think Michelle would feel if she's able to crack this case and find the men who killed her father?"

His eyebrows shot up. "I've wondered about that, too." He fiddled with his glass. "I'm not sure she's thought that far ahead. Honestly, I'm more concerned about what she might do to solve the case."

"What do you mean?"

"She feels so close to finding those men, yet the finish line also feels impossibly far away. She's frustrated."

"Can't blame her for that. You've got a lot of people to sort through, but not much time."

"Right. But people I've encountered in the past like her, folks on a mission . . . they often feel like they've got God's blessing to do whatever it takes to get it done. I worry Michelle is like that." He looked up and away from me. "I worry that she'd be willing to go to any lengths to find those men. Do anything to hold them accountable." He took a sip, set the glass back down, then looked to me. "Anything."

CHAPTER 13

Jefferson left after one drink. "Hoping to get more sleep tonight than last night," he said.

"Lame excuse."

"Whatever, Frank. We ain't young men anymore, you know."

"Like I need you to remind me."

He patted me on the back. "Don't stay out too late now. You're working, after all, right?" He laughed as he walked away.

With Jefferson gone, I started thinking about Deion. I wanted to spend some time with him. Reconnect, like I'd said to him. What had he been up to while I was mired in my own morass of self-blame? He looked as good as ever, too. So damn good. *Stop.* I couldn't go there. When we'd slept together four years earlier, he'd made it clear that he and his partner had a rule: They could hook up with other people, but just once per person. That's it. Was he still with that partner? Had the rules changed? Had Deion changed? Why was I thinking about any of this? We were friends. Period. I needed to accept that, right?

I picked up my phone and texted Deion, hoping his number was the same:

You were terrific tonight. Outstanding!

I put the phone down and ordered another drink. I glanced down at my phone often enough to make my neck sore.

I made small talk with the bartender to kill a few more minutes, but by the time I had finished my drink, I hadn't gotten a reply from Deion. I'd waited long enough. I tipped the bartender and went back to my room.

When I woke the next morning, I rolled over to check the time on my phone and saw I had a text from someone.

Thx! Coffee this morning?

Yep. What time and where?

Meet me at the Bow Bar in half an hour.

"Good morning," Ruby said.

"Good morning to you, too." I sprang out of bed. "I'm afraid I'm going to skip breakfast this morning." I rubbed my eyes. "Just got a coffee invite from Deion. You'll be OK without me?"

"I've been OK without you for over eighty years."

"Sorry. That didn't come out right."

She smiled. "It's OK. I know what you meant." She lightly touched my shoulder. "Clean up and go see Deion. I'll be fine."

I raced through my morning routine and rushed to the Bow Bar. Deion was sitting at a table on the starboard side when I got there.

"Come here often?" I joked.

"By invitation only."

I looked around. Everything was self-service. A buffet of breakfast options spread out over the bar, with coffee stations anchoring both sides. "Need anything from the buffet?"

"I'm good," he said, pointing to a mug presumably filled with coffee already.

"I'll be right back."

I filled a cup with black coffee and put a bear claw on a plate.

"That was a surprisingly good show last night," I said as I sat down.

"Thank you? I'm not sure how to take 'surprisingly good.'"

"Sorry. It's not about you." I sipped some coffee, hoping he wouldn't notice my eyes scanning him from top to bottom. "It's just that I've seen a lot of river-themed shows, and most of them lean heavily into shallow corniness. But yours didn't."

"That's by design. By us." As he leaned back in his chair, I thought how much better he'd look in a sleeveless shirt.

"What do you mean?"

"The company let us, the performers, have input into the design of that show. There were conditions, of course—no coarse language, nothing obscene. The songs had to be about the river—that kind of thing. So, we sat down with the entertainment director and picked out songs we wanted to perform, then worked out how to string them together."

"You make it sound so easy."

"It kinda was. They started us with a list, but then I did my own research and added a few more possibilities."

"Like 'A Change Is Gonna Come'?"

"Yeah." He smiled. "That was one of my additions. I love that song."

"It showed. That was the best moment in a terrific show."

"Thank you." He looked down at the floor briefly, then back up at me. "What have you been up to? You know, in the last four years?"

I sat quietly for a minute, trying to decide how much to tell him. "Writing's going better. When we met, I think I was just getting started?"

"Yeah. You didn't seem very confident about it."

I nodded. "I'm not sure that part has changed much. But at least I'm getting more assignments and making enough money to call it a living now."

"What have you written? Maybe I should look up some of your articles." He pulled out his phone.

"A lot of them have been service pieces. Articles like 'the best places to eat in New Orleans' or 'How to get from place x to destination y on a budget.' Not the most exciting writing, but I try to give them a little something extra, a Frank Dodge *oomph*. To make them more interesting." I shrugged. "At least interesting enough for me to be able to write them."

"So, you're saying I shouldn't look them up?" He tilted his head, then grinned.

"I would never tell you what to do or not do. I'm just saying that most of them are meant to offer practical advice rather than inspire. Although . . . there is one that you might enjoy." I sipped coffee.

"Do tell." He leaned forward.

"A few years ago—before we met, I . . . I did some traveling around the world. For a few months."

"Months?"

I smiled. "Yeah. Months."

"How were you able to pull that off?"

"That's a story for another time. But near the end of those months on the road, I joined a risky expedition to travel through the infamous Darién Gap in Panama."

"Risky?"

"Yeah." I sorted through all the reasons that trip had been a bad idea. "Basically, it's remote, physically difficult to navigate, and full of outlaws." I took a bite of pastry. "In the years since, I've written and rewritten articles about that trip, but I've had a hard time finding someone to publish it. Until a couple of years ago. I finally caught the right editor, so that piece is now out in the world."

"Where?"

"*National Geographic Traveler*. If you search that with my name, it should take you right to the article."

"Now I know what I'm reading tonight."

"If you do, I'd love to know what you think." I finished the coffee while keeping Deion's gaze.

"What?"

"Nothing," I said as I looked down. "I was just thinking . . ."

"That sounds dangerous." He fidgeted in his seat.

"We'll see. I was just thinking, wondering about . . ."

"Yes?"

"Well, when we hooked up before, you and your partner had that one-time-only rule. Is that still the case?"

Deion set down his coffee cup. "Frank Dodge. You ghosted me for four years. We just started talking again . . . after four years. And you already want to hook up again?"

"Well, yeah. Why not? If the rules have changed for you. We had a good connection before." I forced a smile. "Maybe it's still there?"

"Sorry. You short-circuited that connection by ignoring me after we hooked up." He shook his head from side to side. "And here I thought we were going to be friends." He slid his chair back from the table. "Look. I'm glad we're talking again. I genuinely like you. I'd like your friendship. But I'm not interested in another quickie followed by another disappearing act."

"It wasn't exactly quick last time . . ."

He stood up. "Don't try to be funny, Frank." He pointed at me. "You know what I mean. See ya later." He turned and walked out of the Bow Bar. *Shit.*

CHAPTER 14

I needed something to alter the course of my mood, which was spiraling down into the depths of the murky Mississippi. I found Ruby sitting in the auditorium, quietly waiting for the day's first lecture to begin. "There you are," I said.

"Hi, Frank. How was coffee?"

"I screwed up." I sat down and slumped in the chair.

She frowned slightly and put a hand on mine for a moment before pulling it away. "What happened?"

"It's hard to explain without the backstory."

"Well, you have ten minutes before the lecture starts. Is that enough?"

"I suppose." I pulled myself upright. "I met Deion four years ago, when I was working on my first real writing assignment, a piece about a ragtime museum. Deion was an intern at the museum. We hit it off right away. He played some classic ragtime for me, explained what made it ragtime, and told me about his personal connection to the music."

"What was that?"

"St. Louis's Tom Turpin wrote what most experts consider the first rag—the 'Harlem Rag'—in 1892. Turpin also ran the infamous Rosebud Café, where ragtime flourished. Deion is a direct descendant of Turpin, although . . . how do I say this?"

"Just say it."

"Turpin wasn't married to the woman who was Deion's ancestor. He had an affair with a singer in his club, and she got pregnant. Deion is descended from her."

"I see."

"Anyway. That's a distraction. We got along well. Very well." I cleared my throat. "We ended up sleeping together. It felt good. Really good." I smiled. "He had a partner at the time, but they allowed each other some . . . freedom. But it was a one-time-only rule."

"What do you mean?"

"It meant that I could sleep with him once, but that was it." Ruby frowned. "It's OK. I knew what I was getting into and accepted the terms."

"How complicated. The mores today are so different. It's hard to keep up. I don't know how you manage these things."

"Well, I didn't handle it well. He wanted to stay in touch—as friends, you know—which was an entirely reasonable expectation. We got along well. But . . ."

"But what?"

My head dropped. "I just wasn't in a good place back then." I looked up at her. "You remember."

"I do. You were still trying to make peace with what happened with Greg."

"Exactly. I didn't feel like I deserved to be with someone as good as Deion, even if only as a friend. I'd made too many mistakes that had hurt people." As I thought about the past few years, my shoulders sagged. "Besides, we'd had such a good evening. I didn't want to spoil the memory of that night with the inevitable conflicts and disappointments that come along with getting to know someone."

"Oh, Frank." She lightly smacked my hand. "Sometimes you can be such a child."

"Ow. What do you mean?"

"Go on with your story." She was still frowning. "What happened next?"

"Nothing. I mean, nothing from me. He texted me a few times to hang out. I ignored them. All of them." I grimaced. "Eventually, he stopped texting me. I figured I'd never see him again. And then I bumped into him on the boat."

"And how did that go?"

"About as you'd expect. He wasn't exactly thrilled to see me. But I apologized. He accepted. And then . . ."

"What?"

"Then I saw him perform last night." I looked toward the stage. "And I kinda fell for him all over again. Couldn't stop thinking about him. So, I texted him last night about getting together. I didn't hear back until this morning. He was good with coffee. So, we met for coffee."

"That sounds like a good start."

"That's exactly what I should have told myself. But, after a pleasant conversation, I asked if he and his partner still had the same one-time rule."

"Oh, Frank." She sighed.

"I know." I looked down. "I know. Stupid. We had just started talking again after four years. He probably doesn't trust me . . . trust me to be a good friend. And then I go and hit on him so soon. Which may have reinforced his feeling that I couldn't be a good friend."

"Probably so. What did he say?"

"He wasn't flattered." I shook my head. "But it was sincere, at least. I was sincere. I do like him. Not just like him." I swallowed hard and looked up and away from Ruby. "I'd say I have a crush on him."

"Frank. God bless you. I understand what you're saying, but . . . you're usually much smarter when it comes to understanding people." She smiled slightly, and her eyes softened. "You've got a good sense of people, what they think, and you're sensitive to what people feel."

"Thank you."

"It's not exactly a compliment I'm working up to here." She put a hand on mine. "Stop thinking with your penis, Frank."

I nearly slid out of my chair.

"I don't like talking like that," she said. "But you need to hear it." She giggled. "Look. Deion obviously likes you, or else he never would have agreed to have coffee with you. But he's still trying to figure out if he can trust you again. Trust you to not hurt him. Again. You know that, but you ignored it." She scrunched her face, then relaxed. "I understand that maybe you're starting to feel like you're ready to get back out in the world and date again, and Deion is an attractive man. But the two of you have a history of broken trust. Trust you broke." *Ouch.* "If you don't respect that history, you won't be talking to him again."

I nodded. "Yeah, I get it." I exhaled. "I knew as soon as I said it that I'd made a big mistake. But I'll apologize again and see if he'll have coffee with me . . . again. No rushing anything."

"That sounds like the Frank I know."

"Can you do me one favor, though, Ruby?"

"Of course. What?"

"You know I love you. You're like a grandmother to me. Please never say the word *penis* again around me?"

She lifted up her hand, smacked me on the wrist, then smiled. "You can be such a prude sometimes, Frank. I may be in my eighties, but I'll use whatever words I damn well please." She glared at me, then she laughed. "Especially when a good friend needs to be set straight."

The speaker, Sally Crayne, stepped to the podium, prepared to lecture about the history of St. Francisville, the town where we had stopped for the day's excursions.

I leaned toward Ruby. "Thank you. A real friend is someone willing to kick you in the butt when you need it," I whispered. She smiled.

Crayne covered the usual bits of history: the first white settlers, early businesses and industries, St. Francisville during the Civil War. To her credit, she presented the facts of the slavery economy with unsparing detail. The town grew on top of the hills, but down at river level, a place called Bayou Sara was the real boomtown, located about where the *River Voyager* had landed. Like so many places along the Mississippi, the bluffs housed the well-to-do, while the rabble-rousers, card sharks, traders in cotton and slaves, and working women built their homes next to the river. Before the Civil War, Bayou Sara was a hopping place, one of the busiest steamboat ports on the lower Mississippi.

Crayne then detoured to tell a story about the precariousness of river life in that era. In 1848 the steamboat *Clipper* came to an unfortunate end. Late in the night of September 19, the boat's boilers exploded, an accident that happened far more frequently than steamboat nostalgists talk about. Crayne read an excerpt from an account written by one survivor. "The boat," she began,

blew up with a report that shook earth, air, and heaven, as though the walls of the world were tumbling to pieces about our ears. All the boilers bursted simultaneously; vast fragments of the machinery, huge beams of timber, articles of furniture, and human bodies, were shot up perpendicularly, as it seemed, hundreds of fathoms in the air, and fell like the jets of a fountain in various directions; some dropping on the neighboring shore, some on the roofs of the houses, some into the river, and some on the deck of the boat. Some large fragments of the boilers, et cetera, were blown at least two hundred and fifty yards from the scene of destruction. The hapless victims were scalded, crushed, torn, mangled, and scattered in every possible direction; some were thrown into the streets of the neighboring town, Bayou Sara, some on the other side of the bayou, three hundred yards distant, and some into the river. Several of these unfortunates were torn in pieces by coming in contact with pickets or posts, and I myself saw pieces of human bodies which had been shot like cannon balls through the solid walls of houses at a considerable distance from the boat.

"Thanks for that," someone in the audience shouted, then got up and walked out.

Near the end of her lecture, my phone lit up. It was a text from Chuck McDowell, the chief engineer:

> Capt approved Ted Stevens interview. Stick to his career working on riverboats. His next shift starts at 10 but best to catch him on break around midnight.

Since I had my phone out, I texted Deion:

> Sorry! Bad judgment. Terrible judgment. Really, really awful judgment. Can we reset? Continue chatting and catching up? Coffee again tomorrow morning?

After the lecture Ruby and I met Jefferson on deck three and headed outside on the bow to take in some sun. "Any progress with your investigation?" I asked.

"It ain't my investigation, but yes and no."

"Go on."

"The cops and Coast Guard are done with their interviews. They're saying suicide. They think Bucky Jones killed himself."

"Who'd you hear that from?"

"Hopkins, the security chief. I've been chatting with him. He also told me—in confidence—that the captain is eager to get on with his last cruise and put this whole episode behind him. Unless something concrete turns up that contradicts their belief, 'probable suicide' will be on Bucky's death certificate."

"Which means a cloud over his wife and kids," I said.

"And no life insurance settlement for them," Ruby added.

"Yeah." Jefferson said. "That's probably right." He sighed.

CHAPTER 15

"Let me see if I've got this right." I scratched my head. "A man on his honeymoon who has no history before 1975 mysteriously disappears from the world by slipping into the Mississippi as a 'probable suicide.' Nothing suspicious about that, right?"

"Not at all."

"Tell me again." I said. "What's the evidence for suicide?"

"The captain said so. Basically," Jefferson mumbled.

"What does that mean? Did he see Bucky jump into the river with his own eyes?"

"No." He chuckled. "I love how you get all sarcastic when you're skeptical. No. The captain didn't see anything. He apparently heard Bucky had lost his business, got foreclosed on by the bank, and was estranged from his kids."

"That doesn't ring true to me."

"Why? Because you had a ten-minute conversation with him over a drink? Because your superhuman ability to read people picked up some deep truth about his character?"

I smiled. "Something like that." I turned away from Jefferson and scanned the river horizon. The sky was blue and the water uncharacteristically flat. A towboat slipped past us heading downriver, pushing thirty barges filled with grain and cutting a thin path through the mirror-like surface. "I just don't buy it," I said. "Bucky seemed genuinely happy with Mathilda. He seemed excited about it, like he'd finally found 'the one.'" I paused. "He told me he was retired. There was no bitterness, no regret. No sense at all that he'd been forced to retire because of a business failure. None."

"Maybe he wanted to go out happy. You, of all people, Mr. Former Therapist, know this. Sometimes folks who've had it tough, when they finally get a good moment, when the weight they've been carrying lightens somewhat, that's when they end it all. That's when they're most likely to take their own life. Maybe that was the case for Bucky." He looked at me. "It's a possibility we should consider."

"I hear what you're saying. I just don't see how it makes sense here. I don't know much at all about his life, obviously. But nothing about what I know suggests to me he'd been through one hardship after another. Seemed like he'd had a pretty normal life of successes and disappointments." I looked at Jefferson, then Ruby.

"What do you propose we do about it?" Jefferson asked.

I thought about our options. "You've hit a wall trying to find the two killers who are supposed to be on this boat, right?"

"Right."

I shrugged. "Let's talk to Bucky's wife."

"She's already off the boat," Jefferson said. "Might be hard to track her down."

"I bet a hot-shot, big-city detective like you can track down anyone you want when you put your mind to it, right?"

He sighed. "I suppose I could give it a shot. And we definitely need to do something different." He turned to face me. "What would you ask her?"

"I hadn't thought that far ahead." I looked away from him and imagined how a conversation with her might go. "I'd just like to get more of his bio.

Find out what she knows about his life before they met. What she thinks about the likelihood that he killed himself." I scratched my head again. "Would you add anything to that?"

"Sure. I'd like to know more about what happened the other night—the night he died. It looks like he went back to his room after you talked with him at the bar, then left again. And left his phone behind. From what I've been told, he didn't get any messages that might have induced him out. Seems he just left."

"Except I thought he got a text message when I was talking with him at the bar."

"Yeah, but there were no recent texts on his phone, remember?"

"Right. And there weren't any messages from earlier in the day that might have offered clues?"

"From what I've been told, no."

Ruby smiled widely.

"What?" I asked her.

"Oh, nothing. It just makes me happy when you two put your heads together to figure something out. Don't let me stop you." She looked toward the door. "In fact, I'm going back to our stateroom for a short rest before lunch. Come and get me when you're ready to eat."

"Will do," I said.

"Now what?" I asked Jefferson.

"Let's catch up with Michelle."

"Come in," she said, with all the enthusiasm of someone registering a vehicle at the DMV. She stepped back in front of her bed and crossed her arms. "What's up, boys?"

"I just heard from the security chief that the official cause of death for Bucky Jones is going to be listed as a probable suicide," Jefferson said.

Her shoulders sagged. "Do you think that's what actually happened?"

Jefferson looked at me, then back at Michelle. "No." He shook his head. "No. Feels like someone's jumping to conclusions." He slipped his hands in his pants pockets. "But I understand why."

"Why?" she asked.

"There's not much to go on." He shrugged. "No evidence of foul play. Not even any signs of an accident. Nothing. That makes it easier to settle on the idea that he just jumped into the river to end his own life."

"What makes you think that's not what happened?"

He turned to me. "Frank?"

"I used to work as a therapist," I said. "Was good at it, too. I understand people well."

"He does," Jefferson added.

"Thanks." I looked at Michelle, who rolled her eyes. "Look. I didn't know Bucky well. Obviously. But I'd bet anything that he was in a good place. Happy about his new marriage. Glad to be done selling cars, a choice I believe he made voluntarily." She nodded subtly. "I just don't see any hint that he was a man who was ready to die."

Her eyes narrowed. "You feel sure about that?"

"I do."

"Good." She steadied her gaze on me, then moved it over to Jefferson, her right foot tapping furiously. "Fine." She bent down, pulled a suitcase out from under the bed, and opened it. "Let me show you something." She removed a manila envelope, then pulled a piece of paper out of it. "This is a marriage certificate for Lonnie Sims." She handed it to Jefferson.

"'Lonnie Sims,'" he read aloud, "'seventeen years old, married Rebbecca Nash, twenty years old, in Vicksburg, Mississippi, June 1, 1974.'" He looked up at Michelle. "That's the guy who tipped you off, isn't it?"

"Sure is."

"And he got married in Vicksburg a month before your father was murdered?"

"Right." She closed the suitcase and looked over at me. "I had forgotten all about that marriage until you brought it up at dinner last night." She stood up straight.

"Wait," I scrunched my face. "Are you saying you think Bucky Jones might have been Lonnie Sims?"

"Maybe," Jefferson said. "That's what we're circling around."

"But he didn't tell me he would be on this boat, too," Michelle said. "Why not? I could have talked to him directly."

"Maybe that's why," Jefferson said. "Like he told you when he called, he wanted to make amends to you, but he wasn't willing to completely rat out his friends. If you knew he was going to be on this boat, too, you would have dogged him until he broke."

"Got that right."

"He probably knew you had stalked Otis Morris," I said.

Michelle shook her head. "Damn it! Are these guys all going to die before I catch them?"

Jefferson stepped toward her cautiously. "Look. I know you're frustrated, but you came here expecting to find two men who killed your father. The Bell brothers. If Bucky Jones really was Lonnie Sims, it doesn't change anything." He lightly touched her back, then let his arm fall to the side. "We need to do what we can to figure out if Bucky was Lonnie, but regardless, we still have the same mission. Find the Bell brothers."

"Right. You're right." She closed her eyes briefly. "I'm sorry if I was too harsh on everyone last night." She opened her eyes again and looked at Jefferson.

"I respect your passion," I said. "And I don't want to inject myself into a situation where I'm not wanted. But I think I can help."

"Thank you," she said. "My sisters and I have different priorities. Different lives. I'm still trying to hold Papa's killers accountable. They think I should just let go and move on." She flailed her arms. "But I finally feel like I might actually find them. I'm *this* close." She held a thumb and forefinger up to demonstrate.

"I agree," Jefferson said. "I feel it, too." He reached out and held her hands. "Which is all the more reason to let us help you. I . . ."—he looked over at me, then back to Michelle—"we . . . understand that this is your fight. We honestly do. But we can help." He said the last word with force. "We can help you find these men. To serve justice on them. We want to do this for *you*, not for us. Will you let us?"

She stared into Jefferson's eyes, and for a moment, she looked like she might tear up. Then she let go of Jefferson's hands and took a step away from him. "Fine," she said. "Y'all can help. But I'm in charge." She poked at Jefferson's chest. "I'm in charge. Got it?"

"Got it," Jefferson said.

She looked at me.

"Got it," I said.

CHAPTER 16

We stood looking at one another for a minute in Michelle's room. Jefferson broke the silence. "Let's get to work. I'm going to track down a phone number for Bucky's widow. When I get it, Frank'll give her a call, to see if he can sort out just how likely it was for Bucky to kill himself." He looked at me with raised eyebrows. "Sound good?"

"Sounds good," Michelle said.

"What do you know about Miss Rebbecca Nash?"

"Absolutely nothing."

Jefferson looked over at me. "Looks like we've got one more person to track down."

I checked the time on my phone. "Shit. I need to run. Gotta check out a few places in St. Francisville before we push off." I waved quickly. "Gotta get my article done, right?"

"Go," Jefferson said. "Do your work and catch up with us later."

On my way downstairs, I called Ruby. "Hey. I need to run into town for a bit to do some research for my article, so no lunch for me today. Sorry about that."

"It's OK, Frank. Call me when you're back."

"Will do."

I stopped at the Bow Bar to pick up a snack from the lunch buffet, then walked down the gangway and onto land. I had a couple of businesses I wanted to check out—art galleries—but mostly I just wanted to walk around.

The weather was gorgeous: eighty degrees, a few puffy clouds floating by that offered brief respite from the direct sun, a light breeze. I walked uphill from the landing into town. I underestimated how far it was—a full mile into the middle of town, which took twenty minutes and some heavy breathing. Once in town, the sweet scent of gardenias welcomed me. I walked past modest antebellum homes built to resemble their plantation cousins. Gothic brick churches sat serenely, surrounded by live oaks dripping with Spanish moss. Quaint.

It was easy to see why tourism was one of the major industries driving the St. Francisville economy. And all those visitors wouldn't readily know that the other two major industries driving the city's modern economy were nuclear power and incarceration (the infamous Angola prison is just twenty miles from town). Most of those tourists stop for an hour or two to buy antiques or a painting. Or maybe they'd stick around longer to tour one of the old plantations nearby or to meditate in the well-tended gardens of the Hemingbough cultural center.

I had time only for a quick visit, however. No plantations or garden tours were on my agenda. Instead, I found the two galleries that interested me, interviewed the owners, and got a few quotes for my article. The owners were chattier than I expected, so I had to hightail it back to the boat before departure. I didn't need the complication of finding an overland way to Natchez to rejoin my cruise.

"Welcome back, Mr. Dodge," First Mate LeJeune said as I sprinted onto the boat. "I was getting worried. Thought we might have to leave ya behind."

The hotel manager, Barry Riggs, stood next to him. He was shaking his head. "I was just about to run into town to find you," he said. Given his age and frame, I assumed he wasn't being literal. "So happy to have you back with us now. Need anything?"

"No thanks," I waved him off. "I'm good."

Five minutes later, deckhands raised the gangplank, and the boat slowly backed away from the landing and eased into the main channel of the Mississippi.

I texted Jefferson for an update. He called me back.

"Frank. I got Mathilda's number." He sounded excited. "When can you call her?"

"Text me her number. I'll call once I find a place with some privacy."

"Coming right up. And call me right after you talk with her."

"Of course."

I walked up to the Paddlewheel Pub, which was nearly empty. I thought about what to say, how to introduce myself. How to ask "Do you think your new husband really killed himself?" I felt nervous, and that surprised me. I paced around the deck. I got a napkin from the bartender and jotted down a couple of questions. After that, I felt as ready as I ever would. I walked to a quiet spot in the middle of the hurricane deck and dialed Mathilda's number.

"Hello?" She picked up right away. I wasn't expecting that.

"Is this Mrs. Mathilda Jones?"

"Yes. Who is this, please?"

"Hi, Mrs. Jones. This is Frank Dodge. We met over dinner on the *River Voyager*."

"Oh, yes. I remember. What can I do for you, Mr. Dodge?"

"I just wanted to say how sorry I am, to offer my condolences for your loss."

"Thank you. How thoughtful."

"I had a chance to chat with your husband, with Bucky, in the Paddlewheel Pub the other night, before he . . . before he disappeared. He couldn't say enough about how much he loved you. How excited he was to start a new life with you."

I heard some muted sobbing, as if she'd put a hand over the phone. "Thank you. We hardly had any time together, you know."

"I know. I'm sorry he didn't have more time to enjoy with you in his retirement. I imagine he was looking forward to that."

"Bucky was very good at putting his best face forward."

A couple of other passengers walked near me, so I drifted toward the stern to get away from them. "What do you mean?"

She cleared her throat. "Bucky was in a . . . difficult place. He didn't want to retire. I hate to say so, but it's true. His business wasn't doing well. He was forced—the bank forced him to sell it. The car business had changed a lot over the years, but he was still working like it hadn't. So, he sold what was left to pay back the bank."

"I'm sorry. I didn't know that." I was taken aback. Apparently, Bucky had covered up well. "So, I guess you could say he had retired involuntarily."

"Yes. That's what I'd say. And what Bucky said."

"He mentioned that he'd been married before. Did he have children?"

"Yes. A son and a daughter. Unfortunately, they didn't see eye to eye. He hadn't seen them in years." She sniffled. "He invited them to our wedding, but they didn't come."

"He seemed like a personable guy. You probably have to be to sell cars. You must have heard condolences from a lot of his old friends."

"Yes. I've heard from quite a few. And even some old customers. Bucky was easy to like, as you found out yourself."

"Other than his children, did he have any other living family members?"

"I don't think so. He never talked about any family, except for his children, so I can't speak to that." She paused. "I'm sure Bucky would have said something about other family if he'd had any. Family was important to him. But he was also the type of person who lived in the present. He wasn't one to look back. And he certainly didn't talk about his past much, so I don't know much about his life before we met. He told me that the here and now is all we have, so why worry about the then and gone?" I heard some shuffling. "I must be going soon. Is there anything else, Mr. Dodge?"

"I appreciate your time. Bucky's disappearance is so tragic. I don't quite know how to ask this, but . . . it's something that's been bothering me. I've heard speculation that Bucky's disappearance may have been . . . intentional. I find it hard to believe, but I was wondering how that sat with you?"

"I'll be honest with you, Mr. Dodge. No one likes the idea that a loved one might choose to end their own life. I'm no different. But . . ." I heard someone shuffling. "I'm not entirely surprised, Mr. Dodge. Like I said, Bucky had some challenges in his life. And I'm not sure he felt like the good in his life outweighed the bad."

"Even after marrying you? After all, he seemed very happy with you."

She didn't answer right away, but I heard more shuffling. "Who among us wouldn't like to think that our love was strong enough to prevent harm from coming to the people in our lives, Mr. Dodge? I know Bucky loved me. But maybe it wasn't as strong as I thought. Or as powerful."

I felt like I had pushed too hard. "Thank you for taking time to talk with me. I really just wanted to . . . needed to . . . tell you how much Bucky had gushed about you the other night. I feel distraught about his loss, too, especially since I may have been the last person he talked to."

"I appreciate your thoughtfulness. And kindness. The police told me you had talked with him. It makes me feel better knowing he left a good impression on you."

"Of course. I'm sure you have plenty of support, but if there's anything you think I could help with, please don't hesitate to call me."

"Thank you, Mr. Dodge."

She hung up, and I called Jefferson right away.

"How'd it go, Frank?"

"I'm more confused than ever."

"What do you mean?"

"He did lose his business, in a way. Mathilda confirmed it. He was losing money, so he sold it, to pay back the bank. That's not exactly voluntary retirement. And she confirmed he hadn't talked with his children—a son and a daughter—in years. All true."

"Huh."

"Huh, indeed. None of this makes sense to me, Brian." I paced on the deck again. "And I've been around a few suicides. The pieces of his life—the bits we know—well, they just don't match what Bucky told me or the feelings he conveyed when we chatted the other night at the bar. None of it."

"And you don't think he was just putting his best face forward for a stranger?"

"Sure, there may have been some of that." I thought back to our chat at the bar. "But no. I didn't pick up on any depression. No despair. No sense that he might have felt like he was done with it all." I walked to the railing. "No. I just don't see it."

"What are you thinking, Frank?"

"Just that the more I learn, the more confused I get. Makes me think we're missing something here. Something important."

"Me, too. Me, too, buddy. Let's put our heads together after dinner—you, me, and Michelle. Maybe we've overlooked something."

CHAPTER 17

Ruby and I lined up for dinner at six. "I'm in the mood for shrimp tonight,"
I said. "How about you?"

"I could eat shrimp anytime." She beamed.

After we sat down, we scanned the menu for the daily offerings. Shrimp
was an option two ways: as a shrimp scampi appetizer and as an entrée-size
gumbo with shrimp and andouille. "I know what I'm having," I said. "Split
shrimp scampi with me?"

"Sounds good." She scanned the menu a little longer. "I haven't had a
good steak in a while. Filet mignon sounds delicious." She put the menu
down. "Did you talk with Bucky's wife?"

"Sure did." After the server took our orders, I leaned forward so I could
whisper. "She confirmed much of what we'd heard." I shook my head.
"Bucky was forced to retire. He had two kids he never saw. Not sure what
to make of it."

"Maybe he just hid his troubles well." Ruby leaned toward me. "He
wouldn't be the first man to do so."

"I know." I fiddled with my fork. "Sometimes I can get things wrong, but
I can't shake the feeling that something is off with this story." I looked away
from Ruby. "The other night at the bar, my conversation with Bucky. He
seemed like . . ."—I turned to face her—"like a man who had finally settled

into a place where he felt comfortable." I paused. "Like he had something to look forward to. A man like that doesn't then turn around and throw himself into a river to die."

"I would think not. But if he didn't kill himself, then what happened? He slipped off accidentally?"

"Maybe." Our server came by and set shrimp scampi between us. I smelled garlic. A lot of garlic. I leaned forward again and said softly, "Or maybe someone killed him." I stabbed a piece of shrimp and put it in my mouth.

Ruby slid a couple of shrimp onto a small plate. She wasn't smiling anymore. "Do you suppose he could be connected to the murderers that Michelle is trying to identify?"

"You mean, like one of them?"

"Yes. I suppose that's where I was going." She glanced up at me, then back down to her plate.

"It crossed my mind. I know it's crossed Michelle's mind, too." We finished the scampi in silence, then our server came by with our entrées. We didn't waste time before digging into them. Our conversation shifted to Natchez, our next stop on the cruise, and the history we would be stepping into there.

"One of the richest cities in the country, at one time," I said. "At least in terms of the number of millionaires per capita."

"Yes. I read about that. It was a popular place to build a mansion. If you were a plantation owner who owned a lot of human beings."

"Are you going to take the bus tour tomorrow morning?"

"Probably. I have such mixed feelings about these places, especially after our tour of Camellia Crossing." Ruby cut a slice of steak and slid it around in a sauce, releasing the smell of butter-soaked mushrooms. "But I feel like

I should see them for myself." She lifted the fork toward her mouth, then changed her mind and rested it on her plate. "We'll see how long that feeling lasts. I don't need to see all of them. Goodness. I don't understand how people could do that. One or two more will be more than enough for me." She put the steak in her mouth and chewed.

"I know what you mean. But I know you like beautiful buildings, and some of these mansions are impressive, from an architectural perspective." I dipped a spoon into the gumbo and let its savory scent hang in the air in front of me. "I'm sure you'll enjoy the tour. Just don't think about the human suffering that made it all possible." I ate the spoonful of gumbo.

She grimaced. "If I were sitting next to you, I'd smack you on the arm." She smiled. "What's next for you?"

"I'm going to chat with the assistant engineer tonight. He's got a story about another time a passenger went overboard, one of the few other times from what I've figured out. I'd like to hear about it. Maybe I can get another article out of his story." I scooped some gumbo into my mouth. "Not sure what time I'll get to bed after that, so I'll just freestyle it in Natchez. I've got a few places I need to visit for the article. Getting a few quotes would be good, too."

"Will you be going to the show tonight?"

"I sure hope so. I'd love to see what festive singing and dancing they have in store for us tonight."

"Oh. I guess you didn't see the program. There's a guest band playing tonight. Bluegrass, I think."

"So, no Deion tonight?"

"I don't think so." She cut another thin slice of steak. "Have you heard back from him?"

"No. Not yet." I leaned back in my chair. "But in fairness to him, last time he didn't confirm until the morning of. So, I shouldn't get ahead of myself, should I?"

"No. You certainly should not." She grinned as she chewed a piece of the tenderloin.

"Bluegrass sounds fun, too. I've got to touch base with Brian and Michelle. If that doesn't take long, I'll join you in the auditorium."

"OK. I'll save you a seat."

After dinner, Ruby returned to our stateroom for a brief rest while I met Michelle and Jefferson in the Paddlewheel Pub. I found them standing on the far side of the bar next to the railing, drinks in hand, their conversation obscured by the repeated thumping of the paddlewheel. Jefferson saw me and waved me over. The sun had set, and the air was pleasant but cooling quickly.

"I know you already gave me a summary of your phone conversation with Mathilda," Jefferson began, "but I'd . . ."—he glanced at Michelle—"we'd like to hear more. What exactly did Mathilda say?"

"I guess I'll get a drink later."

"Answer our questions first, then you can get a drink. It won't take long."

"Fine. She told me that Bucky hadn't retired voluntarily. That he owned a car dealership, but it hadn't been doing well. He must have had a bank loan, because she told me a bank pressured him to sell the business to pay them back."

"OK. That's good," Jefferson said. He turned to look at Michelle. "We need to find the name of Bucky's dealership. Then it shouldn't be hard to track down the name of the bank that he owed money to."

"You want to verify that part of the story, I assume?"

He turned back to me. "Yeah. Gotta check on every detail, especially with so much we don't know. And given your . . . our . . . suspicions about Bucky's death being something other than suicide. What else did Mathilda tell you?"

"That Bucky had two children he never saw. That he invited them to his wedding—with Mathilda—but they didn't show up."

"Good. We'll follow up on that, too." He looked at Michelle again. "You have a copy of Bucky's first marriage record, right?"

I raised my eyebrows. I knew Michelle had been busy looking up what she could about Bucky, but I didn't know what she'd actually found. "Do you mean you found his first marriage as Bucky Jones?"

"That's right," Michelle said. "I could probably also track down the names of his children. Then what?"

"I'll give them a call. Pretend I'm an insurance agent or something, so I can ask them about their relationship with Bucky." I'd seen this Jefferson before. Focused. Excited. Running all kinds of angles through his mind. I liked this Jefferson. "Anything else, Frank?"

"Let's see." I thought back to my conversation with Mathilda. "She said Bucky had never talked about any other family members." I paused. "Oh. There was one other thing. Something that felt odd in the moment, but maybe I overreacted."

"What's that?" Michelle asked.

"I asked her—delicately—if she thought it was possible that Bucky had killed himself. Her answer was rather . . . what's the word I'm looking for here? Detached?"

"What do you mean?" Michelle asked.

"I don't want to make this into something bigger than it is. Don't get me wrong. But she said something like . . ."—I winced—"maybe he didn't love her enough to want to keep living. I've definitely heard that from people who've lost someone to suicide. But when she said it, she sounded flat. Not much emotion behind it. Maybe she'd already cried herself dry. I don't know." I bit my lip. "I just thought it sounded a bit too . . . pat."

"Well, I think we can give her some latitude in how she expresses her grief," Jefferson said.

"Of course. I agree. But you asked about our conversation and what I thought of it. I'm just being honest."

"Thank you, Mr. Dodge"—Michelle shook her head—"Frank. Sorry. Good job." She reached out quickly to shake my hand.

"Anything else?" Jefferson asked Michelle.

"No." She took a step back and shook her head slowly from side to side. "I just can't believe we're so close." She forced a smile. "You know, I still remember that day, the day we got the phone call from the police that they'd found Papa's body. Like it was yesterday." She cleared her throat. "The tension in that house. Hmm. For weeks, we were in limbo, wondering what had happened to him. I later suspected there wasn't much doubt in Mama's head. Back in those days, when a Black man went missing, he almost never turned up alive."

"What do you remember happening after your mom got the call?" I asked.

"Mama burst into tears. Fell on the floor. I don't think she even got the phone hung back up." She looked away from us. "I didn't understand what had happened, of course, not until a while later. But I knew it meant Papa was never coming home again. I cried about that." She leaned against the rail. "But I also remember wondering who was going to tell me bedtime stories if Papa was gone. I loved his stories." She smiled and nodded subtly. "Every night for as far back as I can remember, he'd tell me a story to help me fall asleep. I had been a fussy child. So my mama said." She sighed. "Papa started telling me stories to quiet my mind. Sometimes he read from a book, but most of the stories, I'm sure, were ones he'd made up or heard from his parents." She shrugged. "It worked. I almost never made it all the way through one of his stories awake." She turned back to us. "After he was gone, I had trouble falling asleep again. So, I did the only thing I could think of that might help. I started telling bedtime stories to Yolanda and Angela." She laughed softly. "I wasn't very good at it, I'm sure. I was still a kid, after all. And it sure didn't make me any better rested. I know that. But it did for them. I could put them right to sleep." She stood up straight. Jefferson wrapped an arm around her. She relaxed into his embrace. "Well, anyway, if we're going to figure out who these two guys are, we've got a lot more digging to do." She looked over at Jefferson.

Jefferson glared at me. "Well, what are you waiting for, Frank? Now would be a good time to get that drink. Or to go watch the evening show."

Michelle's eyes opened wide, and she waved toward the bar. "You probably need to write about it for your article, right?"

I knew when I was being shooed away. I nodded, excused myself, and made my way down to the auditorium.

CHAPTER 18

Michelle had just given me the brush-off, but I didn't mind. She was right. I should watch the show and write something about it. And leave them alone to do whatever they needed to do next. But I didn't have to feel good about it.

When I got to the auditorium, I found Ruby—as promised, she had saved me a seat—and we enjoyed forty-five minutes of foot-stomping bluegrass from a guest band. They were good. Very good. I hoped the boat's entertainment director always chose guest musicians so well. Still, I would've been just as happy to watch Deion and the other on-board musicians do another show of their own.

Ruby retired to our stateroom after the show, and I went back to the Paddlewheel Pub for a drink. By then, Michelle and Jefferson were gone. I didn't feel talkative, so I took out a notebook and jotted down a few questions for the assistant engineer I'd be chatting with—I hoped—in a couple of hours. After a couple of drinks, I slipped back into our stateroom for a nap.

I didn't expect to snooze for long, but when I woke up, it was 11:55. I had only five minutes to get down to deck one and catch the assistant engineer on break. After splashing water on my face, I ran down to the Eads Bar. I wasn't sure how to find him, so I said to the bartender, "I'm supposed to interview Ted Stevens in Engineering about his history on the river. Where might he be?"

"Down those stairs," she said as she pointed. "That'll take you to the engine room. I'll call him and tell him you're looking for him."

"Thanks."

The machines hummed louder with every step down, and the air felt stickier and warmer. I smelled diesel. When I got to the bottom, I stopped at the gate and waited.

I couldn't help but feel claustrophobic while waiting. Machinery took up most of the space below deck, dull steel machines surrounded by light gray walls. Pistons pumped back and forth, producing a rhythmic beat. Gauges and knobs told the Engineering team exactly what was going on with each machine—coded messages I couldn't decipher. A desk with a computer and two screens looked like the control center monitoring it all.

"Are you the reporter looking for me?" I heard someone ask.

I turned to my left and saw a man a few inches taller than me. His face was wan and deeply ridged. "Are you Ted Stevens?"

"I am."

"Then, yeah. I'm Frank Dodge. I'm writing an article about this cruise for a magazine called *Luxe Liners*. But that's not why I'm here. I love talking to experienced river folks about their lives on the river."

He sighed and crossed his arms. "You mean you like hearing old river rats tell a few tall tales?"

I smiled. "Exactly."

His eyes narrowed and locked on me. "You found the right guy." He looked at his watch. "I'm on break for another twenty-five minutes. You have me until then." He looked around. "Follow me."

He opened the gate, and we walked through the engine room to a side door, then stepped outside. "It'll be quieter out here." He leaned against a wall, then lit a cigarette. "What can I tell you, Mr. Dodge?"

He wasn't entirely right about the quiet. The rhythmic splashing from the paddlewheel made it a little hard to hear him, but at least it was more private. The night air was also colder than I'd expected. I shivered as we talked, wishing I'd had the foresight to bring a jacket. "Please, call me Frank. How long have you worked on the river?"

He held the first drag a bit, then exhaled a cloud of smoke that carried a hint of whiskey. "All my adult life, Frank. I started as a deckhand, like a lot of us on this boat."

"Where'd you grow up?"

"Kentucky, western Kentucky. Near the Mississippi, of course."

I chuckled. "So, I assume you grew up fishing, hunting, and so on. Generally spending a lot of time on the river?"

"That's a fair assumption. My granddaddy was a commercial fisherman, in fact. But it got hard to make a living from that as he got older, so none of his kids picked it up. But I guarantee they all grew up knowing how to catch, clean, and cook catfish."

"And I'm sure your family has its own secret recipe for the perfect catfish dinner."

"Of course. But we ate catfish any time of day. Ever enjoyed catfish and grits for breakfast?"

"Can't say I have."

"Well then, Frank, you haven't lived a full life." He took another deep drag off the cigarette. "I keep telling the cook on this boat it should be on the breakfast menu, but she just brushes me off."

"If you shared your family recipe, I'd promise to give it a try. And keep it out of this article." I smiled.

"We'll see. I'm not in the habit of handing out family secrets to strangers."

"Fair enough." I nodded. "What boats have you worked on?"

"Like I said, I started as a deckhand. Did that for a while. The work agreed with me, at least until I threw out my back. Then I started thinking about other careers. I was already pretty good with small motors, so I asked the engineer a lot of questions about the towboat's engines. I saw potential in that. Learned a lot about them and electrical systems from him, then used that to land a job in the engine room of the *Delta Queen*."

"Wow. She's river royalty. That must have been an interesting job."

"A pain in the ass." He flipped the cigarette into the river. "That's what I'd call her. Her engine room looked like a Smithsonian exhibit. Filled with old, outdated equipment." He wiped his hands on his jeans. "We were constantly patching things up to keep her moving." He rubbed his temples.

"That boat's been off the water for a while now. Do you think she'll ever cruise the river again?"

"Don't see how. Unless some bored billionaire wants to throw his kids' inheritance at her to fix her up. There's just too much to replace. Not just fix—replace. Probably be cheaper to build a new boat."

"How long did you work on the *Delta Queen*?"

"Twelve years, I think. There were rumors going around that the company was in trouble. Layoffs sounded real possible. But I got lucky. This boat here"—he waved a hand around—"had an opening in the engine room, so I applied and got hired. Been here ever since."

"I hope this boat's in better shape than the *Delta Queen*."

"Much. But honestly, even if it weren't, I wouldn't tell a reporter." He glanced at his watch.

"We're still good?"

"Sure. I've got a few more minutes."

"There's one other thing I wanted to ask you about. We lost a passenger overboard a couple of nights ago, as you know. How often has something like that happened, in your experience?"

"Almost never," he said quickly.

"Which is a good thing. For all of us." I rubbed my hands together to warm them up. "But I heard a rumor that you might have been on a boat a while back when another person disappeared into the river."

"Yeah. I've told a few people that story."

"Can you share it with me?"

He looked toward the river, although there wasn't much we could see in the dark. "The river has certainly claimed its share of people traveling on these boats. Sure, some of them went over in accidents—boiler explosions, that kind of thing. And sometimes passengers would get in a fight that ended with one of them in the river. Those things almost never happen anymore." He turned back to me. "Not long after I started working on the *Delta Queen*, we had an incident where a young guy disappeared, a passenger. His girlfriend woke up in the morning and noticed he wasn't there. Some women might dream of that day"—he scowled. "Not this one, though. We searched the whole boat and couldn't find hide nor hair of him." He crossed his arms. "We'd been cruising the whole time since he was last seen, so there was no way he'd just slipped off the boat at port. He had to have gone in the river." He tapped his fingers on the rail. "Our security chief, a guy who had worked as a county sheriff, initially figured the missing man had either fallen in the river by accident or had done himself in."

"Sounds a lot like what happened here."

"So far. The chief kept asking around about what the kid—he was in his twenties, which seems like a kid to me now—had been doing on the boat, about his life before the cruise. Lots of questions." He straightened his back. "Come to find out that he and an older guy had been arguing the day before he went missing." He rolled his eyes. "Some other passengers overheard them. The older guy accused the kid of hitting on his wife." He raised an eyebrow.

"So, he killed the kid?"

He waved his hands at me. "You're jumping ahead of the story, Frank."

"Sorry."

He glanced inside the engine room. "But since I've got to get back to work in a minute, I'll cut to the chase. After asking around for a while, the security chief discovered the older guy had lured the kid out in the middle of the night. Got his wife to tell the kid to meet on a port side walkway close to the bow. Like she was setting up a clandestine rendezvous." He took the time to slowly, carefully speak those last two words. "When the kid showed up, the older guy smacked him in the head with a crowbar he'd lifted from Engineering." He simulated the act for me. "The kid collapsed, then rolled into the river. That older guy might have gotten away with it, too." He nodded. "Folks like to believe this river is so dangerous that it can reach out and grab a man off a boat and swallow him up. The chief wasn't one of them. He kept talking to passengers, asking questions. Eventually, another passenger told him he'd seen those two men arguing. I'll spare you the rest of the details on the chief's investigation, but he ended up getting a confession."

He took a step away from the rail. "Once the chief knew where it happened on the boat, he found a couple of blood stains on the railing. A few weeks later, the kid's corpse turned up around the Angola prison landing. He had a big ol' bruise on the front of his head." He pointed to his forehead. "Is that the kind of river story you were looking for?"

"Yeah. That's a good one. But I've also got a twisted sense of fun."

"Good. But that's all you're getting now. I've got to get back to work."

"Quick question before you leave. Do you have a gut sense about what happened to the man who went overboard on this trip?"

"Suicide, right? That's what they're saying? Didn't know the man, but I've had a couple of friends who killed themselves." He looked down and shook his head. "Hard to know what's going on inside a man's head." He tapped on his temple. "And this boat is designed to make it very hard to slip off accidentally, so I don't see that happening."

"Someone could have killed him . . ."

"I thought you might go there. I suppose that's possible, too. But we've got good security on this boat. Cameras in a few places. Crew walking around all the time keeping an eye on things." He paused and looked off into the distance, then back to me. "Still, I could imagine a way a guy might just slip into the water and disappear without being noticed. On the other hand, if there was a confrontation with someone else, I'd think someone would have taken notice. And it's hard to imagine no one hearing a splash." He paused. "Unless . . ."

"Unless what?"

"Well"—he paused and looked around—"I suppose if he went overboard in a part of the ship where there was a lot of noise, maybe you wouldn't hear a splash."

"Where might that be?"

"Well, like here, I suppose." He looked around. "The splashes from the paddlewheel hitting the water over and over might disguise the sound of a body going overboard. I'm sure there are other spots, too." He nodded toward the engine room. "And now I gotta get back to work."

"Thanks for your time, Ted. I appreciate it." We shook hands.

"I hope that gave you what you wanted, Frank." He turned around and walked back into the engine room.

"And then some," I muttered into the night.

<h1 style="text-align:center">CHAPTER 19</h1>

When I got up the next morning, I had a text from Deion.

Coffee at 9?

I replied with a thumbs-up emoji, then breathed a sigh of relief.

"Good morning, Ruby." She was sitting in bed reading, wearing a simple beige dress.

"How'd your late-night interview go?" she asked.

"Good, but quick. May have to track him down again later to get a few more details, but I think he's got a lot of stories to tell."

"Will you be using any of it for your article?"

"Nah. Don't think so. It's just that when I'm around folks who've spent a lot of time on the river, I like to hear their stories. To add to my collection." I sat up in bed and stretched. "Then again, maybe I'll find an angle to write a story about people falling off river cruises."

Ruby nodded. "Well, I'm glad you got what you wanted. Breakfast?"

I scratched the back of my neck. "Um, sorry. Not for me today. Deion invited me to coffee."

She set her book down. "I suspected he'd get in touch again."

"Well, that's one of us anyway. I'm going to take a quick shower, then run down to meet him." I turned and sat on the side of the bed. "What are you doing today?"

"I'm going to take the bus tour around town. I've never been to Natchez, so I should see what I can while I'm here, in spite of my misgivings."

"Sounds like a good idea to me. I know you'll enjoy it. What time are you back?"

"It's all day. I think we get back around three."

"Got it. I need to run into town for my article, so let's catch up after you're back."

"Good morning," I said, as I sat down across from Deion.

He glanced at me, then looked away. "Good morning, Frank."

"Thank you for the coffee invite." I looked at the buffet. "Can I get you something?"

"No thank you. But go ahead and help yourself." He had leaned back in the chair. He'd crossed his arms, and a foot was tapping on the ground. He wasn't keeping time to a song in his head.

"Be right back." I got myself a cup of coffee and an apple Danish and sat down at the table again. "That guest band was really terrific last night."

"Thank you. I heard them when I was on vacation in Tennessee and knew right away they'd be perfect for this boat."

"So, you hired them?"

"Basically, yes. I may not have told you this before, but I'm the music director for the boat."

"Fantastic!" I leaned forward. "What does that mean, exactly?"

His foot stopped moving, and he sat up straight. "It means I do the arrangements for the shows, direct the performers, that kind of thing. I also have a say in hiring the guest performers. It's a lot of work, but I'm loving it."

"How'd you get from intern at the Ragtime Renaissance Museum to music director on the *River Voyager*?"

He inched his chair a little closer. "As graduation day approached, I was having a hard time finding a job that excited me. I thought about going to grad school, but I was tired of classrooms by then." He frowned. "My mom had seen an ad from a river cruise looking for performers, so she passed it along to me. I applied and got hired right after graduation. The pay wasn't great—isn't great—but at least I got to play music. I did that for three years. And loved it!" A big, electric smile spread over his face. "When the music director left, they asked me to take the job. Maybe because I was the only performer who kept coming up with new ideas for shows. They couldn't shut me up, so they made me the boss!"

I smiled. "When we met, I knew right away that you were talented. I'm not surprised they put you in charge." I took a bite of the Danish. "Is this something you think you could do for a while?"

"Don't know yet." He shrugged. "It's been fun, creative, coming up with ideas for the shows and putting new spins on old songs. I can imagine a time, though, when it might be too . . . routine." He leaned forward and rested an elbow on the table. "I've been writing songs on my downtime. Maybe someday, I'll record a few and see what happens."

"What are they like? You were very into ragtime four years ago, and the music you do on the boat is a callback to older styles."

He looked down and drew patterns with a finger on the table. "Yeah, it's not like that. That music is inspiring to me, but what I'm writing now might better fit into what folks call neo-soul."

"Have you shared the songs with anyone?" I hoped he'd volunteer to sing a part of one of them.

"Just a couple and just with family. So far."

"Well, I look forward to seeing Deion Boyd's songs in the Top 40 someday." I took another bite of the Danish, then wiped my mouth with a napkin. "If the Top 40 is still a thing."

"Don't think so, but I appreciate the sentiment." He crossed his arms and sat back. "I read that article of yours. The one you told me about where you tried to get yourself killed traveling through Panama."

I laughed. "That might be just a bit of an overstatement. I don't think I was ever in any real danger. I traveled with a lot of people." Truthfully, we did have a couple of close calls, mostly because of my stupidity. I didn't enjoy talking about it.

"Whatever you say." He grinned and looked down at the floor. "Your writing is good, though." He looked back up at me. "It kept my attention."

"You sound surprised."

"I am! And shouldn't I be?" He waved a finger at me. "Remember, when we first met, you were still getting started as a writer. You didn't seem to believe you'd make it."

"That's true. I was full of doubts back then."

He looked me over, then said, "What other life-threatening adventures have you been up to?"

More than I could tell you about over a cup of coffee. I looked down and away from him. "For one . . ." I faced him again. "For one assignment, I got caught in a bitter dispute between a chocolatier and an ice cream maker."

"Sounds tasty." He smirked.

"You'd think. I got a couple of articles out of it, at least."

"Why do I feel like there's more to the story than you're telling me?"

"Because you're perceptive?" I smiled. "It's a story probably better told over drinks stronger than coffee." I scanned the bar. "And away from this boat."

"Why?" He looked around. "Is there someone on this boat connected to that story?" He quickly leaned forward and dropped his arms on the table. "Is the chocolatier on board?" He glanced from side to side. "Or the ice cream maker?"

"No. Not them." I leaned toward him and rested an arm on the table. "There's another writer on board: Helen Kraft." I whispered her name. "She's part of that story. We don't have a good history." I sat back. "And now she's on this boat. Hired to write a profile of the captain for his last cruise. So, I have to be careful what I say. She has a habit of turning up at the most inopportune times. At least for me."

He gasped. "Frank Dodge has an enemy!"

"A rival, not an enemy."

"Still. Intriguing!" His eyes opened wide, and he rested his chin in a hand. "Were you working on the same story?"

"Not exactly. She's more established than me—at least, she was back then. Got better assignments, with better-paying magazines." I scowled. "But she's also ruthless."

"Like how?"

"When I was getting started as a freelance writer, not long after you and I met, I was researching a couple of story ideas. That's when I met her. She seemed enthusiastic about helping me, so I told her what I was researching.

A few weeks after that, I saw one of those ideas turned into an article for a national magazine. She wrote it."

"She stole your idea?"

"Sure looked like it to me. She disagreed, of course. Insisted that I can't own an idea." I growled. "That she had every right to go after a similar story."

"Feels shady to me." He sat back in his chair.

"Thanks. I sure feel . . . felt that way."

"You don't anymore?"

"Not exactly. Let's just say I've figured out that it's not good for me to hold on to old resentments. What happened happened." I leaned into the table again and whispered, "But I still don't trust her."

"Broken trust is a bitch, isn't it?" He smiled slightly. I fidgeted in my chair. "Well, Frank Dodge. This has been fun, but I need to get to work."

"Of course. Coffee again tomorrow morning?"

"Sure. Same time and place?"

"See you then." He got up and walked away. I leaned back and relaxed in the chair.

Chapter 20

I hadn't been to Natchez in a while, so with the *River Voyager* in port until four in the afternoon, I figured this was as good a time as any to flesh out ideas for future articles. I'd have most of the day to poke around, especially since Jefferson and Michelle had told me to butt out of their investigation until they invited me back in. Besides, I figured the city would still be polished and dressed up after celebrating its tricentennial the year before. And I couldn't ask for better weather, with temperatures in the upper seventies and enough cloud cover to offer relief while I walked around.

On the way to the gangplank, Barry Riggs nearly ran me over. "So sorry! I didn't see you there, Mr. Dodge."

"Are you always in a hurry, Mr. Riggs?"

"Sure feels that way." He laughed, then put a hand on his chest. "But I love what I'm doing." He tilted his head toward me. "Need anything today?"

"No thanks. Just headed into Natchez to check some things out."

"Wonderful! Have fun." He took a few steps from me, then turned around. "Now, don't forget to keep an eye on the time when you're off the boat." He grinned. "That was a close call yesterday."

"Thanks for the reminder, Mr. Riggs. But don't worry about me." He turned and scampered down the hallway. I admired Riggs's dedication to his job as hotel manager. But I was glad I was a writer and not charged with keeping some four hundred paying customers happy.

Right off the boat's gangplank, I stepped into the deep and complicated history of the city. The area known as Natchez Under-the-Hill was infamous in the early days of river travel, the part of Natchez that received passengers when they got off a riverboat, a bubble surrounded by thick forests and the big river. Under-the-Hill offered everything they needed: food, booze, gambling halls, brothels. And they had just as good a chance of finding the supplies they needed as getting robbed or shot. Exciting!

There's not a lot of the original place left today. As rich people built their mansions on the bluff, they frowned on the shenanigans at river level and eventually shut much of it down. Today you'll find few relics from that frontier culture—the river swept most of the old buildings away anyway. What's left suggests little of the infamy of the old place.

Nothing really caught my eye at river level, so I walked up the steep road to the top of the bluff, where most of the city sits today and where the plantation aristocracy built their mansions before the Civil War. I walked along the riverfront park to take in the stunning views. The broad Mississippi brushes up against the tall loess hills that provide a foundation for the city, then drifts to the southwest.

I thought about touring one of the plantation castles, but like Ruby, I was in the mood for history that didn't glorify or excuse slavery and exploitation. I figured I'd keep walking until I spotted an attraction that matched my mood. I walked past a popular riverfront hotel to State Street, then headed east into the business district. It didn't take long to find what I was looking for: a national-park site preserving a complicated story from our history.

William Johnson lived an exceptional life for a Black man in Natchez before the Civil War. He'd been born into slavery, but his master (who had almost certainly been his father as well) freed him at age eleven. Johnson landed an apprenticeship at his brother-in-law's barbershop. It proved to be a lucrative career for him. He eventually ran three barbershops in town. With his earnings, he bought land outside town and farmed it.

Like other top businesspeople in the South at the time, part of his success was possible because he owned several human beings who did much of the labor for him. If you stepped into his barbershop, the person who took care of you could be Johnson himself, one of his apprentices, a free Black person Johnson had hired, or one of the human beings Johnson owned. While exceedingly rare, a handful of well-off Blacks enslaved other Blacks before the Civil War. Their stories say more about the place of slavery in Southern culture than they did about the individuals themselves. Owning human beings was a status symbol in the antebellum South. A sign that you'd made it, like owning a Hummer or diamond earrings.

Ultimately, though, his wealth couldn't protect him from the racial hierarchy institutionalized in the Old South. When a mixed-race neighbor felt displeased with the result of a land survey along their shared boundary, he shot and killed Johnson. In Mississippi at that time (and throughout the South), state law banned Blacks from testifying in court against a white person (a practice that continued into the 1960s, in fact), and Johnson's killer, Baylor Winn, argued that he should be considered a white man, since his being half white and half Native American made him legally "white" in Mississippi. All the witnesses to Johnson's murder were Black. The killer was charged, but after three mistrials over a couple of years, he walked free. A complicated, meaty story.

Back on the street, I felt alternately impressed and distressed by the state of the city. Natchez had some beautiful architecture, but also a lot of decay. Beautifully rehabbed structures stood next to old buildings that looked like they could tumble down at any time. Natchezians may have once held more wealth per capita than just about any place in the U.S., but the contemporary city faced the same challenges as many rural communities: few good jobs and lots of people leaving to look for work elsewhere.

I'd been walking for a while, so I looked for a local restaurant I could dip into for lunch and rest. I didn't see a lot of variety in the food on the menus I'd been checking while walking around. Much of it, in fact, looked straight out of the French Quarter, which made sense. New Orleans is less than three hours away by car, and the two cities have deep cultural ties, thanks to the river they share.

I picked a small place a couple of blocks from the William Johnson house on State Street. At least, it looked small from the street. Inside, tables filled several narrow rooms on three floors. The smell of freshly baked bread reassured me I'd made a good choice. The hostess led me down a flight of stairs to a cozy dining room with little natural light, just chandeliers casting dim rays. It felt like a basement to me, albeit a nicely decorated one. Lace curtains draped over the small, rectangular casement windows at the top of the room. Tapestries and framed oil paintings covered whitewashed walls. The terrazzo floor sparkled, a bone-colored base with dots of gold and green sprucing it up.

I followed the hostess around the staircase to a quiet corner under a window—quiet, at least, until I heard a voice say, "Frank? Frank?"

I looked to my right and saw Helen Kraft sitting at a small table by herself. "What a marvelous coincidence!" She stood up. "Please join me. There's plenty of room at this table."

I quickly scanned the room to assess my options. There was only one other open table, and it was next to Helen's anyway. I considered fleeing and finding somewhere else to eat. "Sure." I sighed, hoping it was shallow enough that Helen couldn't hear it. "I'll join you." I nodded to the hostess and forced a smile.

"How delightful. Please sit."

I slid a chair back from the table and sat down. "So, other than writing about a retiring cruise boat captain, what have you been up to since you got away with murder in Dubuque?"

CHAPTER 21

"You have a twisted sense of humor, Frank." She looked down at the menu. "I hear the gumbo is quite good here."

"And you are very good at deflecting." I watched her scan the menu as I wrestled with how far I should push her to tell me what really happened in Dubuque. She wasn't an innocent bystander when fire broke out at the convention center hosting the Midwest Alliance of Craft Food Producers. I was sure of that much. I was less certain about whether she'd actively sabotaged my writing assignment from *Wandering Gourmet* magazine. "Gumbo sounds good," I said. "How's your profile of the captain coming along?"

"Thank you for asking." She closed the menu and looked up at me. "It's still such a struggle. Getting anything out of him, well—it's harder than catching moonbeams in a jar."

I guessed she knew something about being elusive. "I'm a little confused. Why would he agree to have a journalist follow him around if he wasn't willing to open up?"

Her face lit up. "That's what I thought, too! After the first day"—she leaned toward me—"I had a strong feeling that he didn't want me around. So, I called my contact with the cruise line and expressed my concerns." Our server came back, and Helen sat up straight. After the server left with our orders, Helen continued: "I found out that it was the company's PR person

131

who had pitched the article, and he had done so without asking the captain. That explained some of it."

"You'd think they would have cleared the idea with the subject of the article before pitching it. Maybe the corporate office is in the habit of doing what they want, without running anything past the crew first."

"Yes. That's exactly what I'm beginning to think."

"What have you learned so far?" I leaned back in my chair.

"He's married. Has two children. But he wouldn't talk about his family when I asked. Otherwise, as I said, a lot about boats. That's one thing Captain Smith will talk about. All the boats he's worked on, their dimensions, how much power the engines had." She pressed her lips together. "He spent a full hour in one interview describing—in detail—one diesel engine. Ugh. You know, all the stuff that makes great copy for a personal profile."

I chuckled. And enjoyed knowing she was struggling. The schmaltzy prose she relied on wouldn't work this time. "What do you know about his background? Where did he grow up?"

"Tennessee. He told me he grew up on a farm in Gibson County, Tennessee. That's it." She threw her hands up.

"What did his parents farm?"

"I have no idea. He just told me quote-unquote 'the usual.' Apparently, they were subsistence farmers?"

"How'd he get started working on the river?"

"He tried farming in Tennessee for a few years but didn't like it, so he went to Memphis, where he got hired as a deckhand. As soon as he stepped on board, he said he knew he'd found the place where he wanted to work."

"He must have plenty of stories about working on the river. He's in his sixties now, right?"

"Right. He's sixty-eight." Our server set a bowl of gumbo in front of each of us. Helen leaned forward, waved a hand over her bowl, and inhaled. "Yum. What a delightful smell," she said as she picked up a spoon. "Believe me, I've asked many times about his experiences working on the river. He always defaults to telling me about the damn boats." She dipped a spoon into the gumbo. "Excuse my language."

I swallowed my first taste of gumbo as she talked. "I've heard worse." I thought for a minute about what I had just tasted. "That's delicious. Lots going on with it, but a really nice, meaty broth."

"I agree." She nodded.

Oh, god! Are we bonding? I brushed aside that unpleasant thought. "Have you tried interviewing other crew members about him? Maybe they could give you some insights. Or something for him to react to."

"That's a good idea. I talked to the other pilots, but they didn't have much to say, other than they respected him and wished him well in retirement. But they hadn't been on the *River Voyager* long."

"Ringing endorsements of his character, huh? Maybe you could call your contact at the company again and ask for the names of a few crew members who've worked with him for a while."

"Yes. Yes. That's a good idea. I'll do that when I get back."

"This is a long shot, but late last night, I talked with the assistant engineer, Ted Stevens. He grew up in Kentucky. He's younger than the captain, but he's worked on the *River Voyager* for maybe ten years. I forget exactly how long." I looked down and dipped my spoon into the gumbo again, ready to be done with this conversation. "Maybe he could tell you a few things about working with the captain."

"Thank you, Frank. Those are both excellent ideas."

We finished our lunch, and I was ready for more exploring. "What time is it?"

She looked at her watch. "One-thirty."

"Good. I thought it might be later. Glad I've got time to explore some more. There's a stop I wanted to make before heading back to the boat."

"Where's that?"

"A museum on the edge of downtown—a memorial, really—about the tragic fire at the Rhythm Night Club."

"What happened at the club?"

"In 1940 a fire broke out that killed over two hundred people."

"Oh, that sounds awful. I've never heard about that." We paid our server and stood up. "Would you like some company? I'd like to visit the museum, too." She stiffened her back.

No, I wouldn't. I figured we'd be done bonding after we'd finished eating. I turned away from her and took a step toward the stairs. "As long as you're OK with walking. It'll take at least ten minutes to get there."

"I don't mind. I haven't been getting my steps in since I boarded the *River Voyager* anyway."

Fine. "OK. Let's go." We zigzagged our way through downtown Natchez under increasingly thick cloud cover, stopping occasionally to comment on a building or check out a shop. When we got to the Rhythm Night Club Memorial Museum, a volunteer greeted us and offered to guide us around the exhibits.

"It had been a hot day for April, near ninety degrees," she began, "but the club was hosting a popular Chicago band, Walter Barnes and His Royal Creolians." She directed us to a photograph mounted on the wall. "That's the band there," she said as she pointed. "They drew a young crowd, hundreds of African American Natchezians who dressed up for a night, expecting nothing but good times. Spanish moss hung around the club as a decorative touch. Folks were just out for a good time.

"What we're standing in now isn't the original building, of course. That burned to the ground. The club had been built inside an old blacksmith's shop. Wood timbers, mostly, and covered with corrugated steel. It had a lot of windows—twenty-four of them—but twenty-one had been boarded up so no one could stand outside and enjoy the music without paying."

"Oh, mercy," Helen said.

Our guide continued: "Patrons came in through the front door—the only way in and out. There was a back door, but it had been padlocked and boarded shut." She pointed to a photo of the back door. "Sometime after eleven o'clock, a fire started near the front door. It spread quickly. All that Spanish moss provided fuel, sadly. Some of the burning moss fell on people in the club, setting their clothes and hair on fire. It all happened so fast," she said as she shook her head.

"The fire spread quickly, and because it had started by the front door, hardly anyone could get past it to get out. The club heated up like an oven because of that metal siding. Some folks tried to knock out windows, but it didn't work. Others huddled near the back with the band. A fire engine got to the club within ten minutes, but even that proved to be too late. They might have made the fire worse, actually—at least at first." She must have noticed the confused look on my face. "I'll try to explain. From what I understand, as soon as the water hit that metal siding, it created steam. If you were inside the building when that happened, breathing in that scalding hot steam would have killed you quickly. We think that happened to some of the people in the club." Helen covered her mouth with a hand.

"The official death toll was two hundred and nine. Most died from smoke inhalation, from breathing in that steam, or from being crushed to death.

Nine of the twelve band members were among the dead. Folks said that the smell of burned bodies hung in the Natchez air for months after that." I glanced over at Helen and saw her wiping tears from her eyes with a tissue.

"Afterwards, rumors went around that the fire was intentional. No one ever turned up evidence for arson, though. It was hard for some folks to accept, but the fire was entirely accidental. But maybe that made it harder to deal with."

"Because there was no one to blame," I said.

"That's right. Maybe grief sparked by a tragedy is easier to deal with when we can point a finger at a cause." She walked up to another display of photos. "Thousands of people turned out for the funerals. Practically the whole Black community. I imagine everyone knew someone who had died."

The story was emotionally wrenching. I was ready to get back to the boat and process it all with a beer or two. "We should probably get back," I said to Helen.

"Yes. I agree." She dabbed her eyes one more time, then we left the museum.

We walked in silence through downtown Natchez. When we got to the park along the bluff edge, I walked over to the rail for a last good look at the river. As I scanned the horizon just upriver of us, I spotted the *River Voyager* slowly making its way toward Vicksburg.

"What time is it?" I asked Helen.

She looked at her watch. "One . . ." She looked up at me. "One-thirty." Her arm fell to her side. "Shit!"

"Guess I should have checked my phone."

CHAPTER 22

"Now what do we do?" Helen asked. Her face had turned pale.

I shrugged. "Rent a car and drive to Vicksburg. Meet the boat in the morning."

"Let me see if I can find us a car," she said. "After all, it's my fault we missed the boat."

"I think we share the blame for that. But go ahead. I know an inexpensive place to stay. I'll see if they have any rooms." She bit her lower lip. "Don't worry," I said. "I've stayed there many times. The best Motel 6 I ever stayed at." Her face froze. "Just kidding. It's not a Hilton—it's a mom-and-pop place—but the rooms are modern and clean."

"OK. I trust you, Frank." She looked upriver. "Mostly," she mumbled. "You probably know this area better than I do. We can book two rooms, right?"

"Of course." I called the Southern Breeze Inn in Vicksburg and reserved two rooms. When I finished, Helen was still on the phone trying to find a car, so I called Ruby.

"Hi, Frank. Are you back from Natchez?" she asked.

"If only." I glanced back at the river and watched the *River Voyager* slowly moving away from us. "I missed the boat. Helen Kraft and I were touring a museum and misjudged the time. We're still in Natchez."

"Oh, my. I don't know what's worse. That you missed the boat or that you're stuck with her. What are you going to do?"

"Helen's trying to find us a rental car." I glanced in Helen's direction. She was talking to someone, but her face was flushed. "We'll drive to Vicksburg tonight and meet up with the boat in the morning."

"I guess that means I'm on my own for dinner and breakfast."

"Unless you check with Brian. You may be able to catch him for dinner."

"Yes. I'll give that a try. I don't know if I can sit through another dinner with Michelle sniping at her sisters, though."

"I'm sure you'll figure something out. I'll see you in the morning."

"Good luck with Helen."

After I hung up, I texted Deion and told him I was going to miss morning coffee with him. When I told him what happened, he sent a laughing emoji with tears. I hate fucking emojis. I glanced back at Helen. Her face had returned to its usual alabaster, but she was still on the phone, so I texted Jefferson, too.

> Need anything while we're stuck in Vicksburg?

He responded with a laughing emoji, then with

> Maybe! I'll get back to you.

Helen tapped my shoulder, then cleared her throat. "I found a vehicle." She looked away from me. "Not what I was expecting, but it has wheels."

"What is it?"

"A Ford F-250 pickup. I guess it's big?"

The image of an emoji crying and laughing popped into my head. "Yeah. You could say it's big."

"Do you mind driving?" Her lips curled into a half smile.

We walked seven blocks to the rental car office. Thunder rumbled in the distance. The black pickup parked in front had a grill tall enough to ride the roller coasters at amusement parks. "Good god! Who needs this?" Helen nodded.

Helen went inside to sign the paperwork and get the key. I walked the perimeter of the truck, so I knew what I was getting myself into. *Good thing Vicksburg's only an hour and a half away.*

When Helen came back out with the key, I asked, "Should we stop and pick up a load of compost along the way?" She forced a smile. I climbed up into the driver's seat of The Beast. It actually did smell faintly of mud and leaves. I looked around to make sure I could find the little things, such as how to get the truck in Drive, where the turn signals were, and whether I could reach the gas pedal without attaching a wood block to my foot. The truck roared when I started it. I suddenly felt powerful. I backed The Beast up slowly while cranking the wheel to the right.

"STOP!" Helen yelled.

I hit the brakes, which jerked my head back and forth. "What?"

"You nearly hit the car behind us. I don't need to pay for repairs to this monstrosity." She gritted her teeth.

I put the truck in Park and climbed down out of it. I walked to the rear to judge the distance between the truck and the Toyota Camry behind us, then climbed back into the cab. "There's a good five feet between us still!" I snapped. "Relax already." Then the rain started. I fumbled around the steering wheel, trying to figure out how to turn on the wipers.

"It's not your money on the line." She slammed her purse between her legs and held it down.

I turned to her. "Do you want to drive?"

She scowled. "Just take it easy, Frank. Please." She turned away from me and looked out the passenger window.

I got us out of the parking space and onto the highway with no further panic attacks from Helen, then clenched the steering wheel tightly as the rain picked up. After we'd been driving awhile, I said to Helen, "You've been quiet since we left Natchez."

"You may find this amusing, but I don't." She practically spit the words at me. "I'm mad at myself for screwing up, for making us miss the boat."

"Shit happens," I said. As the rain intensified, I slowed down to forty-five.

"Not to me." She squeezed her purse like she was trying to juice it. "I plan everything out." She looked at me, then back to the road. "And I do it well. And I always have a backup plan." She let go of the purse and rubbed her temples. "This wasn't part of my plan for the day."

My phone lit up. I swiped to turn it on and saw it was a message from Jefferson. "Can you read what Brian texted me?"

She took the phone from me. "Let's see: 'Frank. If you have time, go to the library and vital records office. Find everything you can on Rebbecca Nash. We keep striking out.'" She handed the phone back to me. "That's a strange spelling for the name Rebecca. Who's Rebbecca Nash?"

Lightning flashed in front of us. Wind gusts shook the truck, but it stayed true to the road. "That's complicated." I thought about how to give a quick summary. And whether I should. "We met three women after we boarded the boat. Sisters. They aren't cruising for fun. Their father was murdered in Vicksburg in the 1970s. One sister, Michelle, has spent much of her life trying to find them. She got a tip that two of the killers are on our cruise."

"They got away with it?"

"Yes. Four white guys killed a Black man in Vicksburg in the 1970s. Did you think they'd be held accountable?"

"You didn't mention that the sisters were African American or that white men killed their father. Now that I know, no. I'm not surprised. But it's still . . . shocking." I slid the phone into my shirt pocket. She looked out the passenger window, then turned back toward me. "I assume she—Michelle—knows the names of the men she's looking for?"

"No. Not exactly. She knows the names they were born with, but after the murder, they left Vicksburg and changed their identities. Michelle doesn't know their aliases, and the guy who tipped her off wasn't willing to reveal that detail."

"Then how is Michelle supposed to figure out who the killers are? There are a lot of people on that cruise. And how does this Rebbecca Nash fit in?"

"Aren't you a curious one?" I tapped the brakes to slow The Beast down as we passed through Port Gibson. The rain let up. "Michelle and Brian—my friend who's helping her—don't fill me on every detail, but we think there's a good chance the man who disappeared overboard, Bucky Jones, was one of them. One of the killers."

"What? The delightful man we had dinner with the first night? A murderer? Whatever makes you think that?"

"The short version of the story is we can't find anything about him before 1975. All the killers left Vicksburg and changed their names. If we're right, then Bucky Jones was really Lonnie Sims. And before he got involved in the murder, he married Rebbecca Nash. We're hoping to find her. Find out what she can tell us about him. Maybe even get a photo of him."

"I understand now why you've had trouble meeting your deadlines."

I tested the acceleration of The Beast as we got back on the highway. It was good.

"Easy, Frank."

"It doesn't help when someone—another writer, for example—actively undermines your work."

"And there you go again." She shook her head. "I'll tell you exactly what I told you in Dubuque. I vouched for you with the editor at *Wandering Gourmet*." She turned and pointed at me. She enjoyed doing that. "He was going to assign the story to me, but I suggested he give *you* a chance. I worked hard to persuade him. He had never heard of you. But convince him I did." She dropped her arm back down in her lap and looked ahead. "And then you went and missed the deadline. You made *me* look bad for recommending you. So, I did what I had to do to fix the problem. I volunteered to take over the assignment and finish it. Which I did." She glanced back at me. "If you'd met your deadline, you'd have a credit with *Wandering Gourmet* on your résumé now."

"And why would you advocate for me in the first place?"

She closed her eyes and rubbed her forehead. I heard a soft exhale. "Because you're a talented writer." She cleared her throat. "Better than me. And I felt bad that we'd . . . that we'd had some difficult moments between us. I hoped we might get a fresh start."

In my experience, Helen did a good job of playing sincere, even when she wasn't. "Well, I appreciate that. Sorry it didn't work out. But I got distracted by the turn of events in Dubuque. As you recall."

"Yes. I remember all too well what happened there. But at some point, Frank, you're going to have to decide if you're a writer or an amateur detective. From what you've shown me so far, you can't do both well."

I couldn't argue the point. We didn't talk again until we approached Vicksburg. I kept my eyes on the sky. The clouds were drifting away, revealing brilliant yellows and oranges flooding the horizon from the setting sun. "Can you do me a favor? Check the hours for the Vicksburg library?"

She pulled her phone from her purse. "They're open until eight tonight."

"Good. I'll drop you off at the hotel, then I'm going to spend some time sorting through their archives."

She looked around for a minute. "I can help. I know how to use a library, how to research a topic." She dropped her head slightly to the side and raised her eyebrows. "I'd like to help."

I got off the highway, and as I drove past our hotel, I said, "That's where we're staying tonight." I drove on. "But I guess we'll check in later."

Chapter 23

I parked The Beast on the street next to the library. I didn't want to rack up any repair bills for Helen by trying to squeeze it in and out of the spots in the parking lot. The wind picked up, and the clouds were rolling in again.

"We don't have anything to take notes on," Helen said.

"I still have my reporter's notebook. And we have our phones. Take pictures of what you find." I looked around the library, then nodded toward the reference desk. "Or, we could ask a librarian for paper and a pen to borrow."

"I'm more comfortable with paper and pen." She walked over to the desk and came back supplied. "Where do we start?"

"Good question." I considered our limited time. We had about an hour. "How about this. Let's find city directories or phone books for Vicksburg. Look for Rebbecca Nash in 1973 and '74, and write down her address. We should trace her addresses for a few years. She married Lonnie Sims in 1974. I'll look her up in 1975 under Rebbecca Sims."

We asked the reference librarian to point us in the right direction, then walked to a corner we had to ourselves. "Here we go," I said, then pulled down the bulky white pages for 1973 and '74 and handed them to Helen. I removed the 1975 and '76 editions and set them on a wide table, where we sat down at.

"There's no Rebbecca Nash in 1973," Helen said after rifling through some pages.

"She might not have been old enough to show up. Are there many Nash-es?"

"A few."

"We don't know her parents' names yet." I walked over and took a picture of the page with the Nashes. "Quicker than writing it all down," I said to her.

"Got her!" Helen said. "1974. Rebbecca Nash." Her eyes were wide open. She jotted down the address.

I found Rebbecca Sims in 1975 and gave Helen the address to write down. After a bit: "Hmm."

"What is it, Frank?"

"No Rebbecca Sims in 1976." I thought about it for a minute. "I'm going to see if I can find her in any of the white pages for the rest of the 1970s. Can you check for addresses for the other killers in the books we pulled?"

"Of course. Who am I looking for besides Lonnie Sims?"

"Brothers Ray and Lester Bell and Otis Morris."

I flipped through a few more directories. "Dang. Rebbecca's not listed at all after 1975," I said.

"Maybe she moved away."

"Possible."

"I found Ray and Lester Bell in '73, '74, and '75. Otis Morris is listed in '74 and '75. Addresses noted." She smiled.

"I'm going to take a shot in the dark." On the shelf above the white pages I found an index to obituaries published in the Vicksburg newspapers. I pulled it from the shelves and flipped through pages. The listings were alphabetical by year. Rebbecca Sims wasn't listed in 1975, but I found her in 1976. "Damn."

"What did you find?"

"Looks like Rebbecca died in 1976." My shoulders sagged. "Let's pull the microfilm for the *Vicksburg Free Press* and find this obit."

The reference librarian set us up at their only microfilm reader. I loaded the film and moved it as quickly as I could to the page with Rebbecca's obituary.

"Found it." Helen leaned in over my shoulder.

Rebbecca (Nash) Sims, 22 years old, entered the Kingdom of God early Sunday morning, following an automobile accident. Survivors include her parents, Dallas and Hannah Nash of Vicksburg; and a sister, Ruth Ann (Nash) Bartels of Jackson. A private memorial service was held on Tuesday. In lieu of flowers, the family requests donations to the First Baptist Church school fund.

"Not much there," Helen said.

"Curious. No mention of Lonnie Sims." I rubbed the back of my neck as I wondered what it meant. His absence from her obituary implied that Rebbecca's family had written him off. Not hard to imagine why. He'd been gone for over a year when she died, and they had probably tried unsuccessfully to find him. I glanced at Helen and saw her staring at me. "But at least, it gives us some more names to work with."

I felt a tap on my shoulder. "The library will close in fifteen minutes, sir," the reference librarian whispered. "Did you find what you needed?"

"I'd call it a good start. What time do you open in the morning?"

"Nine."

I rewound the microfilm and set it aside. "I think that's all we're going to get done tonight," I said to Helen.

"Agreed."

"I'm hungry but tired. Mind if we get some takeout for dinner and go back to the hotel?"

"Not at all."

We ran back to the truck to avoid getting soaked in the downpour. "Mexican food OK?" Helen nodded. We picked up dinner, then drove to the hotel to check in. I couldn't say I'd enjoyed the day with Helen. *This doesn't make us friends.* But I hadn't hated getting stuck with her, either. Anyway, we were done for the night. We got our keys and retreated to our separate corners. "See you in the breakfast room tomorrow morning? Eight-thirtyish?"

"Yes. See you then." She took a couple of steps toward her room, then stopped in front of the door. She turned around and said, "Thank you, Frank," then entered her room.

I walked down the hall to room 112. I felt oddly conspicuous checking into a hotel with no baggage. All I had on me was my phone, a notebook I'd been using on the cruise, and a pen. And a bag of Mexican food. I sat at the desk meant for laptops and, in between bites of burrito, searched for Rebecca's parents on the standard Internet genealogy sites. I found a few details of their lives—Dallas was born in 1930 and Hannah in 1931. They married in 1949. Ruth Ann was born in 1951 and Rebbecca three years later. I couldn't imagine being married as a teenager and being responsible for two kids in my early twenties.

I switched to a site with searchable newspaper articles and found what I was hoping I wouldn't: an obituary for Dallas in 1997 and another for Hannah in 2003. The text of the obituaries was behind a pay wall, so I noted the names and dates of the newspapers that had published them. We'd look them up on microfilm at the library in the morning.

Finding anything about Rebbecca's sister was harder. I couldn't find a marriage record online, which probably just meant the state had restricted access to protect their privacy. Hard to argue with that. But I also had trouble finding an address or phone number for her in Jackson—or anywhere else, for that matter. Knowing her husband's name might help, so I made a note to visit the circuit clerk's office at the Warren County Courthouse in the morning, hoping that's where they had married.

I was hitting dead end after dead end and not sure what to do next. Even with so much information available digitally, it could still be difficult to track some people. (Legally anyway.) As I thought about my next steps, my phone lit up. It was a text from Jefferson.

> How'd it go? Any news yet?

> Not good news. Rebbecca Nash Sims died in 1976. Car crash. Her parents are dead, too. Found Rebbecca's obit; not much in it, except for a sister's name. Maybe I can track her down. What do you really want to know about Rebbecca at this point?

> Damn. Was hoping to talk to Rebbecca directly.

I waited to see if he would send another message, then I got:

> If you find the sister, ask about friends of Rebbecca & Lonnie. Anyone they might have hung out with. What does she know about Lonnie's disappearance? Wld rly help to get pics of Lonnie. Maybe the sister has a photo of the newlyweds from their wedding? Good luck.

I turned off my phone to save power and put away my private investigator hat for the night. As long as I was already in Vicksburg, I should finish the research I needed to do here before I boarded the boat again. I flipped through my notes for the *River Voyager* article, but my mind kept wandering back to how I might find something—anything—about Rebbecca Nash Sims. Anything that could help us figure out if Bucky Jones was really Lonnie Sims.

149

CHAPTER 24

After a quick shower I put on the same clothes I'd worn the day before—they were only slightly rank—then walked to the breakfast room. I spotted Helen near the buffet. I nodded at her, then made a beeline for the coffee.

"Did you sleep well?" I asked Helen after sitting down at her table.

"I did. I was out like a light after dinner. How about you?"

"Meh. Took a while to fall asleep. But that's normal for me."

"What's on our agenda today, besides returning that truck and getting back on the boat?"

"A lot. Back to the library. Rebbecca's parents passed away a few years ago. I'd like to look up their obituaries. I didn't have any luck finding an address or phone number for Ruth Ann, Rebbecca's sister, so I'm hoping one of those obits mentions her husband's name. That might make it easier to track her down." I took a sip of coffee, then frowned. It tasted mostly like bitter water, but it would have to do. "If that doesn't work, I'll run to the county courthouse and look up their marriage record."

"We can split up on the obits, right?"

"Unfortunately, no. There's just that one microfilm reader." I took a sip of coffee. "But if you don't mind, you can look up the obits. I thought I'd look through the Vicksburg High School yearbooks. Maybe I can find photos of Rebbecca and of the four killers when they were young men."

"Ooh. That could be useful."

After we'd had our fill of stale pastries, I got a cup of weak coffee to take with me. We checked out of the Southern Breeze Inn and drove to the library.

"What time will the boat be here, do you suppose?"

"Should be here already. Would you mind calling someone on board and asking what time the boat will leave Vicksburg? I'd rather not miss it again."

"How long do you think we're going to be at the library?"

"Not that long. But I have other work to do while I'm here. I need to do some research in Vicksburg for my article." We hit a bump, and I nearly spilled my coffee. "Sorry about that."

"So, you *can* balance work with your hobbies."

"Look who's talking. You're sure having fun not working, too."

"I know. This has been a pleasant diversion." She sounded like she meant it. "But I'm ready to get back on the boat. And back to working on my own piece." She turned and looked out her window.

I parked The Beast on the street again. It was cloudy and much cooler, so we hurried to get inside. The librarian set up Helen at the microfilm reader and pointed me to the shelf with the yearbooks.

Lester and Ray Bell, Otis Morris, Lonnie Sims—and also Rebbecca Nash. Those were the kids I was looking for. I wasn't sure exactly when they were born, but I knew Ray Bell was the gang's leader and therefore likely the oldest. I pulled the 1966 yearbook off the shelf and flipped through it. The content was thin. Only seniors had photos, and there wasn't one for Ray Bell. I flipped to the back. No index. *Great.*

I went back to the shelf and pulled down yearbooks for 1967 through 1971. My best guess was that Ray Bell would have been a senior in 1967. I felt excited as I flipped to the senior photos, but that feeling was quickly extinguished. A page was missing. There were no photos of kids at the front of the alphabet. Someone had ripped out the page.

"Frank." Helen called out from the microfilm reader. I turned to look at her. "I found the first obit. The one for Dallas Nash."

I walked over to her and read the obit over her shoulder. "It's just as brief as Rebbecca's," Helen said. There was no help in the list of survivors: his wife, Hannah, and daughter, Ruth Ann Bartels. No mention of Ruth Ann's husband, but at least it indicated that twenty-one years after Rebbecca's obituary, she was still living in Jackson.

I took a photo of the obit. "OK. On to the next one." I walked back to the table where I'd put the yearbooks and sat down. There were no Bells who were seniors in '68, '69, or '70. I guessed that Lester Bell might be four years younger than Ray, so I crossed my fingers as I opened the 1971 yearbook to the seniors. And once again, my hopes immediately deflated. The first page of senior photos was missing again, ripped out—again. I sat back in the chair. Someone obviously didn't want those photos seen.

I picked up the 1972 yearbook, but this time I expected disappointment. The first page of senior photos was intact (there were no Bells), but the middle part of the alphabet was missing, the page ripped out. No photo of Otis Morris. No photo of Rebbecca Nash. I went back to the 1971 yearbook. Only the first page was missing, but there was no Morris or Nash in that class. The 1973 yearbook was intact, but it didn't have anyone I was looking for. In the 1974 yearbook someone had ripped out the page for *R* through *T*, so no photo of Lonnie Sims.

"I've found the other obit, Frank," Helen said.

I walked over and read Hannah Nash's 2003 obit and wasn't surprised when I saw the only survivor listed as Ruth Ann Bartels of Jackson, meaning she was still there fourteen years ago. I took a photo of that obit, too, then pulled up a chair next to Helen. "This isn't going as I'd hoped," I said.

"Did you find the photos?"

"No. Every page where the photos should have been was missing. Torn out of the yearbook."

"Someone obviously didn't want their photos around for posterity." Helen scratched her head. "But these obviously aren't—can't be—the only copies of the yearbooks."

"No. They can't be. But we also don't have a lot of time to track down others. I guess I'll go to the courthouse and see if I can find a marriage record for Ruth Ann. That would at least give me her husband's name. Did you have a chance to call the boat?"

"Yes. They are here already, as you thought. And they felt terrible about leaving us behind." She frowned. "Or so they said. Anyway, they will leave Vicksburg at five. Promptly, I was told."

"Good. Good. I can use that extra time."

"Frank."

"Yes?"

"I appreciate you giving me the chance to help with your 'research.'" She slid the chair back from the microfilm reader. "But I don't think I can help with much else right now. You seem to know exactly what you need to do, so I'll just be in the way."

"Would you like me to take you back to the boat?"

She looked up at me with her eyes open wide. "Oh, would you, please?"

"Of course. We can go now if you'd like. Do you mind if I hang on to The Beast for a while longer? It'll help me get my work done a little faster."

She hesitated. "Of course." She forced a smile, then stood up. "I'll text you the address where you need to return it. As soon as possible, please, but no later than four."

"That won't be an issue."

I drove to the riverfront and dropped Helen off in front of the *River Voyager*. "This doesn't make us friends, you know," I said. "But I . . ."

Helen smiled. "Yes, Frank?"

I looked down and cleared my throat. "I appreciate your patience and help the past day."

"And I thank you for your patience and assistance, too. Maybe we can find other ways to help each other out again. Someday." She opened the door and climbed down out of the cab.

I was eager to get back on board, too, but that would have to wait. I drove to the Warren County Courthouse first. After a couple of wrong turns in the building, I found the circuit clerk's office. I told the clerk I was researching my family history and was interested in finding a marriage record for my cousin.

She pointed me to a shelf filled with a collection of big, leather-bound volumes with faded covers and loose bindings. Marriage indexes. There was one book per year. Each book had separate indexes for grooms and brides. It didn't take long to find what I was looking for. Ruth Ann Nash married Glenn Bartels on June 19, 1971. Bingo. I requested the full marriage record from the clerk.

"We charge five dollars for an uncertified copy, or twenty dollars for a certified copy. Which would you like?"

"Uncertified, please." I paid the five bucks, and, fifteen minutes later, she came back with a photocopy: Glenn Alan Bartels married Ruth Ann Nash. Both sets of parents' names were also included. I thanked the clerk and went back to my car. I searched for contact information for Glenn Bartels and found a listing in Pearl, just east of Jackson. *Why not?* I called the listed number, and a woman answered. "May I please speak to Mrs. Bartels?" I asked.

"This is she. Who is this?"

"I'm calling from the Medicare Information Network. Did you know you may be eligible for additional savings on your Medicare plan?"

"No thank you. I'm not interested." She hung up, as I expected she would. I plugged her address into Google Maps. I could drive there in less than an hour. I looked at my phone. *Noon. Plenty of time.* I put The Beast in gear and set off for Pearl, Mississippi.

Chapter 25

On the road toward Pearl, I ran through a few ideas for cover stories to justify visiting Ruth Ann and asking her intrusive questions. I settled on an embellished version of the truth.

I parked The Beast in front of her house, grabbed my notebook, and walked to the front door. After I rang the bell, a woman unlocked and slowly cracked opened the door. "Yes?" She asked as she peeked out from a narrow sliver.

"Sorry to bother you, ma'am. I'm a private investigator. I'm looking for . . ." I flipped through a couple of pages in the notebook. I wanted to be convincing as a fake investigator. "Ruth Ann Bartels, maiden name Nash."

"That's me."

"I've been hired to look into an old case that your late sister may have been involved with."

Her jaw dropped slightly. "My sister?" She opened the door wider and stepped into the gap. "Well, she passed away a long time ago." She looked me over. "What did you say your name is?"

"I didn't. Frank Dodge." I handed her my driver's license.

She read it, then handed it back to me. "Yes, so you are. But that was a driver's license, not an ID for an investigator."

"My apologies. The driver's license is the only ID I have for now." She took a half-step back. "Look, I don't want to take up much of your time, so let me tell you why I'm here."

"Go ahead," she said, a hand gripping the door tightly.

"In 1974 a man named Isaac Green was murdered in Vicksburg. No one was ever charged. I've been told the sheriff had identified potential suspects, but they disappeared before law enforcement had a chance to question any of them. Any of that sound familiar?"

She let go of the door handle and slid her body into the door to prop it open. "Yes. I remember hearing about that case," she said. "But that was a long time ago. What help could I possibly be to you today?"

"Tell me what you remember hearing."

"Well, the murder was in all the newspapers, of course." She scrunched up her face and looked past me. "I don't believe they ever arrested anyone, if I recall correctly."

"That's right. No one was ever charged." I looked down and flipped to the next page in my notebook. "Tell me what you remember about your brother-in-law."

"Lonnie?" she stammered. "Well, he was real nice. A couple of years younger than my sister. Friendly. Just about everyone who met him liked him."

I jotted down "friendly" and "well-liked." "How did he and your sister meet?" I shivered slightly.

"She was a waitress at a diner in town." She leaned toward me while keeping her body pressed against the open door. "Would you like to borrow a jacket, Mr. Dodge?"

"No thank you. I'll be fine."

She frowned, then continued. "Lonnie was smitten with her from the first time they met. And, I think it's fair to say, my sister was just as taken with him."

"I guess they didn't feel the need for a long courtship." I kept looking down as I noted how they met.

She laughed softly. "No. They did not. They married soon after Lonnie graduated from high school."

"They were so young . . ." I looked up at her.

"Yes. Indeed they were. But they had big plans." She sighed.

"Like what?"

"My sister wanted to be a teacher. Always loved children. Of course, she wanted children of her own, too. Lonnie dreamed about opening his own business. He had a hard time deciding on exactly what business, though. But he was absolutely certain he wasn't the type to be satisfied sitting at a desk in an office somewhere."

"What happened to Lonnie? He disappeared sometime after they married, right?"

"I don't know if 'disappeared' is the right word, but yes. He left. We never saw him again."

"Why did he leave?"

"My sister told me he had some family business to attend to. She didn't say anything more specific than that. Rebbecca and I"—she winced—"we weren't exactly close. She wasn't in the habit of divulging her secrets to me." She touched the back of her neck.

"Where did he go?"

"My sister said he went to Alabama. He was supposed to be gone for just a few weeks."

"Why didn't she go with him?"

"That's a good question. Naturally, I encouraged her to do just that, to stay by her husband's side. But she insisted she didn't need to. That he'd be back soon enough. She insisted on staying in Vicksburg, where she'd recently started school, to be a teacher."

"How often did you see or talk with Lonnie after he left town?"

"Not once." She shook her head. "Never saw him again."

"You must have found that curious."

"Yes, at first. But my sister passed away the following year anyway. Lonnie would have had no reason to stay in touch with me."

"So, the last time you saw him was at your sister's funeral?"

She frowned. "No. He did not make it back for the funeral. We were unable to find any contact information for him. To let him know about Rebbecca's passing."

"May I ask where you were looking for him?"

"Well, it wasn't me. My parents did the looking. They told me they searched for him in a few places Rebbecca had mentioned. I believe they had called around a couple of places in Alabama, like I said. But they didn't have any luck."

"Lonnie must have heard at some point that his wife had died."

"I would think so. But if he did, he never contacted us." She wiped an eye. "Frankly, we were all so distraught at the time about Rebbecca's passing. . . . We just didn't give Lonnie much thought."

"I can't imagine how difficult that time must have been." I slid the pen into my shirt pocket.

"It still is."

"Of course. Sorry." I felt like I should have offered her a hug, but I didn't think that would be proper PI behavior, so I held back. "One more question, then I'll be on my way. Would you happen to have a picture of Lonnie?"

She hesitated. "Let me see—" She looked over her shoulder. "We took few pictures back then, and we've since cleaned so much out of my parents' house."

I looked over her shoulder and saw several framed photos of people hanging on a wall behind her. "Are those family photos over there?" I pointed behind her.

"Why, yes." She hesitated. "Yes, they are. Please come in, Mr. Dodge." I followed her into the entryway. "There." She pointed at a framed photo in the middle of the photo collection. "That's Rebbecca and Lonnie, from their wedding."

I stepped a little closer for a look. "Mind if I take a picture of this with my phone?"

She cleared her throat. "Of course not."

I took the picture, then quickly scanned the other photos on the wall. "Thank you, Mrs. Bartels." I walked out the front door, then turned around. "I appreciate your cooperation today. If I need to get in touch with you, if I have more questions, what number would be best to call?"

She gave me her cell phone number. As I was writing it down in my notebook, she asked, "What exactly are you hoping to find out, Mr. Dodge?"

"My client is very interested in finding the men responsible for Mr. Green's death." I looked up. "They want closure. I'm trying to help with that."

"Then why are you asking about my sister and Lonnie? Do you think they had something to do with Mr. Green's death?"

"At this point, I'm following every lead I get." I slipped the notebook into my back pocket. "I got a tip that Lonnie Sims was connected to the murder. He might have been a witness, or maybe he was directly involved. I'm not sure, but I believe he's worth a much closer look."

"I can assure you, Mr. Dodge, that Lonnie was definitely not a killer. He was a good man, a Christian man." She raised her voice. "A kind man. He would have never taken a man's life."

"Thank you, Mrs. Bartels."

I went back to The Beast, cranked it up, and checked the time on my phone. Quarter after one. *Good.* I would still have time to visit a couple of shops in Vicksburg before returning to the boat. I opened the picture I'd just taken of Lonnie on his wedding day. A bushy beard nearly hid his young face, and he had hair down to his shoulders. Even after zooming in, I couldn't tell if the Lonnie Sims in the picture was also the Bucky Jones I'd met on the boat. Sure, the Lonnie in the picture was skinny like Bucky, but that beard hid his face, so I couldn't tell how well Lonnie resembled Bucky.

My eyes drifted over to Rebbecca. *Well, lookee here.* I zoomed in tighter on Rebbecca's face. While I wasn't sure if young Lonnie had become Bucky, I was surprised at how much young Rebbecca resembled Bucky's newlywed, Mathilda. Similar facial structure. Same hair color (and style). How could that be? Rebbecca Nash Sims had died forty-one years earlier in a car crash. I'd seen her obit. Did she have a twin sister? Or might there be much more to Rebbecca's story? I needed to call Mathilda again.

CHAPTER 26

Before I got back on the highway, I texted a copy of the photo to Jefferson, with the message:

Wedding day photo of Lonnie Sims and Rebbecca Nash. Anyone look familiar??

I didn't hear back from him until I was pulling into Vicksburg.

Whoa! You back on the boat yet?

Not 'til 4ish.

Hit me up when u r back.

I parked downtown on Washington Street near a couple of businesses I wanted to visit. Over the next hour I got a few salient quotes from the director of a gallery that sells the work of local artists and the owners of a coffee shop and a bakery. Sure, I was writing for a national magazine, but that wouldn't stop me from highlighting my favorite mom-and-pop businesses—or pop-and-pop business, in one case.

I returned The Beast just before four, then the manager of the car rental facility gave me a lift back to the boat. "Welcome back, Mr. Dodge," the first mate said to me as I reached the gangway. "And with a full hour to spare this time!"

Thanks. I nodded to him. I felt relieved to be back on the boat, but I couldn't wait to track down Jefferson and catch up about the preceding twenty-four hours. We agreed to meet at the Paddlewheel Pub.

"Looking a little rough today, aren't we, Mr. Dodge?" The hotel manager must have planted a GPS tracker on me.

"Just need a quick change of clothes, Mr. Riggs. That's all."

He looked me over. "If you say so. Need anything?"

"On my way to get what I need now."

"Wonderful!" He walked away. *That man doesn't have a first gear.*

Back in my stateroom, I changed into a fresh set of clothes. Ruby wasn't there. I freshened up, then headed up to the hurricane deck.

Jefferson was already sitting at the bar, a Beam and Coke in front of him, the older bartender standing, looking at his phone. "There you are," Jefferson bellowed. "You know, Michelle was able to run into Natchez yesterday and get back on the boat in time. How the hell did you screw it up?"

I sat down next to him, ordered an IPA, and crossed my arms. "It starts with a faulty watch," I answered.

"On your phone?"

"Of course not. Helen's watch."

"Helen . . . ? You mean the writer you hate?"

"I don't hate her." The bartender set the beer in front of me. "At least, I don't hate her anymore. But yes. That one." I took a long sip from the glass. "I stopped in a restaurant for lunch yesterday, and she was there, eating alone. She invited me to join her."

"And you said yes? Even though you can't stand her."

"The hostess was about to seat me at a table right next to her. What was I supposed to do? That would have been even more awkward." I took a sip of beer as I glared at Jefferson over the pint glass. "So, we had a civil lunch.

Then she invited herself along with me to tour a small museum. We thought we had plenty of time, but we didn't realize that her watch had died."

"Uh-huh." Jefferson shook his head slightly. I confounded him sometimes. "So, what the hell did you two do for the past twenty-four hours?

"She rented a car . . . a truck, a pickup—a big fucking pickup—that we drove to Vicksburg. We did our library research for you and Michelle, then went back to a hotel—separate rooms, of course.

"I'm not crazy about the fact you involved her in Michelle's case."

"I didn't have a lot of choice," I snapped. "She saw your text message asking me to research Rebbecca in Vicksburg. She read it to me because I was driving."

"I get that." He looked down and paused. "Can we trust her?" He looked back at me. "We're not ready for word to leak out about what we're doing. And she has a history of, you know, screwing you over."

"I remember." I took another sip of beer and wondered if I should have lied to her. "I think we'll be fine. I could be wrong, but I think she's got enough on her hands right now, writing about a captain who doesn't say much." I smiled slightly. "Besides, she really got into the whole subterfuge of what we're doing."

He forced a smile. "If you say so."

This wasn't the conversation I'd felt excited to have. "Enough of that. What did you think of Lonnie and Rebbecca's wedding photo?"

"Yeah." He grinned as he leaned back. "That was a kicker. How did you get a copy of it?"

"I found Rebbecca's sister and drove to her home near Jackson." I smacked my lips after another sip of beer. "I pretended I was a PI."

"You what?" Jefferson leaned forward quickly, and his eyes opened wide.

"I pretended I was a PI—you know, a private investigator."

"I know what a fucking PI is." He slapped me lightly on the shoulder. "Why the hell did you do that? Because it went so well when you tried to figure out what happened to that Scott Joplin document?"

"You're funny. I needed to create a reason I was asking about her family. A cover story. That's what I came up with."

"And she bought it?"

I shrugged. "I'm not entirely sure. But we ended up having a nice chat—at least, I thought so." I tapped the barstool with my foot. "You done with the twenty questions? Tell me what you thought of the photo already."

"A big help." He patted me on the back. "Good job, Frank. Maybe you're better at this than I give you credit for."

"Thanks."

"I'm impressed you pulled off the fake PI thing, but that could have gone south quickly." He raised an eyebrow. "Anyway, Michelle and I looked at that photo over and over," he said softly. "We can't really tell if the man is Bucky Jones. That bushy beard he wore as a younger man covered a lot. On the other hand," his eyes grew wider, "when Michelle and I saw the woman in the photo, we got excited. Sure looked like a younger version of Bucky's wife, Mathilda."

"That's what I thought, too. But she died, according to the obituary I found."

"Oh, she ain't dead." He grinned. "Not at all."

"You're awfully confident of that." *How could he know that already?*

He leaned forward and took a sip of his drink. "That's because we talked to her." He leaned back and crossed his arms. "Technically, Michelle talked to her."

"Already?"

"She didn't see any reason to put it off. Not a lot of time left on this cruise, you know. And she remembered that I'd tracked down Mathilda's number for you."

"What happened when Michelle called her?" I fidgeted in my seat.

"It got a little heated." He laughed softly. "Michelle doesn't fuck around. That's one thing I really like about her. You know exactly where you stand."

"What did she say to Mathilda?"

"She basically said, 'I know who you are. You're Rebbecca Nash Sims.' Should we refer to her as Rebbecca . . . or Mathilda? This is confusing. Let's stick to calling her Mathilda."

I nodded. "I'm surprised Mathilda didn't hang up straight away. Maybe she understood that there'd be no hiding from Michelle."

"Could be. It's possible Michelle said something to the effect of 'If you don't tell me what you know, I will come after you.'" He cleared his throat. "Or maybe Mathilda was just ready to unload what she knew."

"Michelle is good at motivating folks." I leaned closer to him and whispered, "So, what did she find out?"

Jefferson looked around the bar, then said, "First, our hunch was right. Bucky Jones was Lonnie Sims."

"Well, hot damn!" I nearly jumped out of my seat. "Too bad we didn't know that when he was alive."

"No shit. They got married—the first time—right after he finished high school." He leaned close to me and whispered, "According to Mathilda, Lonnie didn't want anything to do with Green's murder. He knew the other three because they'd grown up together. Mathilda said the Bell brothers handled the whole thing."

"That's awfully convenient."

"Sure is. But at least, she admitted Lonnie was there when they killed him and dumped his body in the Mississippi."

"Do you buy her story?"

"I don't know, Frank. I really don't. Like you said, it sure is a convenient story. One that's gonna be nearly impossible to corroborate."

"Except by the Bells."

"Right. Except by them." Jefferson looked down at his drink. "Mathilda said that after the murder Lonnie panicked. The sheriff paid the boys a visit. Seems they didn't do a great job of covering their tracks. The sheriff figured it out quickly. But he didn't like Isaac Green, either. Considered him a troublemaker."

"So, the sheriff told them to leave town."

"Yeah. He told them to leave town. And to never come back. That they should start over someplace far away and establish new identities, new lives."

"The sheriff knew this murder wouldn't be so easy to disappear, I suppose."

"Sure looks like it."

"So, Lonnie left. He told his family he was going to Alabama, but he went to Georgia instead. Out in the country. He got help from a friend of the sheriff's to create a new identity. To start a new life as Bucky Jones. With a new set of papers, too."

"And he just left Mathilda behind?"

Jefferson raised his eyebrows. "He sure did."

"What did she think happened?"

"She was clueless. He'd told her he was going to Alabama for a while to help family but to keep that to herself. Later she figured he didn't want to put her in jeopardy in any way. At that time she was still clueless about what had happened."

"But Mathilda later staged her own death. She must have figured something out."

"Yeah. When news of the murder broke, she put two and two together. She kept dogging the sheriff to find out what had happened to Lonnie. After the initial hubbub died down, the sheriff told her he'd gone to Georgia. He didn't know what Lonnie's new name was, but he gave her the name of his contact down there."

"Gotta admire her persistence." A wind gust blew cold air. I trembled.

"Yeah. I'll give her that." Jefferson finished his Beam and Coke with a long sip. "She didn't want to do anything that could give away where he was, so that's when she staged her death."

"Who knew about it?"

"No one. Absolutely no one. That's what she told Michelle anyway. Her parents went to their graves believing they'd lost a daughter to a car crash. She hasn't talked to her sister since, either."

"Wow." I shook my head. "I hope it was worth it."

"Hard to say, especially since nothing worked out as she'd hoped. Lonnie expected he'd never see her again, and she had a hard time finding him. She searched for twelve years. Got a teaching job in that part of Georgia, but can you believe it? She searched for twelve years."

"She must have really wanted to be with him."

"She did. But by the time she'd tracked him down, he was married again. With children."

"Ouch. I bet Lonnie . . . Bucky? What are we calling him?"

"Let's stick with Lonnie."

"Good. I bet Lonnie was more than a little surprised when Mathilda—the woman he knew as Rebbecca—showed up."

"You know it. But she didn't make a fuss about it. She gave him her new name—Mathilda—and told him how to reach her if anything changed in his life."

"Which it apparently did. They got married again, although it was really their first marriage but under their new names."

"True. Long time to wait to reunite, though."

"So, they reunite and then book a river cruise, one that would also reunite Lonnie with the Bell brothers. What's up with that? Did she know they would be on the cruise, too?"

"No. Not at first. He told her only after they were on board."

"She must know who the Bell brothers are now, though, right? Did she give them up?"

"She said she didn't know any of the other guys. Even though she grew up in Vicksburg, too, she'd never met them. Said she had no idea what they looked like. And Bucky wouldn't tell her who they were. He was firm about that. He worried they'd come after her if they suspected she knew about them." He slid his stool back from the bar, then leaned over very close to me and whispered, "But she did give us one very helpful tip. She was pretty sure both of the Bell brothers *worked* on the boat. Here we've been beating the rugs trying to find these guys among the passengers, when all along they were crew, Frank. Not passengers. Fucking crew."

CHAPTER 27

"I like that our odds of finding these men a lot better now," I said. I checked the time. "I need to catch up with Ruby. Meet for dinner in an hour?"

"Ah . . . not sure. Let me check with Michelle. She's hot on the trail of these men now. Don't know if she's gonna want to slow down for dinner."

"I get it. I'll text you around six."

"Sounds good."

I went back to our stateroom. Ruby was lounging on the bed this time, reading. "Oh, hi, Frank. When did you get back on the boat?"

"Around four. I stopped in to change clothes, but you weren't here."

"I was in the auditorium with Yolanda and Angela. We listened to such an interesting program on the Great Flood of 1927. What a terrible tragedy."

"It sure was. You went with Michelle's sisters?"

"Yes. They are so sweet. We've become good friends, especially with Michelle doing—well . . . you know what she's doing." Her cheeks turned pink. "And you—well, you've been busy, so busy, too."

"Ruby? Are you apologizing for making new friends?"

"No. Of course not." She lay the book on the bed and sat up straight. "Maybe just a little." She smiled. "Oh, Frank. I didn't want you to feel bad about not spending more time with me. When I agreed to come along on this cruise, I knew what I was in for. I knew you'd be busy at times."

"Still, I feel bad about that." I walked over and sat on the edge of her bed. "I've left you on your own far more than I wanted to. I worried you would get bored or feel left out."

"Oh, Frank, you know me. I can take care of myself. I've lived alone most of my life." Her face lit up. "And this cruise—well, I'm just having the best time." She leaned forward and touched my hand. "I haven't felt bored at all. Not once."

"And you've made new friends, too."

"Yes. I have. Would you mind if we all have dinner together tonight? I'm sure you would find them just as interesting as I do."

"Of course. I'd love to. When did you want to go?"

"I'd like a short nap if you don't mind."

"Works for me." I stood up and walked over to my bed. "That'll give me some time to update my notes for the article." I pulled the laptop out of my backpack. "I'm going to work in the library, where it's quieter. I'll come back up here around six?"

"That'll be fine."

I found a comfortable wing chair in the library and set my notebook on the side table. Before I opened the laptop, I texted Jefferson,

> Any idea how many crew members could be suspects?

> Still sorting through that. More than I expected. Older crew on this boat. But fewer than a dozen. I hope.

> Let me know when you have a list. Maybe I can help y'all pare it down.

He replied with a thumbs-up emoji. *He used to hate emojis.*

By six I had caught up with entering notes. I had just about every-thing I needed for the article. Our next stop would be Greenville, where the passengers would have the option of touring the B. B. King Museum in Indianola or taking a literary-and-music-themed bus tour of the area. I'd been to the museum a couple of times before and was already more familiar with the cultural history of the Delta than most folks. I wouldn't need to get off the boat. I texted Jefferson,

Dinner?

Sorry. Not gonna happen right now.

Catch up with you later.

I went back to our stateroom, then Ruby and I walked to the dining room. Yolanda and Angela were already there, waiting for us. When they saw Ruby, they smiled and waved us over. "Let's eat," Yolanda said.

"The best part of the day," Ruby said, smiling.

The hostess led us to a table next to a window, one with a good view. The trees along the river were ornamented with fresh bright green leaves. Watching them gave me a way to mark our steady pace upriver.

"We hear you had an interesting day yesterday," Yolanda said to me, barely concealing a grin.

"I wouldn't call it interesting. Vexing, problematic, baffling, embar-rassing." I slid my chair closer to the table. "Those might be better adjectives."

"What happened, exactly?" Angela asked. "How did you miss our departure?"

"Faulty watch. Helen—the other writer I was with—her watch had died. We didn't figure that out until we got back to the riverfront and saw the boat chugging away upriver without us." I shrugged. "What did I miss? What's been going on here?"

"We saw another terrific show last night," Ruby said. "They performed a medley of show tunes. Your friend Deion took a supporting role this time."

"Ms. Ruby was smiling the whole time," Yolanda said. "And so was I."

"Sorry I missed that one. Was Michelle with you, too?"

"Forgive our sister," Angela said. "She's had this single-minded obsession for as long as I can remember."

"Don't get us wrong," Yolanda said. "We'd love to see our father's killers face justice, too."

"Absolutely," Angela said. "Those were terrible times. Still are, in many ways."

"You know it," Yolanda added.

"The thing is . . . and this is where we . . . where we disagree with our sister. I feel like this whole effort, this obsessive search for Papa's killers, keeps her looking backwards." Angela said and Yolanda nodded. "Ties her to the past. *Keeps* her in the past."

"That's it," Yolanda said.

"I—we . . . Yolanda and I—have always felt we need to keep looking ahead. We'll never forget what happened, though."

"No. Never." Yolanda was shaking her head.

"We know the legal system failed Papa, failed our family. Our community," Angela continued as Yolanda closed her eyes and nodded subtly. "We'll never forget that. But we're just not willing to sacrifice everything we have to fix a past that can't be fixed." She tapped the table with an index finger. "But we *can* change the here and now. We can set our eyes on the future. On living a good life for ourselves, our family, and our friends. And we can go after that. Today."

"We think Papa would have wanted us to do just that, to use what God has given us to forge a better life," Yolanda said. "One that he may have hoped would exist but I suspect doubted would ever be possible." She glanced over at Angela, who gave her a quick nod. "And there's no better revenge against Papa's killers and the racists who abetted them than for us to succeed." She straightened up, her voice louder. "For us to be happy."

"I admire you both," I said. "I've suffered through my share of tragedies, but they rarely left me feeling as determined and . . . as forward-looking as you."

"Thank you, Mr. . . . Thank you, Frank," Yolanda said.

"Well, I'll say this . . ." I glanced around the room, then said quietly, "Finding your father's killers is suddenly looking a lot less like a long shot now."

"What do you mean?" Angela asked.

"Didn't you hear?"

"Hear what?" Yolanda asked, then she looked at Angela. "We haven't seen much of Michelle the last couple of days."

I leaned forward and rested an elbow on the table. "The man who went overboard, the one we knew as Bucky Jones? He was one of the men involved with your father's murder. Lonnie Sims."

Yolanda gasped. Angela's eyes narrowed.

"There's more. Lonnie was the one who tipped off Michelle about two of the killers being on this boat."

Yolanda said, "What?" Her eyes opened wide, then she covered her mouth with a hand.

"And the woman we met as his wife Mathilda was really Rebbecca Nash, Lonnie's first wife. She and Lonnie had married a month before your father's murder. After the murder, Lonnie ran away and changed his name. Rebbecca faked her own death, then went looking for him. It took a while, but they eventually reunited. And remarried."

"How do you know all this?" Angela asked.

"Some good detective work, in part," I answered. "Plus, Michelle talked with Mathilda . . . with Rebbecca . . . who came clean about her past."

"Did she identify the other killers?" Angela asked.

I frowned. "Not exactly."

"Uh-huh," Angela said.

"But she did give us . . . give Michelle . . . a good lead. She said she was pretty sure that the remaining two killers—the Bell brothers—are working on the boat. They're crew, not passengers."

"That narrows it down," Ruby said.

"Sure does," I said. "I don't know what your role is in all this." I sipped my beer. "But maybe this is the right time to check with Michelle. To see if she could use a little extra help before the cruise ends and we lose our best chance to catch these guys."

Angela leaned back in her chair, then looked at Yolanda. They nodded.

Chapter 28

For the rest of dinner, we shared stories about our lives, surprised one another, and laughed a lot. Ruby was right. Yolanda and Angela were a delight. They each had a lot to share, but they were just as interested in hearing about our lives. Ruby's especially. They loved Ruby's stories.

"Never once?" Angela asked. "During all those hard times, you never once missed paying a bill?"

Ruby smiled. "That's right. I always found a way." She leaned in closer to the table and said, "You'd be surprised how many ways you can dress up potatoes and noodles!"

After we finished eating, we all went to the auditorium for the evening show. I checked my phone after I sat down. No messages from Jefferson. Another guest band took the stage again and performed a rousing set of blues and early rock tunes. In the middle of the set, they covered "Hummingbird," maybe the best version I'd ever heard, except for the one by B. B. King himself. I closed my eyes and let the guitar, drums, and singer's voice flow through me.

B. B. King changed my life. I'm not exaggerating. After my family moved to St. Louis, when I was twelve, I fell into a deep emotional hole. I'd lost a lot in the move and needed something to lift me back up. I owned a few records and loved music, but nothing in my collection interested me anymore. Until then, my parents had influenced my choice of music, so I listened to what they liked: a lot of Elvis, Sinatra, and Mitch Miller. Yeah. Mitch Miller. Look him up. It all felt cold to me after we moved.

I found a local record store near home and spent many afternoons wandering the aisles, flipping through bin after bin filled with vinyl records. The clerks who worked there were surprisingly cool with letting a twelve-year-old show up nearly every day and browse without buying a thing. They befriended me after a while, and we'd talk about what I liked. The clerks would smile without making fun of me for my limited range, then took it upon themselves to broaden my musical world. They'd set me up at a turntable with headphones and a gentle "I think you'll like this." They fed me a steady diet at first of pop hits of the past and present, then later they slipped in records totally out of the mainstream. They watched carefully to gauge my reaction. I soaked it all in. When I'd get home, I'd scan the radio dial for stations that gave me more of what they'd introduced me to.

One day, one of those clerks—a guy I knew only as Scratch—handed me B. B. King's *Greatest Hits*. "This is going to change your life, kid." He was right. The record begins with "Hummingbird" and its gentle, hypnotic opening chords. The lyrics speak to the power of love to renew hope and restore a soul. Subsequent songs showed off King's snarky humor (and occasional sexism), his soothing vocal range, and his talent for translating Lucille's—his guitar's—chords into emotions. By the time I got to the melancholy chords and lyrics of "The Thrill Is Gone," I was jelly.

I didn't understand everything I was feeling, but those songs helped me feel what I needed to feel and to let those feelings out. They pulled me out of the emotional muck where I'd been stuck and got me back in the world. I saved my allowance for weeks so I could buy that record. I still own it.

"You OK, Frank?" Ruby's question plucked me out of my head.

"Just fine." I smiled. "Just fine."

After the show Ruby was tired, and Yolanda and Angela begged off to read for a while. "Are you doing any of the tours tomorrow?" I asked.

"Yes," Yolanda said. "We've never been to the B. B. King Museum. Really looking forward to it."

"You'll love it," I said. "Maybe we can meet up again for lunch or dinner tomorrow."

"Of course," Yolanda said. We hugged, and Angela and Yolanda left. I walked Ruby to our stateroom, grabbed a jacket, then went to the Paddle-wheel Pub. I settled on a barstool—most of them were empty—and texted Deion.

> Coffee tomorrow?

> You made it back on the boat??! Sure. See you at 9.

I asked for a gin and tonic, then texted Jefferson.

> How's it going?

While waiting for my drink and a reply from Jefferson, I flipped through my notebook. I found a blank page and drafted an opening paragraph for the article. Looking ahead, I figured it wouldn't hurt to get a few more comments from crew, especially the captain and the hotel manager, about the guest experience they believed they offered.

The bartender came back with my drink. I hadn't noticed earlier, but he was an older guy. *He could be in his sixties.* My phone buzzed before I could chat with him. Jefferson texted:

> Still working it

> Some progress but slow. Check with me again in the morning.

> Will do. Good luck!

The bartender drifted back toward me as he wiped the bar clean with a damp cloth. There wasn't much else to keep him busy.

"Is it usually this quiet up here . . . Carl?" I asked, after looking at his name tag.

He nodded. "You got it right. I'm Carl. And our passengers—well, most of them—are probably getting ready for bed about now. It's busiest up here just before and after dinner."

"If you don't mind me saying, you are a little older than the typical bartender on a cruise, aren't you?"

He laughed. "You aren't wrong. But these boats—river cruises—tend to attract a crew that is . . . let's call us more experienced. That's probably not the case with ocean cruises."

"How long have you worked on the river?"

"A while." He straightened up. "I've been with this company nearly ten years. Time flies."

"You must enjoy it."

"There are worse ways to make a living." He shook his head. "I know. I've tried a few."

I laughed. "I have, too. In college, I worked as a home health aide. Made the same lunch every day—overcooked scrambled eggs—for a diabetic man who didn't get around too well." I tapped the bar. "How about you? What was your least favorite job?"

"Hmm. I've had a few." He turned away for a moment. "Right out of high school, I got a job working at a warehouse in Kentucky. Decent pay, 'specially for someone as young as I was. But it kicked my ass. And I didn't see much hope for moving up to something better."

"When did you start bartending?"

"A few years after that. I bounced around for a while. Didn't want to work too hard or stay put for long. Free and easy. That's how I wanted to live back then." He leaned back against the wall. "I got my first bartending job in Memphis. Maybe twenty years ago?" He rubbed his neck. "I don't know. Like I said, time flies. But that first job, it's hard to forget." He chuckled. "I got hired at a dive bar. Kinda backed into it, honestly. I went there a couple times a week. Good music. One day I heard they were hiring, so I asked about the job. Talked my way into it, really. It helped that they knew me."

"Seems like that could have been a tough place to learn bartending."

"Not really. The drinks were easy—mostly cheap beer—in cans, no taps—and shots. Didn't have to learn many cocktails." He straightened up and moved to the bar. Then he put clean glasses on a shelf below the counter. "The hardest part was really the people. Learning when to cut someone off. Kicking out troublemakers without getting in a fight. Or getting shot at." He smirked. "Little things like that."

"Little things, right?" I nodded. "How'd you find your way onto riverboats?"

"That didn't happen for a while. Bartending was a good job for a wanderer. I could get paid in cash and didn't have to fill out much paperwork. I traveled around—mostly in the South—and always found work in a dive bar or club." He straightened his back. "Hotel bars always seemed to be hiring, too, but if it was part of a national chain, there was a lot more of that red tape to get through. Eventually, I learned about the vacation industry. I was tired of wandering by then, so I signed on with a company that ran resorts along the Gulf Coast and in the Caribbean." He pulled out a box from under the bar. Napkins. He put a few out on the bar. "They were all right. Stayed with them for quite a few years and got to work in some cool places. Loved the warm weather." He smiled. "Learned a lot about cocktails from working in those places."

"A different clientele than in those dive bars . . ."

"That's for sure. But they were all right. Tipped better." He bent down and rinsed a couple of glasses, then put them in the dishwasher. "After a while, though—about ten years ago—I was just ready for something different. That's when I applied here. It's a good gig. Pays well, and I get a bunch of days off in a row. I'm not the wanderer I used to be."

"You got family now that ties you down more?"

"Nope. My folks passed away a while back. I was an only child, too, and never close with my cousins. Never had the desire to marry and have kids."

"You said you grew up in Kentucky?"

"That's right."

"Still call that area home?"

"Nah. I keep an apartment in Atlanta now. It's close enough that I can get to New Orleans or Memphis easily, but not so close that I feel like I'm never away from work. And it's got a lot more going on than Memphis, Vicksburg, or the places closer to where I grew up."

"I had a little time to wander around Vicksburg during our last stop. Seemed like a nice little city, but maybe not many diversions for the person who likes to go out."

"True. I know Vicksburg pretty well." He looked away. "Can't say that I feel a calling to go back."

A party of four sat down on the other side of the bar.

"Excuse me," he said as he went over to take their orders. *About the right age.* I wrote down a few notes about his story: moved around a lot, no family connections, worked jobs that paid more in cash than by check. *Worth a closer look. Much closer.* When I finished my drink, he was still busy with the group. I left a twenty on the bar, nodded to him, and went back to my stateroom.

<h1 style="text-align:center">CHAPTER 29</h1>

"I got something for you," Deion said as I approached his table the next morning. He was grinning. I felt suspicious.

"A cup of coffee? I wasn't expecting anything from you—"

He handed me a small tabletop alarm clock. "I don't need this anymore; I just use my phone. But maybe it'll come in handy for you? The next time you step off the boat, all you have to do is set it to the time you want to return." He winked. "It's like magic. Do you want me to show you how it works?"

"You're a funny guy." I took the black, pyramid-shaped device and turned it around a couple of times in my hand. "Will it count my steps, too?"

"You have to do that yourself. Go get some coffee." He waved toward the bar.

"Need anything?"

"I'm good." I filled a cup with black coffee, picked up a cranberry scone to snack on, then sat across the table from Deion.

"Do I bother to ask how a grown-ass man like yourself can somehow fail to get back on a riverboat before it leaves port?"

"I wouldn't. Let's just say I should have checked the time on my phone instead of relying on a friend's watch. Still, I got back in time to catch last night's show. Loved the band. Especially the B. B. King cover."

"Thanks! They're my favorite of all our guest bands. Can't beat their energy."

"Or their cover of 'Hummingbird.'" Deion smiled. I cleared my throat. "But what did I miss when I was stranded on shore?"

"Besides dinner?" He relaxed in the chair. "Just show-tunes night." He shrugged. "It was a good time. I played the piano but didn't sing. We got to pick most of the songs ourselves, so that makes them more fun to sing."

"What songs did you do?"

"A nice mix of ballads and heel-kicking tunes, with a silly song thrown in. We opened with 'All That Jazz' from *Chicago*. Grabs people's attention right out of the gate. Then we went right into 'We Are What We Are'—"

"With full drag?"

"Eh, no. The company wouldn't let us go all in like that." He slid his chair forward. "But it's possible some cast members might have embellished themselves a bit." He looked down at his hands. "You know, maybe a little color on the nails. Or a something special underneath." He winked. "Not full *La Cage aux Folles*, but we didn't skimp on the tap-dancing routine."

"Wow. That must have taken some practice."

"You know it. Probably our most-rehearsed number. But it comes off really good." He smiled again. "After that, we had to slow it down for a couple of numbers, so we did 'Sunrise, Sunset'—"

"From *Fiddler on the Roof*, one of my favorites."

"Right. And also 'Can't Help Lovin' Dat Man.'"

"That other great song from *Show Boat*."

"You know your musicals, Frank."

I had season tickets for a few years to the Fox Theatre in St. Louis. "Used to anyway. I haven't kept up too well with the newer productions." I forced a smile. "What was the silly song?"

He smirked. "A song called 'It's Amazing the Things That Float.'"

I slapped the table. "I know that song! It's from *The Flood*, an unlikely musical inspired by the Great Mississippi River Flood of 1993." I laughed. "I've never seen it performed live. Not sure how that concept translated to the Broadway stage."

"Not too well, I suspect." He sat back and looked at me. "I should have guessed you'd know that one."

"Knowing you, I'd bet you worked in a number from *Ragtime*."

"Oh, you think you know me?" He rubbed his chin.

"Maybe just a little, especially when it comes to your taste in music." I tilted my head slightly. "Might know a little about that."

"I would hope. If you've been paying attention." *How could I not?* "As it turns out, we did include one song from *Ragtime*: 'Wheels of a Dream.'"

"Good choice. Well, damn. Sorry I missed that show." I nodded slowly. "How's the new show coming along?"

"Great. We debut it tonight, so it better be good."

"Now that I have this handy alarm clock," I waved it in front of him. "I'm certain to be on board for that show."

"What else you been up to? How's your article coming along?"

Deion didn't know about the sisters we'd met and their search for their father's killers, so I said, "Well, I'm in good shape. Don't even need to get off the boat today to take the tours."

"You're not going to the B. B. King Museum? Seems like that would be in your sweet spot."

"It is. But I've already been there. Twice." I shrugged. "I have plenty to do, though. I got an idea for another story."

"What's that?"

"It's a little dark, but that's in my sweet spot, too."

"Is it now?" He tapped a finger on his chin as he looked at me. "Maybe you've gone in a different direction since we met."

"Maybe so."

"What's the story?"

"You remember how a passenger disappeared a couple of days ago?"

"How could I forget?" His shoulders sagged.

"It got me wondering how often something like that happens."

"Not very, I hope."

"No. Not often at all." I raised my eyebrows. "But I heard about one other time. On the *Delta Queen*. A jealous husband smacked another guy on the head with a crowbar, knocked him into the river, where if he wasn't dead already, he drowned."

"Jealous straight men. Figures." He shook his head. "Who'd you hear that story from?"

"A guy in Engineering. Ted Stevens." Deion's face hardened. "What?"

"Nothing." He looked down.

"It's obviously something. What's going on?"

"Stevens in Engineering?" He looked at me. "Seriously? He . . . all those guys down there." His expression hardened. "They're assholes. You sure he's not pulling your leg?"

"I'm pretty sure he's not." I felt confused. "What makes him—all of them—assholes anyway? He seemed OK to me. A little acerbic but OK."

"Of course, he would. You're closer to his age. . . . And skin tone."

"Huh." I leaned back in my chair. "Do you know something about Stevens specifically? Maybe you had a bad experience with one guy in Engineering, so you hate them all?"

Deion crossed his arms. "Are you saying I'm making it up?"

I quickly leaned forward. "No! Not at all." I paused. "Let me try again. I was just wondering if . . . if you've had a bad experience with him directly? Or maybe someone you know has? It might help me figure out how much I can trust him."

He looked from side to side, then leaned forward and rested his elbows on the table. "This isn't a great place for me to talk about them. But yes," he said softly. "I've interacted with him. He was condescending and rude. I've talked with other folks who know him. None of the Black crew have anything good to say about him. Or about anyone in Engineering, for that matter. They all say they get treated rudely by those guys."

"There must be a few Black folks who work in Engineering. What do they say?"

"No." He shook his head. "There aren't. None. Zero." He lowered his voice. "It's all white guys. And most of them are old . . ." He sat back. "Older than you, even."

"Ouch."

Deion cracked a smile. "Look. Sorry for getting all worked up. But you brought them up." He straightened up. "Honestly, I keep my distance from them. Don't trust a single one." He waved a hand at me. "But you go ahead and follow your lead. I just wouldn't trust much of what they tell you."

"I'll be fine." I didn't want to leave our chat on that note. "What's the rest of your day like? Do you get some time off the boat when we stop in port?"

"Depends." He sunk into the chair and let his arms drop. "Sometimes. Depends on the port. I walked around Vicksburg for an hour or so. And found my way back on board on time." He grinned. "But not today. Too much to do. We need more rehearsal time for the new show, so we'll be doing that. And speaking of getting ready—"

"I know. I've taken enough of your time."

"It's been fun, Frank. In spite of you cozying up to those Neanderthals in Engineering." He slid to the front of his chair. "See you again tomorrow morning?"

"Works for me."

"Stay out of trouble." He got up and walked away. I sat at the table a little longer. I understood why Michelle and Jefferson were having a hard time putting together a list of suspects. The crew of the *River Voyager* included several AARP-eligible men. I didn't know how many older guys worked in Engineering, but I was pretty sure Ted Stevens and maybe the chief engineer, Chuck McDowell, were in the right age range for closer scrutiny. And from what Deion had just said, I wondered if there might be others as well. Maybe I needed to pay another visit to Engineering, take a closer look.

Chapter 30

After breakfast I walked back to the Eads Bar, then followed the staircase down to the engine room. I stood at the gate and looked around. A couple of guys passed me without paying me any mind. I guessed they were in their thirties or forties. Both were white, but definitely too young to be suspects.

I stood at the gate, watching the action for a good twenty minutes after that. The machines whirred and hummed, but I saw only those same two guys in the engine room. If Stevens worked nights all the time, he'd have been in bed by then.

"Looking for more river stories, Mr. Dodge?"

I looked to my left and saw Chief Engineer McDowell approaching.

"An insatiable quest," I said. "Just like my desire to understand what the hell I'm looking at."

McDowell looked around. "It's not that hard to figure out, really."

"Not for someone who's spent a lifetime surrounded by it."

"I wouldn't say a lifetime. Not exactly. Feels like it, though." He removed his cap and wiped his forehead. The crew cut made him look younger than he probably was. From a distance, I would have figured he was in his fifties, but now, looking at him closely and with the ball cap off, he could easily have been a decade older. "What's the job of chief engineer like?"

He scoffed. "It's a job." He slipped the cap back on, softening the otherwise sharp angles that defined his face and head.

"What's it take to be chief?"

"A healthy dose of stupidity." He frowned. "Common sense and a good understanding of machines come in handy." Another one of those young engineers walked by. McDowell followed him with his eyes. "Also helps if you're not gullible."

He was obviously thrilled to be the boss. "So, the hardest part of the job is the other people you have to work with?"

"That's about right. Machines I get. More predictable." He paused when the same engineer walked past us again, heading back to where he'd come from. "Give an inch and let out enough slack so they hang themselves." He nodded. "I've found that to be a useful management strategy."

"How long have you worked on this boat?"

"Too long," he said.

"You must know just about everything there is to know about how the boat runs, though, right?"

"I suppose so. I'm probably the only one."

He's a chatty one. "I'd love a tour sometime. A quick overview of the engine room and what the various machines do."

His eyes focused on something out of my sight line. "Gotta get back to it." He took a step away from me, then stopped. "Come back here another time. I'll show you around." He rushed toward the guy who had just passed us.

I thought about pushing that gate open and taking a self-guided tour—seriously, thought it, honestly—but I could see the chief in the distance and figured he wouldn't take kindly to me wandering around his engine room on my own. I climbed the stairs, then texted Jefferson once I was back in a hallway on deck two.

Any updates?

Sure. Come by Michelle's room. I'll fill you in.

Papers covered nearly every available spot in her stateroom: yellow sheets ripped from legal pads, copies of official-looking documents, photos. If there was any pattern to it all, any way they had it organized, I couldn't see it. "Looks like you've been a little busy," I said.

"What makes you say that?" Jefferson asked. "We've been making a bunch of phone calls and looking up what we can in online databases, newspapers, that kind of thing. It's amazing how much info about our lives is out there now, but, man . . . I prefer interviewing folks in person."

I smiled and nodded. "What have you figured out?"

Jefferson looked at Michelle. "Go ahead and tell him," she said, then went back to reading the papers she was holding.

"We haven't been able to get our hands on a complete crew list, so we've had to piece one together."

"A huge pain in the ass," Michelle added. "It better not be a waste of time."

Jefferson looked around the room. "Let's see. Where did I put that?"

Michelle pointed to a legal pad on the bed. "It's right there. How can you miss it?"

"Right." He didn't look at her as he walked over and picked it up. "Here it is." He nodded. "By the way, I found Lonnie's kids and called them. They wouldn't talk to me." He frowned. "As for his business, it looks like much of what he got from selling it went to pay off what he owed the bank. Can't tell from that, though, if he was forced to sell or chose to do so."

"Damn. That doesn't help us much. So, we're still not sure if he killed himself or someone killed him."

"That's right." Jefferson looked down at the paper he was holding. "Anyway . . . let's see . . . we figure there are . . . one, two . . . eight. That's right. We've put together a list of eight people who work on the boat we need to check out. White guys who could be old enough to have been in Vicksburg in the mid-seventies: the first mate, the river historian, a bartender, the hotel director . . ."—he flipped another page—"also, the chief of security, the assistant engineer." He scanned the page. "Oh, and also the chief engineer and maybe the captain."

I raised my eyebrows. "That's a helluva list. Basically, the senior crew on the boat. And a list completely dependent on Mathilda's . . . Rebbecca's comment. Are we feeling confident she pointed us in the right direction?"

"Yeah." He scratched his head. "Mostly." He sighed. "We're running out of time anyway, right? And we weren't making much headway looking over the passengers. We needed a break, something to narrow our focus. I feel good. This feels like the break we needed." He looked at me. "But you're right. There's a chance she's wrong, intentionally or otherwise." He looked down again at the list. "But it's not really that many people. Still daunting, yes, but at least, we've made a list of possibles. Once we dig into these guys more deeply, I expect we'll cross off at least a couple of them quickly."

"I've met some of them."

That got Michelle's attention. She said, "Go on."

"Aside from the captain—Brian and I met him at dinner our first night on the cruise—I've talked with the assistant engineer, Ted Stevens, and a bartender who has to be the one on your list." I looked down at Jefferson's legal pad. "Oh! I also met the chief engineer. Can't say we exactly have great rapport, but we know each other."

Michelle picked up a couple of sheets of paper from the bed and walked them to me. "Any of them look like one of these guys?"

I looked down at a sheet of paper filled with squares of black-and-white photos of young men and women. One photo had been circled. A list of names scrolled down one side of the page. A jagged edge ran the length of the other side of the page. One name had been highlighted: Ray Bell. "Is this from a high school yearbook?"

"Yes," Michelle said. "Do any of the guys you've talked to look like the guy in that photo?"

"How long have you had those?" I asked. Jefferson looked puzzled.

"A while."

"Hours? Months?"

"Years," she snapped. "I got them years ago when I was in Vicksburg."

"Now I know who ripped out the missing pages from the Vicksburg Library's yearbooks," I mumbled.

"It was the only way I was going to get a good, clean copy," Michelle said. "Photocopying didn't work. The images were too dark or too light." She straightened up and crossed her arms. "Besides, it ain't like those were the only copies of those yearbooks. There's plenty of them to be found."

"It wasn't an accusation," I said.

"Why haven't I seen these before?" Jefferson asked.

"You're seeing them now." She cocked her head. Jefferson glared at her. "Does anyone look like that guy, or the one on the next page?"

I flipped to the other page. Same story. A photo circled, and a name highlighted: Lester Bell. I studied it, then went back to the first one and looked again. "I wish," I said. "It's the same issue we had with Lonnie's wedding photo. They're so young in these pictures." I looked over each of the photos again. Nothing stood out about the young people in them. They were nearly indistinguishable from their classmates. Except Lonnie. He wore a beard much like the one he sported in his wedding photo. "So much has changed since: facial hair, bald spots, weight gained." Michelle sighed.

"It's all right." Jefferson sat on the edge of the bed. "It's all right. The photos might come in handy later." He looked at me. "Tell us what you know about the guys you've met."

"Don't know much about the chief engineer yet, other than he's grumpy and hates being the boss."

"What about the bartender?"

"Carl is the guy I met. Is that one of the names on your list?"

Jefferson glanced at the page again. "Yeah. He's one of them. Carl Romero."

"He's worth a closer look. Definitely older than I'd expect the average bartender to be on a cruise. He told me he grew up in Kentucky. Got a warehouse job right out of high school but hated it, so he left. Bounced around for a few years. A wanderer. Got into bartending and worked quite a few jobs that sounded like they paid in cash. Eventually got a resort job, then got hired with this boat. No living family. Or so he said. Keeps an apartment in Atlanta now."

"Good. Good. Thanks Frank." I nodded. "We'll do a lot more digging into his life. What about the other guy, the assistant engineer?"

"Ted Stevens. I talked with him about an incident. He also said he grew up in western Kentucky."

"What's with the Kentucky connection?"

"Not sure." I shrugged. "Maybe just a place young men were eager to get away from. Didn't see much of a future in that, so he left. Got a job as a deckhand on a towboat, taught himself how the engines worked, then landed a job on the *Delta Queen*. In the engine room. When that boat ran into financial trouble, he got a job with the company that runs this boat. Been here since."

"What was the incident he told you about?" Jefferson asked.

"A man went overboard on the *Delta Queen.* I thought I might start collecting stories about people who fall off river cruises."

Jefferson shook his head. "Sounds like something that'd get your attention. What did you find out? What happened?"

"Jealousy. That's the CliffsNotes version. One guy flirted with another guy's wife, then in the middle of the night, the husband cracked the other guy's head open with a crowbar and knocked him into the river."

"Probably not a story that's going to help us here," Jefferson said.

"No. I guess not. What do we do now?"

"I say we get all eight of 'em together and lock them in a room until someone breaks," Michelle said. I didn't think she was joking.

"We can't disappear the entire senior leadership of the boat," Jefferson said.

"We're running out of time, Brian." She threw the pages of yearbook photos on the bed. "We've only got two days left on the cruise, then these men—my father's killers—could disappear. I won't let that happen!" Her hands had curled into fists.

"I understand where we're at." Jefferson got up from the bed and walked over to her. "And the time pressure. But we can't lose our cool. Let's give ourselves a little more time to work this out before we do anything rash." She nodded, but she wasn't happy about it.

He looked back at me. "Since you've already made some contact in the engine room and with that bartender, you should go back. We need you to find out what you can about them." He looked down at his notes. "Maybe you can get them to open up more. See if there are any gaps or inconsistencies in their stories. Do they have a dodgy past?"

"Hey now. No need to use my name as a slur."

"Funny, Frank." Jefferson didn't smile. "Like I was saying, find out anything you can that might point to holes or inconsistencies in their stories. Just do it without making them suspicious." Jefferson's face hardened up. "Remember, Frank. These guys are killers. They killed Michelle's father. They probably killed Otis Morris after Michelle had tracked him down. And who knows? Maybe they killed Lonnie Sims, too." He put a hand on my shoulder and looked me directly in the eyes. "Don't do anything stupid, Frank."

"You always tell me that."

He walked to the door and opened it. "I wonder why?"

CHAPTER 31

I assumed the guys in Engineering would be a lot busier once we got underway again, so I wanted to go back soon. But first I needed lunch and a few minutes to catch up with Ruby. I checked the dining room and found her at a table with Yolanda and Angela.

"Hello. Got room for one more?" I asked.

"Of course," Ruby said. I sat next to her.

"Any news, Frank?" Yolanda asked. "We haven't heard back from Michelle yet."

"Yeah. Some." The server came by and took my order. I said softly, "They've really narrowed down the list of suspects."

"That's encouraging." Angela said. "And surprising."

"And fast," Ruby said.

"How'd they manage to do it?" Yolanda asked.

"The hard way, from what I can tell. They told me they couldn't get their hands on a crew list. I assume that means they had to go around the boat and snoop to create their own list."

"Cut to the chase, Frank," Angela said. "How many people are on their list, and who are they?" They all focused their eyes on me.

"Eight." I looked around the dining room. "I suppose it's possible they missed someone, but there are eight guys on the crew they've identified who fit the profile: White and in their sixties." The server placed plates in front of each of us, and I immediately forked a shrimp and dipped it in grits.

"Eight? That doesn't seem so bad, does it?" Yolanda asked.

"Except the day after tomorrow we'll be in Memphis," Ruby said. "Everyone will get off the boat, including the crew."

"Including the killers," Angela said. Yolanda sat back, and her face went blank.

"That's right," I said. "We have to figure out who they are before we get to Memphis."

Angela set down the fork she had just pierced a tomato with, then said, "OK, y'all. We've got some work to do. Who's on the list?"

I smiled slightly when Angela said "*We* have work to do." I leaned forward and spoke even more softly as I ran through the list of suspects. "I've already had some contact with the two guys in Engineering, so I'm going back down there after lunch."

"Isn't that risky?" Yolanda asked. She looked confused, or concerned. "What are you going to say to them, exactly?" She sliced a piece of chicken, then scooped it up with a piece of blackened shrimp and ate it.

"The chief of Engineering promised me a tour, so I'm going to take him up on that. He knows I'm a writer, so I can get away with asking intrusive questions about his background, like how he got into engineering, where he grew up. That kind of thing. I'm also going to chat with the older bartender again, try to go a little deeper into his background."

"What are you hoping to learn?" Angela asked.

"Brian told me to listen for holes in their stories. Big gaping holes in their bios." I picked up a napkin and wiped grits off my mouth. "We know that these two guys, the Bell brothers, fled Vicksburg after they killed your father, then changed their names. They had to create a new story for themselves, an entirely new bio." I forked another piece of shrimp. "A completely rewritten past. Some do that better than others. Besides, it's been a long time since they left Vicksburg. They might be less, I don't know . . . less thorough about telling the story of their past lives."

"How would we know"—Yolanda looked at me, then Angela—"if they're lying?"

"After I talk with the chief and the bartender, I'll pass along my notes about their stories to Brian and Michelle. They said they'd try to verify the details."

"So, that's it?" Angela asked, then ate a biteful of salad. "You're just going to ask for their life stories, then see if you can prove any of it?"

"I'll be listening for a couple of red flags, too. Were there any sudden changes in their lives in the mid-seventies? Did they work cash jobs, especially when they were younger, or jobs that didn't require a background check?"

"In the seventies? I bet most jobs didn't require a background check then," Angela said.

"True," I said. "But if one of these guys got a government job in the seventies, for example, we can probably rule him out."

"Anything else, Frank?" Ruby asked.

"I suppose if they know a lot about Vicksburg, especially from the seventies or earlier, then that might also be a red flag. But if these guys have worked on the river a long time, they'd probably know a fair amount about Vicksburg anyway. And they probably would feign ignorance."

Angela tapped the table, then asked, "How can we help?"

"That's a good question for Michelle and Brian," I said.

Angela and Yolanda looked at each other. "Michelle hasn't talked to us in a couple of days," Angela said.

"We left her a message after we talked with you yesterday, but she hasn't responded." Yolanda glanced at Angela. "She's so deep in it right now, I feel like we might be a . . . distraction. I fear she wouldn't exactly welcome our help right now."

I sat back and ran some options through my mind. "How about this?" I leaned forward again. "We've got eight people to scrutinize and limited time. Let's split up some of it, at least some of the initial screening. What if you—Yolanda, Angela, Ruby—whoever wants to, spend a little time getting to know the hotel manager and the river historian?"

"We can do that." Angela's face brightened up. "Ruby, you would be especially good with the river historian, given how much you love history."

Ruby nodded slightly, but her face had gone blank. "Yes. I suppose I can do that." She swallowed hard. "I'll just need a little time to think about how to approach him."

"I'll help you as much as you'd like, Ruby," I said. "Naturally."

"Thank you. I'll take you up on that." I couldn't tell if that had reassured her.

Yolanda shifted in her chair. "I think I understand what we should do, but I don't know how convincing I can be. I'd be so nervous." She laughed, nervously.

"Then let me handle it," Angela said. "Him. The hotel manager." She sat up straight. "I can figure something out."

"I'm not saying I won't," Yolanda said. "I'm just nervous about it. What do we do if, you know, he gets suspicious?" She whispered, "These guys are killers, right? We have to be careful." Angela rolled her eyes.

"Of course," I said. "If you feel like you've pushed your luck at all, if you get any hint he doubts your sincerity, back off. Just back off and apologize for being too curious. Something like that. We'll find another way to probe."

"We have options, just not much time," Angela said. "Did Frank's advice make sense, Yolanda?"

She fiddled with her hair. "I suppose. Maybe we can practice on each other before we talk to him? I'd feel better if I had a . . . I don't know . . . a clearer idea of what I might say."

"Then, we'll practice," Angela said. "Right after lunch." She looked across the table. "And Ruby can help us. She can play the role of the hotel manager."

"And you can pretend to be the river historian for me," Ruby said.

They all laughed, but I don't think it was because they found the whole thing funny. "I'm glad you can help." I looked at each of them. "But I want to reinforce what Yolanda said, what Brian said to me. These men are dangerous. That's not an exaggeration." I glanced at Angela. "Don't push too hard. Don't let on that this has anything at all to do with your father's murder. You're just curious tourists. Keep it at that. Understand?"

"Clearly," Yolanda said. Angela and Ruby nodded in agreement. Their smiles melted away.

"If word gets around that we're on to them, we're cooked." I finished the last bite of grits and slid the plate away from me. "I should get on with my part. We'll be in port for only a couple more hours. I was hoping to get my tour of the engine room in before then." I slid my chair back and stood up.

"You be careful, too," Ruby said. "You have a tendency to . . . to—"

"Do stupid things?" I grinned.

"Yes, but I wasn't going to put it like that."

"It's OK. Brian already reminded me." I put a hand on her shoulder. "Don't worry. I'll be fine."

"I'm sure you will," Ruby said, looking entirely unconvinced.

Chapter 32

"Back so soon?"

"I figured you'd be too busy to give a tour once we got underway again. Am I right?"

"Mostly." Chief McDowell opened the gate and waved me into the engine room. "I've got a few minutes to show you around. For a good cause, right? Make sure to write flattering things about me in that article of yours."

"Of course." I pulled out a notebook and pen.

The engine room was quieter and not as hot as the first time I'd walked around it. "Our steam engine was salvaged from an old, decommissioned dredge. A four-cylinder beast with tandem pistons and double-acting reciprocating motion." I had no idea what that meant, but I wrote it down. I figured I'd look it up later.

"How'd you get interested in all this?" I asked.

"Kinda fell into it, I suppose. Grew up tinkering with machines and engines, so that helped."

"Did you grow up near the river?"

"Nah. My people are from Alabama." He paused in front of a panel with several gauges and told me what each one measured. I jotted down a few notes as he talked and pointed—safety this, temperature that—but I was more interested in asking questions about his background.

"What was your path to the river, then?"

"Like a lot of the guys on this boat, especially us older ones, I started on a towboat. Honest work, but hard. Didn't pay great. From day one, I was looking for a way out." He may have broken free from the work of a deckhand early, but his face, even dusted with a couple days of stubble, suggested otherwise. His cheeks looked dry and wind-blown, his wide nose red.

"So, you found your way into the engine room?"

"No." He waved me to follow him, and we walked toward the stern, passing a metal cabinet with drawers full of hardware. "I left river work for a while. Worked construction."

We stopped in front of the pistons that pushed the giant paddlewheel in circles. "This here is the heart of the boat." He stroked the pistons' housing like it was his pet dog.

"I guess the two of you have become well-acquainted."

He smiled. "You could say that. Keeps me on my toes. And easier to figure out than people." He glared at a guy who walked past us as he talked. "We did a lot of work restoring this old engine"—he turned back to me—"but you can't change the fact that it's an old soul. It does its best to keep up, but sometimes it just gets tired and needs a rest. Or a little attention."

"Sounds more and more like me," I said. He smiled. "This isn't the only way the boat moves, though, right?"

"Right. We've also got what's known as a Z-drive." He pointed toward another part of the engine room. "Powered by diesel. It gives a boost when we need an extra push, but we also use it to maneuver."

"I remember. When we were pulling out of . . . where was that? Maybe Camellia Crossing? The captain turned the boat a hundred and eighty degrees on a dime. I guess he used the Z-drive for that?"

"That's right. Couldn't spin around like that with a single paddlewheel in the back."

"You said you learned about engines when you were a kid. Did you learn on anything like these?" I waved a hand around the engine room.

"No. Nothing so big."

"Maybe working construction?"

"Not exactly in the way you might guess. Working construction day after day is hard on the body. I got laid up a few times with back pain, so I started looking around for something else to do." He stretched his back." I'd heard riverboats were coming back strong on the Mississippi—cruises, not barges—so I looked into it. Saw a posting for an entry-level engineering job on this boat and applied. Been here ever since."

"Your experience working construction helped get that job?"

"I suppose. Truth be told, though, you don't need much skill to start down here. Gotta be willing to listen and learn." He looked over his shoulder toward another crew member. "Work hard. Do that, bring that with you. We'll teach what you need to know."

"Can't ask for much more, I suppose."

"You'd think. We get a lot of guys, though, who can't even do that. I've lost track of the number of 'em that have come and gone. Doesn't take us long to figure out who's going to make it, so we don't mess around." His voice got lower, his teeth clenched tightly. "If you can't cut it, we'll kick you to the curb and find someone else who can. No shortage of guys willing to try."

"I didn't realize you had a lot of turnover."

"More than I wish, but no one is willing to work hard anymore. Sign of the times, I guess. People have gotten soft and expect to have things handed to them." He looked down and shook his head. "Anyway, let's move on."

As we walked away from the pistons, I said, "I was wondering." I paused. "Seems like the boat's crew—the *River Voyager*'s crew—is pretty mixed: Black and white, men and women, older and younger. Down here, though, I've seen only white guys. Mostly older white guys at that."

He stopped and turned to face me, his eyes narrowed. "Is there a question in that?"

"Why doesn't the crew down here look like the rest of the boat's crew?" I paused. "That's the question."

He rolled his eyes and started to say something but stopped himself. "Just the way it is now. We've had Negroes—"

"That's not a word I hear much anymore."

He glared at me. "Coloreds." His blue eyes looked like they could burn a hole in me. "Blacks, if you will, have worked down here before. They never worked out. Just a fact. Can't think of a single woman I've ever met who could do this job, either." He turned his back to me. "Boiler's down there," he said, pointing to a stairwell. "Follow me." He glanced back. "But watch your step. Filing injury reports is a pain in the ass."

We walked down and into a room visitors don't normally get to see. Not that it was all that exciting. Just a big iron box and lots of pipes and gauges. Felt claustrophobic. And hot.

"In the old days, these machines"—he pointed at the boiler—"were quite temperamental. Had a tendency for pressure to build up too quickly and explode." He scanned the boiler. "Killed a lot of people. Thousands." He looked at me, raised his eyebrows, then looked back at the boiler. "'Course, much safer today. Plenty of fail-safes built in." He glanced over at me. I wiped a bead of sweat off my forehead. "Still, if one of these pipes somehow came loose while we were under steam, it'd scald a man to death. Or leave him in the kind of pain that'd make him *wish* he were dead."

I looked at him and couldn't tell if he was relating a fact or serving a warning. "I'll make a note to stay out of this room when we're moving."

"Wise man." He looked at his watch. "And that's the end of today's tour. I hope that satisfied your curiosity, Mr. Dodge, but now I gotta get back to work. Time to get this beaut ready to move on to Memphis. Follow me." He walked back up the stairs, then toward the stern. "The exit is this way." I lagged a couple of steps behind. "Don't dilly-dally, Mr. Dodge."

I caught up. We didn't talk. When we got to the gate, he opened it. I stepped inside the visitors' area, then turned around. "Thanks for the tour, Chief McDowell. I appreciate your time. Hope I didn't offend you with any questions."

"I'm not one who's easily offended, Mr. Dodge." He closed the gate, took a step toward the stern, then looked back at me. "Just remember. You promised to write nice things about me." He forced a toothy smile, then walked away.

I walked up the stairs to the Eads Bar, sat on a stool, and ordered a drink. A whiskey.

Chapter 33

Chief McDowell hadn't taken kindly to my question about his hiring practices. In fact, he'd answered my question about those practices with a veiled threat. At least, that's how I took it. I couldn't tell if that made him a murder suspect, a racist, or just someone who doesn't take well to criticism. Regardless, I made a few notes about his life story—family from Alabama, tinkered with machines as a kid, worked in construction—and looked forward to poking holes in it.

As I sat at the bar, I felt a faint shake as the pistons fired up and churned the paddlewheel behind me. We were pulling out of Greenville and beginning the last leg of the trip. We'd be cruising overnight and all the next day until we reached Memphis the following morning.

I felt anxious. Finding two guilty men in a pool of eight didn't seem impossible, but could we do it in less than two days? And even if we identified the right two men, what then? Would they quietly give themselves up to the authorities? Which authorities? Had Michelle and Jefferson thought that far ahead, or were they so caught up in the search, they hadn't thought through what might happen when they had their suspects cornered?

I needed to ask Jefferson about that at some point. But I could wait. We needed to shorten our list of suspects as quickly as possible, or the rest didn't matter. I called Jefferson and relayed what I'd learned about Chief

McDowell; it wasn't much, but maybe he and Michelle could do something with it.

The whiskey was going to my head, so I left the bar. I hadn't gotten five steps from the door when someone came up from behind and tapped me on the shoulder.

"Need anything today, Mr. Dodge?" Barry Riggs asked.

The hotel manager sure seemed eager to please. Maybe too much so. *I feel like I'm being stalked, not helped. Is his act just a thinly disguised way of keeping tabs on me?* "I'm good. Just on my way to do some writing."

"Wonderful!" He walked away, and I wondered if Angela and Yolanda could get him to slow down long enough to have a conversation.

I popped into our stateroom to get my laptop—Ruby wasn't there—then found a quiet corner in the library to write a first draft of my article about the cruise. Every time I'd get a few paragraphs done, though, my mind would drift back to the engine room, to Chief McDowell and Ted Stevens. And I'd rehash my conversation with the bartender, Carl. When I saw them again, what would I say? How could I get them to say something more? Anything that might betray their past?

I eventually finished a full draft, but it took all the rest of the afternoon. I flagged a couple of places I could use an additional quote or two, then closed the laptop and went looking for Ruby. It was time for dinner, but I wasn't in the mood for another sit-down meal. I scanned the dining room and didn't see Ruby, Angela, or Yolanda, so I went up to our stateroom. Ruby wasn't there, either. When I called her cell phone, I heard it ringing loud and clear; she'd left it on the nightstand next to her bed. I shrugged. The three of them were practicing ways to approach the hotel manager or river historian, or they were already in the middle of quizzing them.

I went down to the Bow Bar and filled a plate with salad and slices of bread from the buffet. Carl wasn't stationed there, so I figured I'd try to find him after dinner at another bar. I sat at a table near the side, as close as I could get to the wide river. The sunlight was softening, and the air still smelled of fresh blossoms and damp earth (with a hint of béarnaise sauce). The *River Voyager* cut a narrow path through the umber waters of the Mississippi, a river colored not by the detritus of humanity but by dirt and sand from the Rockies and Great Plains recycled by Mother Nature. Water touched the levees in places. In others, it spilled over banks, blanketing the bottoms of trees in the floodplain and on islands. Still, those trees had fully leafed out and were gloriously green. The sky was a clear blue. High in the sky, flocks of ducks and pelicans occasionally passed us on their way north. So much life!

I couldn't understand how nineteenth-century Europeans traveling the Mississippi had been so dismissive of this river. Charles Dickens described the Mississippi as "an enormous ditch, sometimes two or three miles wide, running liquid mud, six miles an hour." British travel writer Frances Trollope wrote, "For many a wearisome mile above the Wolf River the only scenery was still forest—forest—forest." Captain Frederick Marryat, who traveled the river in the 1830s, wrote he "could only regret that life was so short, and the Mississippi so long." Grumps. Every one of them.

Dinner over, I walked up to the Paddlewheel Pub. Carl was there, but he was busy. The post-dinner crowd had him running from one end of the bar to the other. I sat at the end of the bar in the last empty seat and looked for entertainment on my phone while I waited for the crowd to thin. Most folks wouldn't stick around for more than one drink, I assumed. I was right, and little by little, customers left.

"What can I get ya?" Carl asked.

"How about a beer? Got a good stout?"

"Sure." He turned around and pulled out a bottle from the cooler, then showed it to me. "Siege Brewing Company. We got some of this when we stopped in Vicksburg."

"Not a brand I know. Let's give it a try."

After serving me he moved to the other end of the bar to clean up after three people who had just left. Then he drifted back down to my end.

"What d'ya think?"

"Tasty." I took another small sip. "Full body. More than a hint of chocolate. A bit malty but not too much, but also a little hoppiness on the back end." After still another small sip: "Good flavor. Balanced. Impressive. I like it."

"I wasn't expecting a full review, but I appreciate it. You sound like someone who's drunk a beer or two in his life." He leaned against the bar.

"You could say that. I've also written a few food and drink reviews, so I've had to learn the lingo."

"Ah. You must be the writer I heard about." He stood back up. "Maybe I shouldn't have talked so much the first time we met!"

"Nah. You're good. All off-the-record stuff."

"Cool." He reached down and washed a glass in the sink below the bar. "Getting paid to ride cruises, eat, and drink? Sounds like a good way to make a living."

"There are worse things to do. If only I'd been smart enough to find someone to show me the ropes early on, this might have been an actual living instead of just a collection of paychecks."

"And yet, here you are. Here we are, a couple of guys who found ways to put together paycheck after paycheck doing what we wanted to do. Life could be worse." He pulled out a pair of shot glasses. "Care to toast with me?"

"I thought drinking on board was forbidden—"

"I won't tell if you don't." He turned around and scanned the bottles on a shelf behind the bar. "Tequila?"

"Wouldn't turn that down!" He poured two shots, then looked to his left and right to make sure no one was watching. We clinked glasses and drank the tequila.

"Tasty. Thanks." He slid a glass of ice water in front me, which I appreciated. "You ever look back and wish you'd taken a different path?" I asked.

"Nah." He dropped the shot glasses into the sink. "Sure. It's been tough at times. The fates didn't always deal me a good hand. But you could say I got dealt the freedom card and have done my best to make the most of that."

"What do you mean?"

"I grew up in Kentucky. I may have mentioned that."

"Yeah. I remember that."

"When I was fifteen, my parents got killed in a car accident."

"That's horrible."

"Yeah, well, it got worse. I was an only child. Too young to live on my own, so the state sent me to live with my mom's sister. She was what we used to call a spinster."

I smiled. "Yeah. I don't hear that word too often anymore."

"It's not too polite, I suppose." He picked up a rag, then wiped the top of the bar. "Anyway, she lived nearby, alone, so I didn't have to change schools. But she was a devout Christian and a fucking control freak. She let me out of the house only to go to school, or, if I was lucky, maybe for a school event. But only if she knew adult chaperones would be there." He shook his head.

"Not much space for a teenager to do what teenagers want to do."

He chuckled. "True. Which is why I ran away. Just couldn't live under those conditions." He let go of the rag and stood up straight. "Looking back on it, that car accident really messed me up."

"How could it not?"

"True. Anyway, maybe under other circumstances, my aunt and I might have made peace. But not then. I wasn't in any frame of mind to live under those conditions."

"Where you'd go?"

"I found my way to Paducah. Got a job in a warehouse moving shit around. Hard work, but they paid cash and never asked how old I was. I stayed there awhile. Made enough to rent a room in town and feed myself, then eventually got tired of that job and moved on." As he talked, he moved a couple of glasses from under the bar to a shelf behind him. "Back then, it was easy to find cash jobs, especially for a mobile young man who didn't mind working hard. Kept that going for quite a few years: cash jobs, cheap rooms."

"Sounds like freedom. But maybe a bit lonely, too?"

"Not as bad as you might think. You'd be amazed how easy it is to make friends when you're a young man with cash in your pockets." He forced a smile. "Anyway, I eventually found my way into more stable work, if you consider bartending stable."

"You ever go back to where you grew up?"

"Once." He leaned back against the cooler. "I was what? late twenties? The town was on a downhill slide. Didn't look at all like I remembered. Some businesses had closed. Found our old house empty and abandoned." He looked down at the floor. "Looked like a lot of people had left. My aunt had passed a couple of years before."

"No reason to stick around."

He looked up at me. "None whatsoever. Never went back after that. Never looked back, either. Like I said, I got dealt the freedom card. And I've been doing my best to bet with it again and again."

"Nothing to tie you down."

He shrugged. "I married once. Didn't work out. We split after a couple of miserable years, for the both of us. I'm better off on my own. And so was she."

I felt sad for him, if his story was true. And it sure felt like it was to me. Yes, he had a lot of freedom, but I couldn't imagine a life with no strong ties. No family around. Transient friendships. No one to share life's burdens and joys with. Maybe it worked for him. It wouldn't for me.

My phone lit up. Jefferson was calling. "Excuse me." I stood up and answered the phone as I walked away from the bar. "What's up, Brian?"

"The Coast Guard found Bucky's body. He'd washed up just outside some place called Plaquemine. Deep bruise on the back of his head."

"Maybe he hit his head on the side of the boat when he went in?"

"No. Not likely. Someone hit him, hit him hard. He probably fell in the river after that."

"So, he didn't kill himself."

"No. He was murdered."

CHAPTER 34

"Everything OK?"

Carl the bartender must have read the concern on my face. "Yeah. Just a quick call from a friend going through a hard time." I sat down again. "Hey, I've got a random question."

"What's that?"

"You said you were from Kentucky. A couple other guys on the crew also said they were from Kentucky. What's up with that?"

"Did they ever work on towboats?"

"Yeah. I think both of them might have gotten their first job on a towboat."

"That explains it there. The tow companies used to recruit a lot of deckhands from a couple of counties in Kentucky. I hear they had their favorite bars, where they'd hang out, strike up a conversation, then offer a bonus to lure them onto a tow."

"But that wasn't the case for you?"

"Nah. I never took the bait."

"Huh. I had no idea." I checked the time on my phone. *Shit. Gotta go now. Deion's new show is about to debut.* I thanked Carl for the tasty stout and the shot, tossed a ten-dollar bill on the bar, then excused myself and hightailed it down to the auditorium. I spotted Ruby in a middle row and slipped into a seat next to her.

"Oh, good. You made it," she said. "I was getting worried."

"Lost track of time upstairs." The lights went down and the curtain up. Deion sat at the piano, dressed in a well-fitted gray pinstripe suit, white dress shirt, and a bright red tie decorated with musical notes. The suit looked tailored to the early 1900s. The tie was definitely Deion's personal touch. A spotlight zeroed in on the piano, and Deion deftly played the opening notes of Scott Joplin's "The Entertainer." As the tempo picked up, other cast members danced onto stage dressed in Jazz Age attire.

The show was an absolute treat to watch, mixing classic ballads (Billie Holiday's "I'm a Fool to Want You") with blues standards ("St. Louis Blues"), a deep cut ("Levee Man Blues"), a toe-tapping favorite ("It Don't Mean a Thing [If It Ain't Got That Swing]"), then wrapping up with "When the Saints Go Marching In."

The show earned a standing ovation, although I wasn't sure how much of that was because the passengers got up to jockey for position at the elevators. Still, I loved the show, and Ruby was beaming afterward, too. "I could sit through that a dozen times and never tire of it," she said.

We left the auditorium and stepped outside to the deck. The night air was crisp but not cold. We were in the navigation channel close to shore, and the scent of humus drifted across the water from the riverside forests. Stars filled the sky, and the Milky Way painted a wide, faint line across it. "Did you have a chance to talk to any of our . . ."—I looked around the deck to make sure we were alone—"to any of our suspects?"

"No. Not yet." A couple walked past us and relaxed next to the railing to look over the river. Ruby leaned toward me. "Angela and Yolanda are going to find the hotel manager tomorrow. By the time I'd worked out a few things to ask the river historian, I couldn't find him." She laughed softly. "I'm still not entirely confident about how to do it. I get nervous when I think about it."

I thought for a minute. "One angle, I suppose, would be asking about his job." I scratched my head. "You could say you have a nephew who's really interested in the history of the Mississippi. What would he have to do to land a job like a river historian? You could ask him what his path into the job was like: Where did he go to school? What did he study? Was the river part of his childhood? Things like that."

"Yes. Yes. I think I could do that. Thank you, Frank."

I put an arm around her shoulder. "You're so good with people, Ruby. So natural. Just be yourself. Roll with the conversation. You'll be fine."

"Thank you. That helps." Ruby shivered slightly. "It's getting a little too chilly for me out here. It's about time for me to retire anyway. What are you going to do the rest of the night?"

"I need to catch up with Michelle and Brian. After that, I thought I might pop back into the engine room around midnight and chat again with that assistant engineer, Ted Stevens. Still need to get more details about his life."

"Of course. You're going to be a tired one tomorrow."

"Probably so." I walked her back to our stateroom, then texted Jefferson.

Got a minute?

Sure. Come by Michelle's room.

"Housekeeping will not be thrilled with the state of this room," I said after I entered. "No wonder you keep the 'Do Not Disturb' sign on the door."

"You're funny," Jefferson said. "What's up?"

"I've got a little down time. Thought I'd see how you two were coming along."

Jefferson looked at Michelle.

"We can rule out that bartender you talked to," she said.

"Carl?"

"Yeah. We found an obituary for his parents. Died in a car accident when he was fifteen, right?"

"Right," Jefferson said.

"That's what he told me. Did the obit mention any other family?"

"Just a couple of aunts," Michelle said. "Looks like Carl was an only child."

"That's also what he told me."

"Good," Jefferson said. "We also verified that he worked for a resort company, like he told you, worked there before he got hired on this boat."

"I found his name in a couple of Memphis phone books in the 1970s, too," Michelle said. "And no criminal record, right?"

"Right," Jefferson said.

"He left a good paper trail. I think he's telling the truth," Michelle said. "I don't think he could have planted all that retroactively."

"What if he assumed someone else's identity? Isn't that possible?" I asked.

Jefferson shrugged. "I suppose, Frank. If he killed the original Carl and stole his identity, memorized the details of Carl's life. Maybe he could get away with that. Do you think that's what happened?"

"No, actually. I don't. I think he was telling the truth about his background."

"Then let's strike him off the list and move on," Michelle said. "We can always circle back to him again later if we need to."

"What about the chief engineer, Chuck McDowell?" I asked.

"The guy you pissed off?" Michelle asked.

"Yeah. That one." I crossed my arms.

"He's a harder one. More than a few McDowells in Alabama." Jefferson looked at the bed. "Where did I put those notes on McDowell?"

"On the dresser."

"Right." He picked up a legal pad and looked down at the notes on it. "We found a birth record for a Charles McDowell that would be about the right age. Born in Birmingham. A Charles McDowell graduated from a high school in Birmingham. It would help a lot if we knew our McDowell's exact date of birth. Still working on that. We've found a few other bits on him, but it's spotty. He didn't tell you much about his life that we could check on, so we're still looking for more." He looked up at me. "But based on what I've seen, I don't think he's one of the killers. Not impossible, but a long shot."

"Damn. I really want him to be guilty. Don't like him."

"Yeah, well, that's not how it works. Being an asshole, even a racist asshole, doesn't make you a criminal. If you come up with anything else about his background that might lead us to change our minds, let us know." He tossed the legal pad back onto the bed. "Any other news?"

"No. Not yet. I'm going back to visit with Ted Stevens tonight. I'll let you know how that goes. And I expect to have something to pass along to you tomorrow about the hotel manager and the river historian."

"I sure hope so, Frank," Michelle said.

"Clock is ticking, you know," Jefferson said. "The cruise will be over in less than thirty-six hours."

"I know." *I know.*

CHAPTER 35

I left Michelle's stateroom and took the stairs up to the hurricane deck, then walked back to the Paddlewheel Pub. A few people sat at the bar, enough to keep Carl busy pouring drinks. I nodded at Carl, asked for a stout, then sent Deion a text.

> Absolutely loved the new show. Terrific! My friend Ruby said she'd happily sit through it over and over.

He replied right away with an emoji, a face with a hand over its mouth, then a brief message.

> I've got some down time. Finally! Meet me on deck three, outside?

> Sure! When?

> Ten minutes?

I sent him a thumbs-up emoji, then got Carl's attention to cancel the beer. I scanned my news feed for a couple of minutes, then walked back down to deck three. Deion was leaning on a rail on the port side of the boat when I got there.

"How's it feel to have a hit on your hands?"

He turned and smiled at me. "I don't know if a standing O on a cruise ship counts as a hit, but . . . not bad. Not bad at all." He shivered. "It's colder than I expected. Maybe we should go back inside. How about the library on deck two?"

"Works for me." We walked down a flight of stairs, then found a couple of well-padded wing chairs in a quiet corner of the library.

"I assume you were happy with how the show went?"

"I am. Super happy." He looked down at the floor. "Everyone—the whole cast—was amazing. So proud of everyone."

"It helps when you've picked the right songs to work with."

He cleared his throat and looked at me again. "Yeah. That's the point, right?"

"I like how you slipped in some hometown love with 'St. Louis Blues.' Then followed it up with an obscure river-themed tune."

"You mean 'Levee Man Blues'?" He grinned.

"Yeah. That's the one."

"I thought you might recognize that one. A while back, I went deep into Jelly Roll's catalog. That song jumped out at me. The simple piano chords. The feeling of desperation. I thought it would make for a good tempo change in the middle of the show."

"Worked for me."

"What's up with you, Frank? How'd your chat with the asshole engineer go?"

I chuckled. "Which one?"

"What do you mean?"

"I guess I haven't updated you yet. I've talked with Ted Stevens and with the chief, Chuck McDowell."

He raised his eyebrows. "What did you think?"

"You're right. I mean . . . they're both hard to like."

"Let me help." He leaned toward me. "Stevens is a prick. McDowell is a cranky old man."

"Can I quote you on that?"

He nudged me on the shoulder. "Seriously, sometimes I think there's a secret cabal on this boat. These old white guys seem to stick together and avoid anyone who's not like them."

"If they're just pricks and bitter men, then maybe you should consider yourself lucky."

"Nice try, Frank." He sat back in the wing chair. "At least we'll be rid of the captain soon. That guy is just terrifying. Thank God someone talked him into retiring."

"You get along swimmingly will all the senior officers, don't you?"

"Hush." He slid back in his chair and crossed his arms. "How's that article of yours coming along?"

"Better than expected. I finished the first draft today. Guess I'll need to go back and add a few words about the new spectacular musical revue."

He slapped my hand lightly. "Enough. We've still got a full day ahead of us tomorrow. What're you going to do with your time if you're finished?"

"I've got a couple of little things I still need to do. Mostly just getting another quote or two." I looked away and debated whether to tell him about the case I'd gotten pulled into. "There is one other thing taking up a lot of my time." I looked at him without facing him directly.

"What's that?" He crossed his arms.

"This has to stay between you and me." I looked him square in the eyes. "I'm not kidding about that."

He nodded. "OK. I promise not to tell." He leaned slightly closer to me. "What's up, Frank?"

I told him about Isaac Green's murder. How his daughters, Michelle, Yolanda, and Angela, were on the *River Voyager* because they believed two of the killers were on the boat. How I had tiptoed my way into their search to do my part to help find the killers.

He looked away from me, his lips curled tightly. He seemed lost in thought. "I'm glad you didn't tell me about this sooner," he said. "I would have had a hard time concentrating on my show."

"We've been keeping it very quiet, as you might guess. We can't afford to tip anyone off."

"Do you have any ideas about who it might be?"

"We're betting they're both part of the crew. And we've narrowed it down to seven men." I ran through the list.

He ran a hand through his hair. "You're sure about that? That two of those guys . . . two of them are killers? Murdered a Black man some forty years ago and got away with it?"

"Yeah." I flinched slightly. "I mean . . . sure, it's possible that we're on the wrong track completely. But I don't think that's the case. Or maybe we've overlooked someone else who works on the boat?"

"What makes someone a suspect?"

"Basically, a white guy in his sixties."

"There's a bartender who fits that description."

"Carl?"

"Yeah."

"We already ruled him out. What do you think about the other seven? You know them?"

"Sure. It's not that big a boat. We all know one another. Even if we don't like each other." He rubbed his forehead. "Excuse me, Frank. I just feel a little overwhelmed. This is intense." He shivered again. "You know I don't care for those guys in the engine room. I told you that before."

"I remember. What's that about?"

"They're racist, homophobic Neanderthals. That's what."

I smiled slightly. He didn't pull punches. I liked that about him. "All of them? Or just the ones I mentioned."

"All of them. The engine room feels like—to me anyway—feels like a step back in time. To the Old South. Not a place I care to visit. I've never felt comfortable around any of those guys." He frowned. "Plus, in case you didn't notice, there's not a single brother working down there, and I don't think there ever has been. At least, not since I've been working on this boat."

"I'm sorry you have to put up with that shit. I've already figured out the racist part from the conversations I've had with Stevens and McDowell. Especially McDowell." I leaned closer to him. "What do you know about them? I assume you aren't having heart-to-hearts with them—"

"Got that right."

"But have you ever heard anything about their backgrounds? Like where they're from? Do they have families? Nicknames? Anything?"

"I really don't know." His face lit up. "But maybe I can find out? Ask around about them?"

We needed help, but I was worried about tipping our hand. We didn't know who they were, and I didn't want them to know we were looking for them. "Who could you ask?"

"Well, let me see. A couple of the women I perform with, they've worked on this boat longer than me. I could start with them. Confide in them about the way one of those guys treated me and see if they have anything to add."

"That sounds OK. You just have to emphasize that you're telling them in confidence." I leaned toward him. "Understand? Tell them you need to vent but don't want to jeopardize your position on the boat. Tell them to keep it to themselves."

"I can do that." He nodded, then pulled his shoulders back.

"What about the others on the list? Know anything about them?"

"The river historian? He's pretty new. I think he started after I did. Maybe he worked as a captain or pilot or something like that for most of his career. The hotel manager? Well, he just keeps to himself. Way too cheery. But rarely hangs out with the rest of the crew. I figured he must get worn out by spending all day tending to the passengers. Needs some alone time to refresh. They'd wear me out."

"And the first mate?"

"Don't have much to do with him, either. He's busy bossing around the deckhands and placating the captain, I assume. Don't think I've ever said anything more than hi to him."

"And what about the chief of security?"

"Hopkins? Eh, no." He waved his hands in front of him. "I keep my distance from anyone in law enforcement. Don't trust 'em."

I sighed. "Seems like you all live in your own bubbles on this boat."

"Yeah. We do." He shifted toward me. "And I don't mind it that way. Just because we work in the same place doesn't mean we have to be best friends." He sat back and crossed his arms. "What now?"

I knew we could use more help. Seemed like a minor risk for Deion to poke around a bit. "I like your idea. Talk to those women you work with, tell them about how the guys in Engineering treated you like shit. See what you can find out from that."

He nodded. I stepped forward and hugged him. We were in no hurry to let go.

"Don't push too hard," I said, then took a step back. "Don't go asking a ton of questions about them. We absolutely have to keep a low profile with this." I looked him directly in the eyes. "Clear?"

"Clear." He kissed me on the cheek and hurried away.

CHAPTER 36

After Deion left, I went back up one deck and stood outside. No one else was around. With some time to kill before I could go back to the engine room, I wanted to linger near the river, without distractions. It helped me clear my head. Light from the boat reflected off the water, unveiling the boundary between river and boat. Looking toward the horizon, though, I couldn't tell where the river ended and the sky began.

Ted Stevens. We'd hit it off OK the first time, but mostly because I was looking for a good river story or two. I'd try the same tactic again. I was bored and finished with my assignment, I'd say, and needed some fresh material to write about. Maybe he could help with that. After all, he said his grandfather was a commercial fisherman. Men like that collected stories as eagerly as they netted fish.

I felt good about what I wanted to say to him, so I walked back down to the library—I had the place to myself—where I read and warmed up until just before midnight. I enjoyed the quiet, and the gentle, steady low hum of the engine—a sensation I felt more than heard as the boat glided across the water—nearly lulled me to sleep.

I reluctantly got up and made my way to the Eads Bar and the stairwell down to the engine room. The bartender was cleaning up when I entered. "We're closed," she said.

"Just making my way to the engine room. Hoping to catch Ted Stevens."

She pointed. "Stairs are over there."

I stood at the gate at the bottom of the stairs and looked around. The room hummed as usual, and smelled of oil, as usual. "Back again?" I heard someone ask.

"I haven't been around talented storytellers in a while. Thought I'd come back for more."

"Chief know you're here?"

The question surprised me. "No."

"Guess we won't tell him, then." He grinned, then opened the gate. "This way. Just about to take a smoke break."

I followed him as he loped toward the same place where we talked before, toward the stern but outside of the engine room. Once we were outside, he used a wall as a windbreak, cupped a hand, and lit a cigarette. The flash spotlighted his face, which had more lines than *Macbeth*. "What would you like to know?" he asked without taking the cigarette out of his mouth.

"You've been on the river awhile. Ever had a moment when you were afraid the river might take your life?"

He turned to me and blew smoke toward the river. "More than once." He leaned against the wall. "My first year as a deckhand, we were coming into Baton Rouge, downriver. Heavy thunderstorm. Blinding rain, except for these flashes of lightning that gave me a quick look at what was going on. We pulled into the berth, and me and another fella raced to get the barges secured in place." He flicked ashes off his cigarette. "Well, we got one of the lines around a bollard when a big gust of wind pushed us back out toward the channel. The pilot tried to correct for it, but it was no good. The pressure on the line was too much. It snapped. *POP!*" he yelled. "The barge I was on swung away from the dock. I got knocked off my feet. I fell on my ass and rolled to the edge of the barge, but I reached out and caught hold of something. Don't even remember what exactly. Pure survival reaction. If I hadn't done that, we wouldn't be talking today." He took a long drag.

"A moment like that can make a man question his life choices."

"Ain't that a fact. Of course, that don't happen until after the shit's hit the fan and you have time to think. I still had to get back up on my feet and secure the barge."

"What happened next?"

"Lucky for us, we didn't get another wind gust that strong. The pilot got us back in line with the dock, and we got everything tied down securely." He cleared his throat. "Never needed a cigarette and a shot so bad in my life."

"Damn. That was a close call. But it sounds like everything worked out OK."

"Not exactly. That's when I hurt my back. Laid me up for a few weeks. Lots of time to think." His eyes opened wide. "To question those life choices."

"What did you take from the experience?"

"That I needed a different job."

"What about when you were a kid? Any close calls on the river growing up?"

"Not really. Didn't really spend much time on rivers until that first deck-hand job."

He confused me. "Oh. I thought you said your grandfather was a commercial fisherman. I assumed that meant you spent a lot of time on the river."

He stood up straight. "Oh. Right. I thought you meant later." He flicked his cigarette into the river. "Yeah. My dad and granddaddy were commercial fishermen. But they gave it up when I was pretty young. I wasn't part of that. I was born in '54. They were out of fishing by then."

"Sorry. I must be confusing your story with someone else's." I wasn't. He'd told me before that only his grandfather had worked in commercial fishing. "Where'd you grow up then, if not near the Mississippi?"

He looked down as he exhaled again. "Tennessee. Outside of Knoxville."

"So, near the Tennessee River, then. What was that like?"

"We didn't live all that close to the Tennessee, truthfully."

"Must have been hard to leave behind so much family history in commercial fishing. What did your family think when you went out to work on the river?"

"My dad had passed on by then. My mom was just happy I found a job."

"How old were you when your dad passed?"

"A teenager." He squinted. He straightened up, took a drag off his cigarette, then blew it lightly in my direction. "You know, I heard about your . . . disagreement with the chief."

"How's that?"

"You made some snarky remark about his hiring practices." He flicked the cigarette into the river, then immediately lit another one. The flame reflected in his eyes. "He doesn't like being second-guessed. Or someone implying that he isn't properly . . . open-minded. Maybe you noticed."

"I made an observation about the composition of the Engineering crew. That's all. No disrespect intended." Changing the subject would have been a good way to short-circuit the chance of escalation. I wasn't in a deflecting mood. "But that doesn't mean my observation was wrong. I just find it odd how, you know, the guys working down here are so . . . uniform."

He fixed his gaze on me but didn't respond right away. "Where'd you grow up, Frank?"

"Wisconsin. And St. Louis." I held his gaze.

Another drag, then he exhaled smoke at my face. "You've got to be careful in these parts, Frank. Careful about sticking your nose where it don't belong. Into a culture you know nothing about."

"Ted. We've been getting along so well. We're both river rats. Let's not get riled up because of a little disagreement I had with the chief. That's got nothing to do with you."

"You got that wrong, Frank. It's got everything to do with me, too. He and I, we've worked together for years. We both have say about who gets hired to work down here. You criticize him, you're criticizing me, too."

I hadn't realized that McDowell had a cooperative approach to management. "Like I said, Ted. It was just an observation."

He flicked the second cigarette into the river. "I'll take you at your word. But we're done here." He straightened his shoulders. "Gotta get back to work." He turned around and walked back into the engine room. I followed.

"Hope you got all you needed for your story, Frank. We're gonna be busy down here until we reach Memphis." He turned back to me and rested a hand on my shoulder. His eyes opened wide. They burned red and looked irritated. "Can't imagine I'd have time for any more of your questions."

"I appreciate your time. And patience, Ted." I stepped toward the stairs. His arm dropped. "I suppose if I have any more questions for my article, I'll just ask the chief directly."

"Good luck with that." He opened the gate, I stepped through, and he closed the gate behind me. He walked away, shaking his head.

I dashed up the stairs, through the Eads Bar, and back to the library. I was sure he'd told me earlier that only his grandfather had been a commercial fisherman, that none of his kids had wanted to go into it because the money was so poor. And he'd definitely told me he was from western Kentucky, not

Tennessee. One would think basic facts like where you grew up would be easy to remember. Unless you were making it all up.

CHAPTER 37

By the time I rolled out of bed the next morning, it was nine. Guess I was tired. Ruby wasn't around, so I assumed she'd given up on me and had already gone down for breakfast. I showered quickly and went to the dining room. When I didn't see Ruby there, I went to the Bow Bar for a quick breakfast.

I sat down and shot off a text to Jefferson.

I have news.

He answered with a phone call. "Give it to me quick. We've got a lot going on this morning. Waiting on a couple of phone calls."

"I talked with Ted Stevens last night, the assistant engineer. He changed some details about his childhood." I walked to the front railing. I hoped the sound of the boat moving through the water might be just loud enough to give me some cover as we talked.

"Like what?"

I looked around. The bartender was busy clearing plates. Just a couple of other people were still eating, and they were at least thirty feet away. Still, I kept my voice low. "The first time we talked, he said he grew up in western Kentucky. Last night, he said he grew up near Knoxville, Tennessee."

I could hear Jefferson talking, but the sound was muffled, like he'd put a hand over the phone. "Sorry about that, Frank. Needed to ask Michelle where we were at with Stevens. We haven't had much luck with him so far. What else you got on him?"

"He said he was born in 1954. I told you before he worked on the *Delta Queen*, but this time he changed some details about his past. He told me during our first chat that only his grandfather had been a commercial fisherman. This time he said his father had also been one. And instead of growing up near the Mississippi—like he said the first time—he told me he lived in eastern Tennessee as a kid. Pretty big changes. Makes me wonder if he's making up a past on the fly."

"Yeah. That seems shady to me, too. Anything else?"

"His father died when he was a teenager, but he wasn't any more specific than that."

"Did you get his father's name?"

"No."

"All right, then. At least that's a little more to work with. Any other news?"

"Have you heard anything from Angela or Yolanda?"

"Just a minute." I heard the muffled voice again, then a door opening. "That's still a touchy subject with Michelle," he whispered. "She got their messages the last couple of days, but she's not ready to talk to them yet. Doesn't want to be distracted by dealing with them."

"I know there's tension among the three of them, but Angela and Yolanda are trying to help."

"How?"

I scanned the deck again. "They volunteered to talk with the hotel manager, to see what they could learn about his background."

"Well, I hope they do it quickly. We need to strike some names off this list and now. We've lost a lot of time trying to find out anything about Stevens and the first mate—what's his name?"

"Kenny LeJeune?"

"Right. I'm losing track of names. Sorry."

"Easy to do. Hopefully, we'll have fewer names to deal with soon. Ruby also volunteered to chat with the river historian. I may have more news for you by lunch."

"I hope you're right. What're you going to do next?"

"I thought I'd track down LeJeune, the first mate. See what more I can learn about him."

"Then you should get to it. And I need to get back to Michelle. Thanks, Frank."

"I'll be in touch."

I poured coffee into a paper cup, then took the stairs at the bow down to deck one. I liked the spot, not just because it was a convenient place to catch crew coming and going but also for the close-up views of the river. I could stand next to the railing and practically reach out and touch the water. The smell of grilled meats and baking bread coming from the nearby galley were an unexpected bonus, too.

I watched the bow cut through the river's current, and I sipped coffee as I waited and hoped that the first mate would pass by. The clouds were back, and the forecast called for rain later in the day. My patience paid off about fifteen minutes later, when Kenny LeJeune came down the stairs with a deckhand.

"Enjoying the view, Mr. Dodge?"

I turned to look at him but kept an arm against the railing. "Sure am. This is my favorite spot. I almost feel like I'm in the water." I finished the last sip of coffee.

"We'd prefer if you stay on this side of the railing, of course." He looked over at the river. "One of my favorite spots, too."

"I intend to stay perfectly dry." I stood up straight. "Say, I was hoping to catch up with you. Do you have a few minutes? I'm working on a sidebar for my article that'll describe some of the jobs on the boat." I wasn't, but it made for a good cover story. "Just a few quick descriptions about the work and the people who do it."

He looked at the deckhand. "You go on ahead. I'll catch up in a few." Unlike the chief engineer, the first mate seemed to show a casual rapport with the folks he worked with. "Sure. I can make a few minutes. We're basically on cruise control for a while." He grinned. "Sorry for the pun."

I grinned. "Not bad."

"What would ya like to know?"

I pulled a notebook from my back pocket and flipped to a blank page. "Let's start with the basics. What's the job of the first mate? Not sure I even know that myself."

He laughed. "Might be easier to tell ya what I *don't* do." He scratched his head. "Well, I'm basically the captain's assistant. His eyes and ears on the boat. I look out for the safety of the passengers . . ."

"I remember. You taught us how to put on life jackets and jump off the boat in case of emergency."

"Hopefully no one would ever need to jump off the boat, but yeah, safety. When we get to or leave port, it's my job to communicate with the captain, so we get in and out safely."

"And I guess you're the one making sure everyone gets back on board before we leave."

"Yeah, well, I do my best. But sometimes we get a passenger or two who can't tell time and exceed our ability to wait."

I cringed. "Yeah. That wasn't good. Sorry about that."

"It all worked out OK. For us anyway. Let's see." He tilted his head to the side and squinted. "I also supervise the deck crew. Work out schedules, make sure they're doing their jobs. That kinda thing." He looked around as he thought. "If a passenger complains about something, I'm probably going to be involved in fixing the problem, trying to keep it off the captain's radar."

"I imagine the captain has enough to do without worrying about passengers who run out of toilet paper." I was certain the captain wanted nothing to do with passenger complaints.

"Yeah, well, thankfully that almost never happens. But sometimes things quit working. Showers back up. TVs won't turn on. Gators in the bathtub. That kinda thing."

I laughed and looked up. "I assume an alligator would have a hard time finding its way onto this boat."

"You'd be surprised." He patted me on the shoulder. "Yeah, that's probably not the best example. Let's see. What else do I do?" He rubbed the back of his head. "Oh. I check a lot of the equipment on the boat and make sure it's all running and properly cared for."

I jotted down some notes. "Even in the engine room?"

"Well, not usually. The chief engineer takes care of most of that, but I'll sometimes pop in for a look over myself."

"What's it take to be a first mate?" If other first mates were like him, I'd guess tall, well-groomed, polite, and handsome.

"Helps to be organized. Attention to detail. Also, good with machines and people."

"I don't imagine there are many people who are good with both."

"I won't argue that point."

"How long have you worked on this boat?"

"Ten, maybe eleven years. I came here from the *Delta Queen*."

"Seems like that's common. Assistant Engineer Ted Stevens told me he also came here from the *Delta Queen*."

"Teddy? Yeah. We worked together there for a while."

"So, you're another one with a lot of years on the river."

"Yes, sir. Just another aging river rat."

"Was it something you grew up with? The river?"

"Sure. I grew up with folks who loved and feared this beast."

"Where was that?"

"Louisiana. From a small town in the swamps you've never heard of."

"I might be way off, but I thought I heard some Cajun country influence in the way you speak."

"Yeah, but a mixed marriage in my case. My daddy was Cajun. Mom wasn't. She came from Georgia."

He glanced at his watch, so I figured it was time to go a little deeper. "You mentioned safety was part of your domain. You must have been a busy man after Bucky Jones went missing."

He looked away from me. "Yeah. That was a mess."

"When you learned he was missing, what did you have to do?"

"The obvious stuff. Searched high and low on the boat. Looked back through security tapes. Talked with crew on duty."

"What do you think happened to him?

His face turned light red. "It's not my place to speculate, Mr. Dodge. I'd bet he went in the river. There's no other explanation, really. But it's beyond my pay grade to figure out how—or why—that happened." He looked toward a deckhand checking the lines on the starboard side of the deck.

"I heard they just found his body."

He turned to face me. "That so?" He crossed his arms.

I couldn't tell if he knew already. I assumed he did. "I heard the back of his head had been flattened." LeJeune didn't blink. "Hard to imagine how a guy jumping in the river to kill himself had his skull cracked."

"Like I said"—his arms dropped—"it's beyond my pay grade to figure out what happened." He waved his hands in the air. "But maybe his body crashed into something, like a boat or a rock."

"Maybe so."

He turned again to look at the deckhand near us. "That's about all I can give ya right now, Mr. Dodge. Gotta get back to the grind."

"Of course. Thanks for your time." I reached out to shake his hand. "This helped a lot. Maybe now I can explain to someone else exactly what a first mate does."

"I'm looking forward to seeing just what you figured out."

I laughed. He didn't.

"See ya around, Mr. Dodge."

I watched LeJeune walk around the corner, then I climbed the stairs so I could get far enough away to pass along to Jefferson what I'd learned.

CHAPTER 38

Judging by the dozens of people all moving in the same direction, the clanking plates, and the smells coming from the galley, I figured lunch had started. I swung over to the dining room and found Ruby, Angela, and Yolanda just as they were being seated.

"Oh, hi, Frank," Ruby said. "We were just talking about you."

"Then it's a good thing I showed up to put a stop to that." I pulled out a chair and joined them at the table. "What's the word? Got any news?"

Ruby smiled. I looked at Angela and Yolanda, and they were smiling, too.

"We did our part," Ruby said. "We talked to the two men you asked us to visit."

"Already?"

"We don't have time to waste, remember?" Angela said.

We placed our food orders, then I said, "Let's get right to it. What did you find out?" I leaned in toward the middle of the table. "But keep your voices down."

"I had an enlightening conversation with the river historian, John Mathews," Ruby said softly. "He's new on this boat, but he used to work as a pilot on riverboats. For a long time. One of his jobs was working on—what did he call it? A dredge boat? Is that right?"

"Yeah. That's right," I said. "So, he must have worked for the Corps of Engineers?"

"I believe he did mention that. He told me about some places he took that dredge boat on the Mississippi. Sounded fascinating. He knew those places so well, but he told me he'd always been interested in river history. He grew up in Jeffersonville, Indiana—"

"On the Ohio River," I said.

"That's right. So, he heard a lot of stories about rivers and riverboats."

"Anything else?"

"He said he grew up on the Ohio River, but he's worked all over. He's married, but I don't think it's his first. He also said something about a daughter who also works on the river, but I didn't ask about her or any other children he might have."

"Thanks, Ruby. That helps."

I turned to Angela and Yolanda. "What did you two find out?"

"Angela was so clever," Yolanda said. "She came up with a story about—"

"Let's not get too deep in the weeds, Yolanda," Angela interrupted, glancing in my direction. "Let's just tell him what we learned. We can tell him how we did it some other time." Yolanda nodded. "The hotel manager, Barry Riggs, hasn't worked too long on this boat. Just two years. But he's worked on ocean cruises before."

"He spent most of his career working as a manager for the Hilton chain," Yolanda said. "He was the guy the company would bring in to clean up a mess."

"What kinds of messes?" I asked.

"It sounded like it was mostly underperforming properties," Angela said. "Hotels that weren't profitable but probably should have been."

"So, he'd go in and shake things up?" I asked. "Figure out who to fire and who to keep?"

"Something like that. I'm sure he'd have more than personnel to deal with, but it was mostly that." Angela looked at Yolanda. "Did I miss anything?"

"Oh. Just one. We visited him in his office. On his wall I saw a certificate of commendation from the Hilton Corporation. And on his desk I saw a picture of him and another man. Maybe his partner or spouse?"

"That's a fair guess." I sat back. "Thanks so much. All of you. Excuse me for a minute. I'm going to step out of the dining room so I can call Brian and pass along what you learned."

There were too many people coming and going around the dining room, so I walked back to the library and found a quiet corner. I called Jefferson and told him what Ruby, Angela, and Yolanda had learned, then described my chat with the first mate. He promised to get back to me if he needed anything more. I went back to the dining room to finish lunch. The conversation turned lighter, but I couldn't get my mind off what we still had to do.

"A little distracted, Frank?" Ruby asked me softly as she set down a fork. Angela and Yolanda continued to eat, but they looked at me as they chewed.

"Yeah. Trying to figure out what I can still do to help. Anything we might have missed." She nodded.

Angela said, "That thought has crossed my mind, too. But I doubt much has slipped past Michelle." Yolanda nodded in agreement.

Before we left, I got a text from Jefferson.

Ruled out the historian and hotel manager. Not sure yet about LeJeune. Stevens looks damn shady.

"Job well done," I said to the women. "Just got a text from Brian. They've ruled out the hotel manager and the river historian. We're down to five." They all smiled, but their faces quickly turned serious. I figured they, like me, couldn't get past the reality of what was still ahead of us.

We went our separate ways after lunch. They were off to the auditorium for the afternoon lecture. I was ready to keep digging. The captain was technically one of the five remaining suspects, but we hadn't given him any serious thought. Thinking about him, I realized I hadn't seen Helen since we'd gotten back on the boat after our land-based adventure. I sent her a text:

> Hey. How's it going?

She replied almost right away:

> Not well!

> Got time to meet in the library? We can catch up.

> On my way.

I made my way back to deck two and slipped into a wing chair in a quiet back corner. Helen found me just a minute later. "Thank you for contacting me," she said, then she sat down. "I didn't want to bother you after we got back on the boat. I know you have your hands full."

"I've been busy. But not so busy that I couldn't make time to listen to what's going on with you. What's up?"

"I'm so tired of hitting dead end after dead end with this man. I feel like I'm profiling a uniform, not a person."

"You haven't had any more luck getting the captain to talk?"

"Not at all. Whenever I get a minute with him, he reverts to talking about the boats he's worked on. Over and over." She cleared her throat. "But I already told you that."

"Have you had any luck interviewing other crew? Find out what they have to say about him?"

"I have. I've talked with senior staff, mostly. The hotel manager, the first mate. A couple of other pilots, like I mentioned before. They were all very polite. They told me how efficiently the boat runs under his command. Always on time." She snapped her fingers. "Few mechanical problems. How he sets clear expectations. Thrilling stuff, huh?"

"He runs a tight ship. An old-school captain. That's what I hear. But no one would say anything at all about his personality? No one has a good or funny story about how he screwed something up or what makes him laugh?"

She shook her head. "I don't think he ever laughs."

"Hmm. At the very least, it sounds like the crew doesn't feel any warm fuzzies for him." I rubbed my chin. "What do they think about his upcoming retirement? Are they worried about who they'll get for the next captain?"

"They just say something about how much he's earned it. Retirement. And they wish him the best."

"How about crew members who've worked directly with him for a while? Any luck interviewing them?"

"No. Not really. The pilots are new. I've tried to talk with the chief engineer, but he's always busy. There's another guy—the one you told me about who works in the engine room . . ."—she flipped through her notes—"Ted

Stevens. He's worked with the captain for a few years, but he works nights, and I'm not staying up late to hear another person tell me how efficiently Captain Smith runs the boat."

Based on what I knew of those two men, she was probably right. They weren't going to tell her anything new. "Tell me again what you know about him? Where did he grow up? When did he start working on the river?"

"Ha! Almost nothing. He said he grew up in western Tennessee. On a farm. Tried farming for a while but didn't like the work. He got hired as a deckhand on a barge—"

"A towboat?"

"Right. Sorry. I keep getting confused about the terms. He got hired as a deckhand for his first river job. I think he said he got hired at Memphis."

"When would that have been?"

"He didn't say. Let's see." She pulled out a notebook. "He's sixty-eight now, so if he farmed for a few years before working on the river, he could've gotten hired as a deckhand in what, the early seventies?"

I thought about everything I knew about the captain, most of which came directly from Helen. There were a lot of holes in his background, too. "Or a little later," I said. "Like the mid-seventies—?"

Helen looked at me. The color drained from her face. "You don't think he could be one of the . . ."—she looked around—"one of the men you're looking for?" She covered her mouth with a hand.

"I don't know. He hasn't given us a good reason to rule him out. And the haziness of his background does raise a lot of questions." I leaned toward Helen and whispered, "If he started as a deckhand like he claimed, he would have done so when it was easy to get a job with no questions asked. The tow companies back then weren't exactly known for rigor in their hiring processes. They needed bodies. Not saints." I leaned back in the chair. "I need to call Brian."

Chapter 39

"Maybe I'll just have to take some creative license with his story," Helen said before she got up to leave and return to her room. I called Jefferson.

"What's up, Frank?"

"How much have you found out about the captain?"

"A lot, I think. Why do you ask?"

"I just talked with Helen Kraft—"

"Your new buddy?"

"Funny. Frenemies, maybe. I don't know." I cringed. "Anyway, she's supposed to be writing a feature article about him and his illustrious career on the river. But he's exceptionally tight-lipped about his personal life. Hasn't given her hardly any details about where he grew up, anything that would add character to her story. Or story to his character. And none of the crew she's talked with has been willing to say much, either."

"OK. Let me grab my notes." I heard footsteps, then paper rustling. "We've got a lot of detail about his career. The boats he worked on. Promotions. Looks like we can pretty much trace his whole career."

"When did he get his first job on the river?"

"I've got that here . . . Looks like 1977. Hired as a first mate."

First mate. *Probably the first job where he'd have to do real paperwork.* "What about before that? What do you know about him before he starting working on the river?"

"Well . . ." I heard more papers rustling. "Give me just a minute, Frank." He said something to Michelle. "Born August 20, 1949, in Gibson County, Tennessee. We have his parents' names. They owned forty acres in that county. What are you thinking, Frank?"

"Huh. I'm surprised. That's more than I expected." Maybe the captain just doesn't enjoy talking about himself. But I wanted to be sure. "Just a feeling, but maybe we should dig some more. Do we know much about the time from when he was born until 1977?"

"Don't think so, but can't say we've tried all that hard."

"That first-mate job wasn't his first. He said he started as a deckhand. Back in the seventies, companies hired deckhands with no questions asked, so maybe that company didn't require any real identity verification until they wanted him to work as a first mate."

"Honestly, Frank, we haven't thought much about him. I assumed with all the personnel records he's got, that he had to be who he said he was. We've had to make some quick decisions, you know, since we're running out of time. When you told me, for example, that the river historian had worked for the Corps of Engineers, I knew we'd be striking him off the list. Hard to get hired in a government job with a fake identity. Too many background checks."

"But maybe it wasn't so hard to fake an identity for a private company back in the seventies?"

"Probably not." He sighed. "I guess we could see if we can find any traces of him before 1977."

"How can I help?"

"Keep asking questions. Work some Frank Dodge magic."

"Where do I start? We've still got five guys we're looking at."

"Four. Don't worry about the chief of security. Michelle and I are working on him. See what more you can do with the others. And since the captain probably won't talk to you directly, keep asking around about him. Maybe someone will be willing to say something."

While I sat in the library considering my options, my phone lit up.

Got a minute?

Deion was texting me.

Sure.

Meet me in the Bow Bar in 5.

I made my way back down to deck two. Lunch was over, so the Bow Bar was empty. I got some coffee, then sat at a table as far I could get from the bartender. When Deion arrived, he hurried over to me, then sat down.

"What's up?"

He was out of breath. "I may have screwed up." He bit his lip.

"What do you mean?"

"I did what you asked me to do," he whispered. "I asked around about the guys in Engineering." He slid his chair closer to me. "No one"—he scanned the Bow Bar—"has anything good to say about them. No one I talked to anyway. They all do what I do—keep their distance from them."

"What's that about?" I tried to make eye contact, but he was restless and looking around. "Did they give any examples of something that happened?"

"Yeah. Condescending attitudes. Sexist comments. 'Come here and show me that ass.' That kinda thing."

"They say that to you, too?" I smiled. He didn't.

"Not funny, Frank." He whispered forcefully, "They don't talk to me directly. But when I've been near them, I've heard them say to each other, 'What's that fag doing down here?'"

"Sorry about that. But it doesn't surprise me. They don't seem like the most open-minded people."

"You're good with understatement, Frank." I heard a *tap-tap-tap* from his foot hitting the floor. "But that's not what I was going to tell you."

"You think you messed something up—" I scooted forward in the chair until I was sitting on the edge.

"Yeah. I do." He grimaced. "There's a woman on the boat, another performer—Judy—who's basically my best friend. On the boat anyway." He shrugged. "She kept asking why I was so interested in the guys in Engineering. 'Do you want to fuck one of them?' she asked me. I got annoyed, so I told her why." He bit his lip again. "About the murder in 1974. About how two of those killers are on the boat right now. That you and your friends have narrowed down the list to just a few crew—" He hesitated. "And that two of them were in Engineering."

"OK." I felt my stomach tighten. "What did she think of that?"

"She looked curious. Maybe a little scared. It was hard to tell. She confused me, so I told her the first mate was another one of the guys under suspicion. Man, did she get pissed at me!" His eyes opened wide. "'How could you think that?' she hissed at me. 'Kenny wouldn't harm a bug. You guys are all nuts.'" He put a hand on a hip as he imitated how Judy had talked.

"That shocked me, her reaction. Obviously." He leaned in and practically whispered, "Turns out she's dating him, Kenny LeJeune. The first mate." His face scrunched up.

"Oh, shit." I flopped back in my chair. *So much for having the advantage of surprise.* "So, our secret's out." I looked past Deion toward the river. "If he's one of the killers, he knows we're on to him."

"Afraid so." He covered his face. "Although, honestly"—he leaned forward—"he's only gonna know *you're* on to him. I don't know any of your friends or the sisters. Haven't met any of them."

"Lucky me." My mind raced. *Am I in danger? Can I take advantage of this somehow?* "Do you think she told him already? When did you talk to her?"

"This morning. And yeah, given how she reacted, I bet she couldn't wait to tell him." He reached across the table and rested a hand on mine. "I'm sorry, Frank. I had no idea she was dating him. No idea." He sat back and crossed his arms. "The bitch never told me. If I'd known, I—"

I sat up straight. "It's OK, Deion. It really is. I'm surprised we didn't get exposed sooner. I need to let Brian and Michelle know right away, but don't beat yourself up." I nodded. "Thanks for sticking your neck out for us."

"What do I tell her if she asks me anything else?"

"Nothing. Just say you've already told her all you know. Let me deal with the fallout." He nodded and stood up. "I'll let you know how it goes." I smiled, walked around the table, and hugged him.

When he left, I called Jefferson. "We've got a problem, Brian."

Chapter 40

I went up to Michelle's room to deliver the news. "Well, shit," Jefferson said. He paused and paced back and forth, then said, "That's OK. I'm surprised something like that hasn't happened already."

"Right now, he only knows I'm part of it. He doesn't know anything about you or Michelle."

"Yeah. Good point. But if he—if the Bell brothers—really wanted to figure out who you were working with, it wouldn't be that hard, would it? I mean, I came on this boat with you. And Michelle and her sisters are just about the youngest women on this boat."

"And there aren't many other Black women," Michelle said. "What do we do now? We can't stop. Not at this point."

"Harder." Jefferson's hands curled into fists. "We've got to go at them harder."

"How?" I asked.

"You're gonna go back and talk directly to that first mate," Michelle said. She glanced at Jefferson out of the corner of her eyes as she talked to me. "And you're going to press him. You're going to threaten him if you have to."

I couldn't imagine how that would work. "Threaten him? With what? Writing something nasty about the boat in *Luxe Liners*? Shoving him into the river if he doesn't spill everything?" My voice got louder as we talked.

"Now, Frank. Calm down." Jefferson slowly pressed his hands toward the ground. "We're all on the same side here."

"Don't roll out the kumbaya talk now, Brian," Michelle said. "I've come too far to let them slip away from me. We're so fucking close." She pointed at him as she talked, her finger shaking. "We've got them trapped on this boat. We're down to just a few people it could be." She clenched her fists. "We go after them quick and hard. And we do it now."

Jefferson stared at her. "OK. We'll ramp it up." He turned to me. "Frank, you've got to go back to the first mate, to Kenny LeJeune. You've got to figure out a way to put some pressure on him. Stick it to him."

"How?"

"I don't know, Frank!" he yelled. "I don't know!" His voice dropped back to normal, and he paced in the room. "Look—we're all going to be exposed soon. That's why we can't wait any longer to confront him directly. I can't believe I'm about to say this—"

"What?"

"Go. Now." Jefferson stopped pacing and faced me directly. "You're the one who's been talking to him. I trust you to figure something out. You've got to get him to give up something that'll help us figure out if he's one of the Bell brothers." He walked over to me, put a hand on my shoulder, and looked me directly in the eyes. "You've been playing at being a detective here and there. Now you need to do it for real. I know you can do this."

I took a deep breath. "I'm not exactly sure what to do—"

"Take a minute to think about it." His voice softened. "A few minutes even. Or figure something out as you're walking around trying to find him. Tap into those people-reading superpowers of yours." His face hardened. "But push the fucker to the edge if you have to. He's not likely to come after you right now. Too many potential witnesses." He walked over to the bed, picked up a legal pad, and looked over his notes. "We still have a couple more things we're waiting to hear back about. I'll call again and try to speed them up." He looked back up at me. "You got this, Frank. But be careful. Very careful. And call me right after you talk to him."

I nodded, then turned around and walked to the door. I opened it a crack, then turned around and saw them huddled next to the bed, looking at their notes, so I crept out.

I went back to the bow, to deck one, and stood near the railing and behind a post that shielded me from the wind. I assumed it would be a while before LeJeune might come by.

Wrong. I'd no sooner rested an elbow than he came flying down the stairs. "Dodge?"

I turned around. "Yeah. What's up, LeJeune?"

He stopped a few feet away from me but faced me directly. "You know what's up. I heard what you're up to. Thinking I murdered some Black guy forty years ago." His face was bright red. "Are ya out of your fucking mind?" He reached around and rubbed the back of his head.

"Might be." *Damn, he's pissed off. Does he think I've already pegged him as guilty?* I played along. "Tell me why I'm wrong. Why wasn't it you?"

He stepped toward me and pointed a finger at my face. I wasn't sure if he was going to pick my nose or hit me. "I ain't never killed no one." His eyes were wide open. "But right now, I feel you could be the first." I straightened my back, then he squared his shoulders, too. "Just one quick push, and you'd be at the mercy of the river."

"Sounds like something a person with a guilty conscience would say." I held his gaze, but I felt my stomach churning.

We stared at each other like two wolves circling, teeth bared, wondering who was going to make the first move. His nostrils flared. "Ya gotta be careful about digging through the pasts of guys like me. Some of us came to the river for a fresh start. But that don't make us crooks or killers." He took a couple of steps back.

"Is Kenny LeJeune your real name?"

He rubbed his chin, glared at me, then looked away. "I started working on the river as a young man. Not long out of high school. Back then, to get hired on a boat, a guy just needed his word about who he was."

A loud thump diverted our attention for a moment. A piece of driftwood had bounced off the hull. "Who did you tell them you were?"

"Kenny LeJeune." He raised his chin. "That's who I told them I was."

"And who did you leave behind?"

He looked down and kicked at the floor. "Nathan Landry." He frowned. "I left behind my life as Nathan Landry."

"Why?" I relaxed my shoulders. "What did Nathan Landry do that was so bad you had to leave him behind?"

He shook his head. "It wasn't about Nathan. It was his family." He moved over next to me, then leaned against the railing. "My dad was a career crook. In and out of prison when I was a kid. Robbery, assault, moonshining, illegal fishing. You name it. Could've killed someone, for all I know." He scowled. "Laws meant nothing to him. My mom wasn't much better. She had a hand in most of what he did. But when Dad got caught, he went to prison. When Mom got caught, Dad went to prison. I think she was playing both sides."

"I'm sorry to hear that, but why would that be a reason to change your name and identity?"

"My daddy had big ideas about how the two of us were going to team up to lighten the loads of rich folks and big companies in Louisiana. I didn't share his enthusiasm for the idea." He turned to look at me. "He made me go along on a couple of house break-ins. We barely escaped getting caught the second time. I didn't want that life. When I told him that, he smacked me." His face was blank. "Broke my nose and practically knocked me out. Screamed at me: 'You'll do whatever the fuck I tell you to do.'" His jaw clenched.

That wasn't the story I'd expected. I felt for him. Felt bad for him. But I didn't have time to be his therapist. "So, you got out of there."

"That's exactly what I fucking did." His face turned red again. "If I'd stayed, I'd have either ended up in prison like him, or ended up dead. So, in the middle of the night in early June, just after high school ended, I slipped out of the house."

"And you became Kenny LeJeune?"

"Yeah. Maybe not the most creative choice of names." He smiled slightly. "Iry LeJeune was a popular musician back then. I figured no one outside of Cajun Country would know who he was, so I borrowed his last name for an alias." He looked down. "I hadn't planned on staying Kenny LeJeune, but about a year after I'd left home, I called to let my folks know I was still alive. Mom answered, but in the background I could hear Daddy swear that he'd track me down and kill me if I didn't come back right away. After that, I became Kenny LeJeune permanently."

"How'd that work exactly? At some point, an employer must have asked for proof of identity, a Social Security number, something like that."

"Yeah, but not right away. When I started as a deckhand, the company didn't care much about those things. But after I'd stuck around awhile and got promoted, the company's HR person dogged me for a birth certificate and Social Security card. Turned out it was easy to get fake papers made up. Expensive, but easy. I got myself a birth certificate made for Kenny LeJeune that's filed in the state of Louisiana. And even a new Social Security number."

I believed him. I didn't want to, but I did. "Let's assume you're not bull-shitting me."

He glared at me. "I ain't lying, Dodge."

"Fine. You're not lying. What exactly did Judy tell you I was up to?"

He stepped away from the railing and stood again in front of me. "She said you're trying to track down a couple of guys who killed a Black man in Mississippi in the 1970s."

"What else?"

"Not much. Just that you thought I might be one of those men."

I stepped toward him. "Who else on this boat isn't who they say they are?"

He chuckled. "Now, that's something I can't help ya with. It's generally not good for one's health to go around asking old guys on riverboats who they murdered when they were younger."

I stepped close enough to smell coffee on his breath. I pointed a finger at his face and did my best to channel John Wayne. "You better not be holding back on me, Kenny."

"What are ya going to do, Dodge? Break a pencil over your leg and try to stab me? You don't seem like much of a fighter."

So much for John Wayne. "You're right. I'm not." I let my arms fall to my side and took a step back. "But I'm also not very good at keeping secrets. And what do you suppose your bosses in this company would think if they learned you've been living with a fake identity for so long?"

He gritted his teeth. "What I told you is between us."

"Did you hear me promise to keep any secrets?" I held up my hands. "Maybe they'd have to check and see what your parents have to say about your new identity." He didn't respond. I took a step closer to him again. "Who else on this boat is hiding their past? Stevens? McDowell?" I paused. "The captain?"

He crossed his arms. He tapped his rib cage rapidly. "Look, I wouldn't be surprised if all of them ain't who they say they are." He dropped his arms, turned around, and took a few steps away from me. He rubbed his forehead for a minute, then turned back to look at me. "I ain't got no affection for any of those men," he said. "Especially the captain. That man's a mean son of a bitch. Everyone on this boat would agree with me." His jaw tightened. "But this is a brotherhood out here. Especially among us older guys."

"I get it. But are you part of a brotherhood where everyone is really looking out for one another? Or is someone counting on that brotherhood to shield himself from being held accountable for the terrible things he's done in his life?"

He shook his head, then looked around the deck.

"You want to be part of a brotherhood like that?" I added.

After a minute, he sighed, then stepped closer to me again. "The night that guy went in the river—"

"Bucky Jones?"

"Yeah. That guy. Well, I'd been restless. Couldn't sleep. Chief McDowell had told me about a couple of minor issues in the engine room they hadn't been able to fix. So, I figured as long as I couldn't sleep, I might as well go down and see if I could solve them out myself. When I got down there, no one was around. Stevens must have been down tending to the boiler or working on something somewhere else. I walked over to the computer to check a couple of gauges, then I heard some guys arguing. I peeked outside, out on deck just in front of the paddlewheel. I saw three men standing there and yelling at each other. Man, were they pissed! They were pointing and screaming—"

"One of them was Bucky?"

"Yeah. One of them was Bucky."

"Who were the other two?"

"It was dark, so it was hard to tell. I wasn't thinking about that anyway. I was about to go out there to break it up." He rubbed the back of his neck. "At least until one of them swung a crowbar and smacked that Jones guy in the back of the head. Knocked him out cold." He paced in front of me. "After that, they both looked up and around them. When they turned toward the boat, light from the engine room showed me their faces."

"And?"

He stopped pacing and looked at me, his face losing color. "It was McDowell and the captain."

My heart raced. "That must have caused you some panic."

"Fuck yeah, it did!" He looked around to see if anyone had heard him yell.

"Did you see them throw him in the river, too?"

"Hell, no. I'm no idiot," he hissed. "There was no way was I going to stick around after I saw the captain hit Jones. I slipped out before they could see me. I didn't want to be next."

"You sure they didn't see you?"

"Yeah. I'm sure. If the captain knew what I'd seen, he'd have let me know. One way or another." His voice dropped off.

"How do I know you're telling me the truth?"

"Ya don't." He shrugged, then stood in front of me again. "But if ya search under my birth name, Nathan Landry, I'm sure you'll find a few records—including, I'd guess, an old missing person report." He stepped closer to me and kept his voice down. "I ain't lying, Dodge. I saw what I saw. Now leave me the fuck alone."

My phone rang. "Fine. We're done here." Then I added, "But I believe you." He walked away quickly, and I answered the phone. "What's up, Brian?"

"You won't believe this. We found a high school photo of William Smith, the captain. It took a while. We looked through yearbooks for every high school in Gibson County, Tennessee, where the captain said he was from. We had to go through them all a second time with fresh eyes, because we didn't find him the first time through." I heard a muffled giggle. "Did you know he was a Black man when he was eighteen?"

"What?"

"Yeah. Imagine our surprise, too."

"I don't know what to say about that, but I've got news, too." I glanced around me to make sure I was alone. "I had a revealing chat with First Mate Kenny LeJeune. He saw Jones get hit in the head with a crowbar the night he disappeared."

"Who'd he see do it?"

"Captain William Smith and Chief Engineer Chuck McDowell."

"Goddamn. We've got them!"

Chapter 41

I raced up to Michelle's room, equally excited and terrified. We'd found them. We'd found the two surviving men who killed Bucky Jones, and they were almost certainly the same men who'd killed Isaac Green in 1974. After Jefferson let me in, I looked around at the piles of paper, the empty coffee cups, and the relief on their faces. No joy or self-satisfaction. Relief.

"What now?" I asked after I told them about my conversation with LeJeune.

"We're gonna confront the killers," Michelle said.

Jefferson frowned. "Of course. Of course." He rubbed the back of his head. "Give me a minute to think about how we might do this."

"We don't have to act immediately, do we?" I asked. I felt nervous about what might come next. "Maybe we should get a quick dinner and talk about our options?" They didn't react to my idea, so I added, "They aren't going anywhere. We won't reach Memphis until tomorrow morning. We have some time to figure it out. To do it right."

Jefferson nodded. "Right. Good idea, Frank. Thanks for the reminder. We've still got some time." He turned to Michelle. "Let's go eat. Think more deeply about what's next. Whad'ya say?"

She sat down on a corner of the bed, then closed her eyes. Jefferson walked over and rubbed the back of her neck. She pushed his hands away.

When she opened her eyes and looked up at him, she said, "I'm not hungry, babe." She smiled slightly. "You go ahead and eat. Talk with Frank. I could use some time to think about it all. I need a minute for it all to sink in." She stood up and touched his face. "Alone. Please." She flashed a half-smile.

"You sure?" Jefferson asked. "We have a minute to catch our breath. Really plan this out."

"I understand. But like I said, I just need a few minutes alone. You go ahead." She waved him toward the door. "Work out a plan, then come back here and tell me how you think we should handle this. Just leave me be for a little while." She tilted her head and smiled. "Please?"

"OK." He took a few steps toward me. "We won't be long. You want me to bring you something back?"

She closed her eyes again and rubbed her temples. "Sure. Just something light. Maybe a sandwich."

"Will do." He scratched the back of his head. "You're sure you want to stay here alone?"

She sat on the bed again with her back to us. "This has been exhausting, Brian." She turned to look at us. "Right?"

"Right."

"I'm exhausted. Just give me some time to get myself together. I don't need long." She pushed some papers to the side and lay flat on the bed. "It's OK. I'll be OK. Just give me a minute."

"Let's go, Brian," I said. Michelle closed her eyes. "We won't be long."

We walked out of Michelle's room. "Bow Bar?" I asked. "We can eat quicker there."

"Sounds good."

We didn't speak as we walked. I didn't mind. My mind was racing any-way. *How do we get Smith and McDowell in custody? Who do we even turn them over to? How are they going to react? Would they growl like cornered dogs or play dead like possums?* And even though we were sure Smith and McDowell were the Bell brothers, did we have the evidence to get a conviction forty-three years after their crime?

When we got to the Bow Bar, we walked right to the buffet and filled our plates, then sat down at a table where no one would be close enough to hear us talking. "How are you doing?" I asked.

"Michelle's right. Exhausted. We haven't slept much the last couple of nights." He cracked a smile. "But honestly, pretty jazzed, too."

"What now? How do we finish this thing?"

"Good question. We can't just walk up to the captain and accuse him of murder." He swirled a couple of french fries in ketchup. "We're going to have to show him some of our cards, tip our hand somewhat. Tell him we have a witness who saw him kill Jones." He ate the fries as he continued to think. "We don't want to say who the witness was. Not yet."

"I'm not sure LeJeune would be thrilled to be identified anyway."

"Well, he's going to have to talk at some point. But it's better in the short term if we can roll out enough of the details of Jones's murder without naming the first mate." He sat back briefly. "We'll want to corner him someplace around other people, too. Make it hard for him to get away, but it'd also be nice to have another witness or two who could testify to his reaction."

"So, we go after him for Bucky's murder, but how do we tie him to Isaac Green?"

"Then we tell him we know his real name. Show him the yearbook photo of the real William Smith." He nodded slightly. "Lay out the facts we have about his life."

"Sounds so easy." I took a bite of hamburger.

He chuckled. "Sorry. Like I said. I'm tired. I might be oversimplifying this."

"Would it make more sense to start with McDowell? Confront him first?"

"Not a bad idea. But we'd need to keep him corralled. Can't give him a chance to tip off the captain."

"We could still do it like you described. Lead with Bucky's murder. That we found a witness who saw him and the captain arguing with Bucky on the night he disappeared. Who saw the captain hit him in the back of the head."

"I like that. Get him nervous about Bucky's death, then call him by his birth name—Lester—and press him about Isaac Green's murder in Vicksburg."

"So, what . . ." I scratched my head. "So, we're basically hoping that he confesses? To one murder or another?"

Jefferson forced a slight smile. "I suppose that's where we are. It would make our lives a lot easier if he'd confess, that's for sure."

I picked up my burger, then set it down again. "Do we have anything that's likely to stick in court?" I looked at Jefferson. "Do we have enough solid evidence for a prosecuting attorney to pursue charges against Smith and McDowell for Isaac Green's murder?" I picked up the burger again and took a big bite.

Jefferson frowned. "Honestly? Probably not. Not yet. We know that Captain William Smith isn't who he claims to be. Maybe we could probably prove he stole the real William Smith's identity." He winced. "It would help if we knew what happened to the real William Smith." He leaned back in his chair. "We're in a better place proving he murdered Jones, though. Don't know if that would be enough." He pursed his lips. "For Michelle."

"So, even if we can prove that William Smith is an assumed identity, it doesn't prove that he's really Ray Bell. Or that he killed anyone—except, of course, maybe Bucky, as you said."

"That's right. Doesn't matter how sure *we* are. Proving that case in court just with what we've put together so far . . ." He sighed. "Well, that might be a big ask."

"So, we're back to Bucky Jones. Our best shot"—I said, wiping ketchup off my mouth—"is tightening up the case that the captain killed Bucky Jones. Shoring up the evidence for that."

Jefferson nodded. "We have an eyewitness. When his body turned up, it had a deep bruise in the back of his head, and our witness saw Smith hit him in the back of the head. That's not too bad. As long as LeJeune is willing to testify in court, we'd have a shot."

"I admit, after all the work we've done, after all the crap we've—you've—sorted through . . ." I looked down. "It feels entirely unsatisfying—incomplete, even"—I looked out toward the river—"to feel so confident we've found the men who killed Isaac Green but, at the same time, to feel so uncertain about whether it'll be enough to hold them to account." I looked over at Jefferson. "Deflating. Maybe that's the right word."

Jefferson nodded. "I hear what you're saying. And I'd be lying if I said I didn't feel the same." He slid his chair back from the table. "But we can't afford to feel deflated, Frank. We're almost at the finish line." He wiped a napkin across his face. "I'm tired. Michelle is tired. Exhausted." His voice rose. He cleared his throat. "We need to stay sharp . . . and believe that we can get it done. We don't have a choice. There's no way I'm gonna let these guys walk away now." He clenched his teeth. "One way or another, we're going to finish this and hold them to account. One way or another."

I nodded. "We start with McDowell, then?"

"Yeah." He leaned back. "We start with McDowell."

We walked back up to Michelle's room. Jefferson knocked on the door and said, "It's Brian and Frank." When he didn't get a response, he handed me the sandwich we'd brought back for her, then used a key to open the door. "Michelle?" We looked around. "You in the bathroom?" Jefferson walked over to the bathroom door and knocked. Again, no response. He opened the door and looked in. "Shit." He turned to me. "She's not here." He struck the wall with the palm of his hand. "Shit, shit, shit!" he yelled. "I knew I shouldn't have left her alone."

"What's going on, Brian?"

"She's going after Smith and McDowell on her own."

Chapter 42

"We need to find her. Now!" Jefferson said. "Where do we start?" He paced back and forth, taking short, quick steps.

"The pilothouse?" I asked. "That would be the logical place to start."

Jefferson slammed the door to Michelle's room behind us, and we raced up the stairs to the hurricane deck.

"What do you think she'll do if she finds them?" I asked.

"Don't want to think about that," he said, panting.

Once we'd reached the top of the staircase, we sprinted across the open deck to the pilothouse, then put the brakes on. We peeked through the windows. Nothing looked out of order. The two pilots on duty were chatting casually as their eyes moved between the navigation maps and the river ahead of the boat. We tapped on the window, and they turned around at the same time. One of them walked over to the pilothouse door.

"Everything OK, gentlemen?" He rubbed his beard.

"We're looking for the captain," I said.

"His life may be in danger," Jefferson said, then pulled out his St. Louis police ID.

The pilot looked back and forth at the two of us, then he turned toward the other pilot, who said something I couldn't make out. "We haven't seen him. He's off duty for a few more hours."

"Where should we look?" Jefferson asked, his voice pitched higher than usual and cracking.

I jumped in and asked, "Where are his quarters?"

"Deck four. But you'll need a badge to get to that section." He walked over to the other pilot and whispered in his ear, then came back to us. "Follow me." He shrugged.

We backtracked down the stairs—my mind raced as he took his time—then down a hallway until we reached a secured door. Or, rather, a door that had been secure at one time. Someone had busted the lock apart. "That can't be good," the pilot said.

"Which one is the captain's quarters?" Jefferson asked as he pushed his way past the pilot.

As I walked through the hallway, I spotted blood on the carpet. "Brian," I said. "Look down."

"No, no, no!" he repeated.

"Right there," the pilot said as he pointed to an open door. "That's the captain's quarters." Someone had forced their way in there, too. Jefferson barged in first. I followed. I saw another splash of blood on the bed. Jefferson swept the room. "Nobody's here." His face grew paler. He looked around, then said, "Look down. Follow the blood trail as far as we can."

We went back into the hallway and to another staircase. The blood drops led us down to deck three, then disappeared. Jefferson and the pilot crept down the hallway. I slowly descended the staircase.

"Here!" Jefferson yelled. I raced back to the hallway and followed Jefferson. The trail led to the outdoor lounge. Jefferson looked through the window. "There they are!" He pulled out his phone and made a quick call. "Now would be good," I heard him say. "Deck three outdoor lounge." He pushed the door open, and a blast of cool air hit me in the face. We raced across the deck, which was empty except for Michelle and the captain, maybe because of the uninviting weather. The captain was pressing his back against a railing. He was holding a bloody hand close to his chest. Michelle was pointing a gun at his head, her hands swaying slightly in the wind. The gun had a long tube attached to the end—a silencer, I assumed.

"Don't come any closer, Brian!" Michelle yelled. "I'll kill him now. You know I will." She threw a sideways glance at Jefferson. "I already shot him in the hand. Won't be any harder to shoot him in the head." She stretched her arm and stared down the gunsight.

Jefferson stopped cold. "I believe you," he said. "I just don't understand what you're doing."

"I think you do. This man—this is Ray Bell. The man I've been searching for all my life." Wind blew hair around her back. "Now that I've found him, I'm gonna make him pay for what he did."

"I don't know what you're talking about, you crazy woman!" the captain yelled. "My name is William Smith, not Ray Bell. And I'm the captain of this boat." He looked over at us. "Tell her to put the gun down."

"Shut the fuck up, liar!" she yelled at him. "You killed my father. In 1974. In Vicksburg, Mississippi. You remember Vicksburg, don't you, Ray Bell?" The captain didn't flinch. "Isaac Green!" she yelled. "My father . . . You—Ray Bell—killed Isaac Green. My father."

"You're making a big mistake, lady." He pressed on his bleeding hand. "I grew up in Tennessee. Never lived in Vicksburg. You've got me confused with someone else."

"You lying sack of shit. If you come clean now, admit who you are and what you did in front of all these people"—she waved the gun toward us—"then maybe I'll let you live." She pointed the gun at his head again.

"You've got the wrong man," he said, raising his chin. "I'm William Smith." His voice was strong and defiant. "And you're going to pay for this!" He raised his wounded hand.

"William Smith, huh? William Smith, born in Gibson County, Tennessee? Went to Stonewall Jackson High School?"

A gust of wind unsteadied him. He reached for the railing, then yelled, "Yes! That's me."

Her mouth slowly widened into a big smile. "That William Smith, sir, was a Black man. A Black man, Ray! How do you explain that?"

His eyes narrowed. Before he could respond, the door to the outer lounge opened up, and two more people came toward us: Security Chief Bo Hopkins with Chief Engineer Chuck McDowell. Hopkins nodded at Jefferson. The captain turned to look at them, and his eyes focused like a hawk zeroing in on a field mouse.

"What are you doing here, Charles?" the captain yelled. "Go back to your station. Back to the engine room. Now!"

"Go on," Hopkins poked McDowell. "Tell him."

The captain spoke first: "You'd best think long and hard about what you say next, Chief McDowell." He straightened his back and covered his injured hand again.

"They got us, Ray," said the man I'd met as Chuck McDowell but who was really Lester Bell. The captain's face turned red. "Someone on the boat saw us . . ."—he clenched his jaw, then he continued—"saw *you* hit Lonnie." The captain glared at him. "*Kill* Lonnie. We got nowhere left to run to."

"You always were a weak man," the captain said. "Weak and dumb!"

"Maybe so, but I ain't no killer. And I'm done with all this . . . all this pretending." Lester Bell took off his cap and threw it down. The wind picked it up and blew it across the deck. "Done looking over my shoulder wondering when it would all catch up with us." He stepped closer to the captain. "Well, it finally has, brother. Caught up with us. I'm fucking done, Ray!" he yelled.

As the captain stood mute, staring at Lester, I shot off a text to Angela.

"Well, looks like your own brother has given you up, Ray," Michelle said. "That's gotta sting." She smirked. "Still gonna try to tell me you're not Ray Bell?" She gripped the gun tightly.

"McDowell is a liar." The captain looked away from Lester and back at Michelle. His arms fell to the side, and he leaned toward Michelle. "His word against mine. And believe me, no one's gonna believe an engineer over a captain." He grinned. "And that man with him?" He pointed toward the security chief. "He answers to me. No one else." He waved at him dismissively. "He's got no authority over me. And good luck to him if he tries anything. He's not even armed."

"But I am," Michelle said as she steadied the gun in the wind.

"And I've got some options," a fresh voice added. I turned and saw First Mate LeJeune. I'd been so focused on the gun pointed at the captain's head, I hadn't heard him come in. And he wasn't alone. Ted Stevens was standing next to the pilot who'd led us to the captain's quarters—I hadn't noticed when he left the deck—and a couple of other men I didn't know stood next to them.

"Get back to your post, LeJeune!" The captain scowled. "All of you!" he screamed. "Or you'll never work on the river again."

"Looks like it's your river career that's over, Captain." LeJeune stepped toward the captain. Michelle turned her head slightly to watch him.

"What are you talking about, LeJeune?"

"I saw ya kill that passenger. Bucky Jones." LeJeune's face turned red. "I saw ya clock him in the back of the head with a crowbar."

The captain glared at him. "You need to get your vision checked, LeJeune."

"No. I don't. I know what I saw." He looked over at Lester Bell. "And you were there, too, when he killed Jones."

Lester glanced at the captain but didn't respond.

"Your career is over, LeJeune," the captain declared. "You are relieved of duty."

LeJeune shook his head. He took a couple of steps back to stand next to Stevens and the others. "You've got that backwards, Captain. You're the one who's relieved of duty. No one here considers you their captain anymore."

The captain's jaw clenched. "Your gonna deeply regret what you're doing, LeJeune."

"Maybe. But we can sort it all out when the Coast Guard gets here. They're on the way."

The captain stared at LeJeune. His face grew pale, and his shoulders sagged. Then the man who'd been known as Captain William Smith but was really Ray Bell turned to Michelle. "Your father was a fool," he said. "Didn't know his place. Thought the world was changing. But it wasn't. Not my world!" He smacked his chest with his good hand. "We warned him, but he wouldn't listen. He was a prideful bastard. A fool." He turned his head and spit over the railing into the river. "He got what he deserved."

Michelle's hand shook. She opened her stance to steady herself against the wind. She locked eyes with Ray Bell, and I think, for a moment, she forgot she wasn't alone.

"Babe. Michelle," Jefferson said. "He ain't worth it. If you kill him now, you let him ruin your life all over again. Don't give him that much power."

"He has to pay!" she said through clenched teeth. "My family lost a brilliant man. We lost a father! This scum, this sorry excuse of a human being"—she was waving the gun at Ray Bell—"he got to live a full life. A career. He married. Had children. He's in his fucking sixties, for God's sake.

How is that fair? Or just?" She looked down the gunsight again. "And you heard him. He's got a respectable job—a fucking riverboat captain. He could slip away from justice again. I won't let that happen."

"Michelle. Dear sister," Yolanda said. Yolanda, Angela, and Ruby must have slipped in after LeJeune. Michelle looked at her out of the corner of her eyes. "We love you so much, Michelle. I know we've fought over the years about this . . . about finding Papa's killers." Yolanda took a step closer to Michelle. "But you were right." She nodded as she stepped still closer. "You were right," she repeated. Tears rolled down her cheeks. "You found the men who killed Papa. You did it!" She made a fist, then took another step closer. "He would be so proud of you. Of your persistence. Of your intelligence." She pointed at her head. "For keeping him alive in our hearts." She put her hands together, then laid them on her chest. "But your work is over now. Done." She nodded. "These men, these two men"—she pointed to Ray and Lester Bell—"just admitted in front of all of us . . ."—she waved an arm toward LeJeune, the crew with him, and Security Chief Hopkins—"admitted their guilt. You caught them." She clasped her hands together in front of her. "Don't taint it—all those years of searching and sacrificing—by stooping to their hateful level. You can't fix the violence done to us by doing violence to him." She took another step closer. "Put down the gun, sister. Put down the gun. It's over."

Michelle looked back and forth between Ray Bell and Yolanda. She snarled, fidgeted, then took a step toward her father's killer. "I could end your life right now, you know." Her eyes opened wide, and she steadied the gun with both hands. "Just a little more pressure on this trigger"—she smiled wryly—"and your worthless life would be over. And I wouldn't feel any more guilt about killing you dead than I do when I step on a cockroach." Her hands shook. She stared intensely at him. "You deserve to die." She dropped her hands down in front of her. "But I won't be the one to take your life."

Jefferson darted up to Michelle and eased the gun out of her hands. She looked at him, cried, then steeled herself again. "And just for the record"—she turned back to Ray Bell—"I don't forgive you or any of the others who killed my father! I don't forgive you. I curse you." She spit in his direction. "I curse you, your family, and everyone you've ever loved. May you all rot in hell!"

Jefferson put an arm around her and walked her away from Ray Bell. Hopkins walked over to the man. "We don't have much of a brig, as you know," he said. "But it'll hold you and your brother good enough until the Coast Guard gets here."

"I'm bleeding here," Ray Bell said, "in case you couldn't tell."

"I noticed that," Hopkins said. "We'll find someone to patch you up."

LeJeune and the other crew walked over to Ray Bell. LeJeune grabbed his arm. "I can walk on my own," Bell snarled, then he walked toward the door. The security chief shoved him in the back and said, "Let's go."

Angela and Yolanda rushed over to Michelle. Jefferson let go of her, and the three sisters held on to one another and cried.

Chapter 43

Hopkins, LeJeune, and Stevens escorted Smith and McDowell—the Bell brothers—off the lounge and out of sight. After the sisters' group hug broke up, I walked over to them.

"You did it," I said to Michelle. She ran a hand across her eyes, then sniffled. "No," she said. "We did it." She looked around at her sisters, at Jefferson, at Ruby, at me, then sniffled again. "*We* caught them." We hugged, then I walked over to Ruby. She was smiling, but her eyes were red and damp.

"I don't remember seeing 'solve an old murder' on the itinerary for this cruise," she said as she pulled a tissue out of her purse.

"Guess I forgot to mention that. But you know how it goes around me."

"Yeah. Shit happens." She laughed, then wiped her eyes. I walked back to Jefferson and Michelle just as Angela and Yolanda came over to Ruby.

"There's one more show tonight," Yolanda said to Ruby.

"God, it would be nice for a distraction right now," Angela said.

Ruby added, "Let's go, then. Let's just hope they're not doing a murder mystery tonight!" She walked over to me and tapped me on the shoulder. "Frank, we're going down to the auditorium for the last show. Do you want to come along?"

"I do." I looked at Jefferson and Michelle. "But I'll be along in a few minutes. I'd like to stay here a little longer."

"OK," she said with a slight nod, and the three of them left.

"How does it feel to have finally caught the men who killed your father?" I asked Michelle.

She didn't answer right away. "I feel relieved, I suppose." She looked off toward the river. "I don't know how I expected to feel," she said. "I guess I never really believed I'd catch them. This search, it's consumed so much of my life. Night and day. Night and day, year after year." She shook her head. "It's all I've thought about." Her voice became soft. "It even cost me a marriage." She looked back at me. "Yes. It sure did. And it almost cost me my job. I passed the tenure test, but just barely. My chair, he scolded me. Scolded me good. Said he'd never worked with such an underachiever." She forced a smile.

"Was it worth all that?" I asked.

"Was it worth it? I don't know how to begin to answer that question." She walked over to the side of the boat and rested an arm on the railing. "Justice isn't free. It requires sacrifices. And I've paid my dues. I would've had a very different life if those men hadn't killed my father. A life more like my sisters'."

"And as normal as anything could be for you," Jefferson said as he nudged her.

She smiled slightly. "You're right. I'm sure I would have found something else to obsess about." She laughed until the laughter slowly faded away. "I thought this moment would feel more satisfying, honestly. I don't feel that at all."

"What do you feel?" I asked.

She looked down. "I feel empty. Honestly, that's what I feel. Empty." She wiped a tear from her cheek. "Sure, I've spent all of my life chasing these men down. But it gave my life a purpose—and a righteous one at that." She looked at me and Jefferson. "Chasing justice! Now that the search is over, who am I? What do I do with myself?"

She looked back out over the river. The sun hung just above the horizon, a glowing yellow ball exploding reds and oranges. I'd seen a lot of sunsets over the Mississippi. This was one of the most colorful. But it didn't move me. I don't think it did anything for Michelle, either.

Jefferson walked over and put an arm around her waist. "You're still the same smart, determined, perceptive person you were before." He rested a hand on her back. "That hasn't changed. It might take a while to figure out exactly what your next mission will be, but I'd bet continuing to fight for justice will be part of it. And if you want me to, I'd be honored to go along with you as you find out."

She hugged him. Jefferson glanced at me. I nodded at him and left. I heard Michelle sobbing again as I left the lounge.

I wanted to catch the end of Deion's last show, but I really wanted a drink first. I ran up to the Paddlewheel Pub and ordered a whiskey from Carl. He filled a rocks glass with a generous pour, then said to me, "Thank God we're rid of that bastard."

"Sorry?" I asked

"The captain. That mean, no-good, bitter son of a bitch." He slid the glass over to me. "I hear you helped expose him. For killing someone."

"I had only a small part in it," I said, then took a sip of the whiskey.

"No matter to me. I'm just fucking elated he's gone. And hope that he'll be as miserable now as he made his crew." A couple showed up and took seats on the other side of the bar. Carl nodded at me, then walked over to take their orders. I dropped a twenty-dollar bill on the bar and left with my glass of whiskey.

Before making my way back down to the auditorium, I swung by the pilothouse. First Mate LeJeune was talking with a couple of pilots. He must have glimpsed me from a corner of his eye, because he excused himself and came out to talk. "Looks like ya got what ya wanted," he said. He crossed his arms.

"I wouldn't put it that way, exactly. I just wanted to relax on a cruise and write a fluff article about it." LeJeune almost smiled. I glanced toward the pilothouse. "Your timing was awfully good earlier . . ."

He nodded slightly, and his shoulders sagged. "After that little chat you and I had, I came to terms with the fact I wouldn't be able to keep my mouth shut. Couldn't live with myself if I did." He straightened his shoulders. "I went to Hopkins, the security chief, and told him what I saw. We agreed we needed help, that we weren't equipped to do what needed to be done. So, we called the Coast Guard to come help, then I called HQ and told them what we were doing."

"How'd that go over?"

"Not well. They wanted to wait until we got to Memphis to turn the captain in. Didn't want to do anything that might draw media attention. I didn't think we could wait. And when your friend Michelle Green did—well, you know what she did—there was no chance we'd be able to wait until Memphis."

"Hopkins must have contacted you? Told you to come up to the lounge when he saw Michelle pointing a gun at the captain?"

"Yeah." He sighed. "I've never been a mutineer, Dodge. Don't especially like how it feels, either."

I nodded. "It's not exactly something you train for. But it had to be done."

"I know." He looked away. "I know."

"What happens now?"

"That Coast Guard boat should be here soon. I assume they'll take the captain and the chief —excuse me. I mean Ray and Lester Bell. I'll feel better once they're off this boat."

"Amen to that. I'm guessing we won't be going on to Memphis?"

"We might. That's still up in the air. We'll keep it all running like normal as long as we need to. It's kinda hard to continue on after your captain and chief engineer get arrested, but we're not too far from Memphis. Might be just as easy to finish as planned. And our crew can handle it. The pilots will get us there just fine, and Stevens is acting chief engineer. We can manage."

"Personally, I wouldn't object to going on to Memphis. You're in charge now, right?"

"Yep."

I nodded. "That's good." I nodded, then grimaced. "I'm sorry about earlier. About threatening you."

"I get it. Not saying I approve, but I get what you were doing. Now." He leaned back against the pilothouse. "I just didn't believe the captain would ever face the music. Heck, I would'a been happy just to send him off to retirement and never see the bastard again. I didn't want any more trouble."

"I know you weren't a fan of the captain."

"Hated that man. With a passion. Never had a good word for anyone, but quick to tear ya down when ya messed up." He straightened up. "But when ya work closely with someone, ya have to make do as best ya can. I'd learned to keep a low profile around him. Stay off his shit list. Just do the job and ignore the rest. Can't say it made me happy, but it didn't make me unhappy, either."

"Well, that's over now. May your next captain look after you better." I raised my glass of whiskey like I was toasting, then took a sip. He nodded. I turned to walk back to the stairs, then turned back to look at him. "I hope you know this—but I still feel the need to say it out loud. What you told me, stays with me. End of story."

"I appreciate it, Dodge. But if you'll excuse me for saying so, I wasn't too worried about that. Ya don't strike me as the type of guy who would rat someone out."

He had no idea how desperate I had felt in that moment, but I wasn't about to disabuse him of his insight. "Glad you think so." I grinned, then walked down to the auditorium to catch the show. I stood near the back, sipping my whiskey and enjoying the last moments of the final show. The cast was paying tribute to the music of Memphis. Deion had just started singing Otis Redding's "The Dock of the Bay." The song's themes of feeling lost and helpless felt strikingly relevant as I stood there.

The show wrapped up with Neil Diamond's "Sweet Caroline," a song Diamond recorded in Memphis in 1969. The cast took turns singing verses, then the crowd joined in when the refrain came around, each time with a little more enthusiasm. By the last verse, everyone was singing and waving their hands in the air. I saw a lot of smiling faces as folks exited the auditorium.

I wasn't sure when I'd get the chance to talk to Deion again, so I slipped backstage to congratulate him in person. "Great show!" I said when I found him putting props away.

"Thank you, Frank." He walked over to me. We hugged. He squeezed me tightly, then let go and stepped back. "I hear you got your man."

"A couple of them. And by 'you,' I assume you mean Michelle and Brian. They did most of the work."

"Whatever." He gently pushed me in the chest. "I just know you were deep in it, too. And I'm thrilled to be done with that fucking captain."

"Seems like a common feeling around here."

"You have no idea."

"I just wish folks had said something sooner."

"Fear is a powerful weapon, Frank. And that man deployed it liberally."

"What happens now?"

"Rumor has it this cruise could be done."

"Last I heard, the company hadn't yet decided. You know something different?"

"No. I just assumed it would be hard to keep the spirit of it all going when your captain and head of Engineering turn out to be murderers." He grinned. "Couldn't have happened to nicer guys. But hey—we got all our shows in."

"What's next for you?"

"Work, then more work. I'm supposed to get right back on at Memphis and ride back to New Orleans. I'm sure that'll still be the plan. Capitalism doesn't take a day off, so neither do I." He slipped off his shoes. "How about you?"

"I've got some work to do. I expect the magazine will take the article I wrote about this cruise, but I'm also going to pitch a piece about the Green family's successful search for justice."

"Yeah, well, we'll see about the justice part. At least they found the killers."

"Right. Good point." I didn't want to part the same way we had before. "Keep in touch this time?"

"Are you capable?" He crossed his arms and tilted his head slightly. Then he smiled. "I'd like to. Of course, *I* wanted to last time as well." He dropped his arms to the side. "You have my number. Shoot me a text from time to time. Let me know you're still alive. Who knows? Maybe one of these days we'll both be in St. Louis at the same time, and we can get coffee or something." He winked.

"I look forward to it." I grinned. "You really are talented, you know. I expect big things from you."

"Thanks! Maybe you can talk a big-time producer to book a trip on one of my cruises. Now, that would be helpful." He pointed at me, then said, "But right now, I'm gonna change out of these work clothes." I went back into the auditorium, then took out my phone and texted Deion:

> I'll let you know as soon as I make any producer friends.

I caught up with Ruby just outside the auditorium. She was talking with Angela and Yolanda. "Nice show to end on, huh?" I said.

"It sure was!" Ruby said. "I didn't know what to expect from the entertainment on this cruise, but honestly, I didn't expect much. What a pleasant surprise that turned out to be!"

"What's going to happen now?" Angela asked.

"Last I heard, a Coast Guard boat was on the way to meet us. I assume they'll take the Bell brothers to the FBI. The cruise may or may not continue after that."

"Oh, it would be such a shame if we had to stop early," Yolanda said.

"After all"—Angela shrugged—"what's done is done."

"And they'd still have to get us to Memphis somehow, right?" Ruby asked.

"Yes," I answered. "They would."

"Then I'd much rather get there on this boat than a bus, which is almost certainly what they'd have to use, right?"

"I would think so," I said.

"In that case, let's get a drink while we can," Ruby said.

"But you're not a drinker," I said.

"And it's your bedtime," Angela teased.

"Pshaw," Ruby said. "I may never go on a cruise like this again. Especially with people I like so much. So, let's get a drink. I want to enjoy whatever time we have left together."

EPILOGUE

We had more time than we thought, after all. In the end, the cruise company determined it was in everyone's best interest to finish the cruise as planned. Most of us would sleep away the last few hours anyway. While I'd been watching the last show on the boat, the Coast Guard arrived and took the Bell brothers into custody. They also detained Michelle. Turns out shooting the captain of a riverboat is generally frowned upon.

We got to Memphis under thick cloud cover with no more drama, then left the cruise like it was any other. Sure, some passengers exchanged giddy remarks about printing T-shirts that read "I survived the murder cruise!" But most seemed unfazed by it all and eager to get back to their senior living communities and retirement condos.

"Thank you for choosing the *River Voyager*," Barry Riggs said to me just before I left the boat.

I sighed. "But I didn't. It was an assignment."

"Sorry. You're right." He took a deep breath. "Now that the captain is gone . . ."—he leaned close to me and whispered—"I hated that man, but please write nice things about us. I love my job." He took a step back and stuck out a hand. "And come see us again sometime." He beamed. I shook his hand and exited the boat.

I didn't know it at the time, but Helen Kraft had slipped off the boat as soon as we'd reached Memphis. No goodbyes or even a farewell text to me. Two weeks after our cruise had ended, though, I saw an article in a national magazine about a riverboat captain with a secret past. Helen wrote it. (And in typical Helen fashion, by emphasizing the drama and personal conflict without getting too caught up in petty things like details.)

In the article she described Isaac Green's murder in 1974 and how the four men had fled Vicksburg shortly afterward. The sheriff knew they were guilty, but rather than prosecute the four white men for killing a Black man, he gave them the chance to start over somewhere else. Three of the men—Lester Bell (Chuck McDowell), Otis Morris (Michael Johnson), and Lonnie Sims (Bucky Jones)—bought forged papers to carve out a new identity. (Helen hadn't done enough reporting to learn that the sheriff himself had personally connected them with the people who forged their fake identity papers.)

Ray Bell—the captain—took a different approach, however. He settled for a while in New Orleans, which is where he met a Black wanderer named William Smith. They were near the same age, and Bell figured out that Smith had few ties in the world. So, he killed him, then assumed his identity. Why would Ray Bell, who killed a Black man to shut him up, assume the identity of a Black man when he was running from the law? He's never said, but I have a couple of ideas: For one, I think he believed no one would notice the real William Smith's death. The man had no ties. No close family. Who was going to report him missing? But I also think Bell got a kick out of it. A secret—maybe even a joke to him—that he expected to quietly enjoy the rest of his life.

By all accounts, Ray Bell had taken the lead in killing Green, had planned it, and then had killed him. It's not clear how much the others knew what they were signing up for. Lester Bell, for example, later swore under oath that he thought they were going to only scare Green—maybe rough him up a bit—but not kill him. But he also admitted that he believed Green got what he deserved.

While Ray Bell remained defiant and unrepentant, the men who'd helped him seemed weighed down with guilt and regret to varying degrees. Lester Bell later claimed that Otis Morris wanted to come clean after Michelle had tracked him down. Morris called Ray to tell him so, but he promised he would only admit to his role and wouldn't give away the other three men. That wasn't good enough for Ray Bell, though, who arranged a face-to-face meeting with Morris, then killed him.

Lonnie Sims (Bucky Jones) also wavered. He'd found Jesus and wanted to take responsibility for his part in Green's murder. When he told Ray Bell his plans, Ray invited him onto the *River Voyager* cruise (at a discount) so they could talk it out. He gave Lonnie a burner phone to communicate with (and that was the phone I'd seen light up when I talked with Bucky—Lonnie—the night he was killed). Then, late at night, he and his brother lured Lonnie onto a quiet part of the boat, out of reach of the surveillance cameras, struck him in the head with a crowbar, then dumped his body into the river. Lonnie, of course, had gone so far as to tip off Michelle that the Bell brothers would be on that cruise. But while he felt remorseful, he wasn't willing to completely give them up by divulging their aliases. If he had, maybe he'd still be alive.

Helen attributed the ultimate resolution of the crime to the persistence of Michelle Green. She wasn't exactly wrong, but Michelle couldn't have succeeded without the assistance she got on the boat. Jefferson's help, of course, was critical. He used his detective skills and law enforcement connections to collect and verify crucial details about the backgrounds of each suspect. But even Ruby, Angela, and Yolanda contributed in their own ways. I suppose I did my bit, too.

Helen's account was, typically, far from complete. She didn't know that Lonnie's widow was actually his first wife, too, so she couldn't have known how shocked Ruth Ann Bartels felt when her long-dead sister showed up at her house. I called Mathilda after I got home, hoping to satisfy my curiosity about a couple of details. Some parts of Lonnie's story were, in fact, true. When he'd sold his business, it wasn't entirely voluntary. A bank hadn't pressured him, but his competitors had. Revenue had been slowly declining, and he didn't have the enthusiasm to find a way to reposition his business for a more competitive market. So, he sold it and retired.

And he did, in fact, have an estranged relationship with his children. They rarely talked. "I wasn't a good father to them," Lonnie had told Mathilda. He didn't blame them. Those details made suicide seem more plausible to the investigators. She went along with the story, though, because Ray Bell had threatened to come after her if she didn't. She knew from experience that Bell was a man of his word.

Lonnie, Mathilda said, had never been happier in his life than in those months after they'd gotten back together. He told her so—over and over. He was ready to make amends for his past, to come forward and tell the authorities what he knew about Green's murder, and to rebuild relationships with his children. But he ran out of time. Ray Bell took it away from him.

Helen also wrote an oversimplified portrayal of Michelle Green and her lifelong quest. Helen gushed about Michelle's character and persistence and the deep sense of satisfaction she must have felt by solving the case. She celebrated Michelle for exacting justice and achieving "closure." She lauded Michelle for forgiving the killers and moving on with her life (even as she glossed over Michelle's arrest for shooting Ray Bell in the hand with a gun she'd purchased when the boat had stopped in Natchez).

Forgiveness. It makes for a good story. A neat ending. In 2006 a gunman raided a school that served an Amish community in Pennsylvania. He ultimately shot ten young girls, killing five of them, then himself. The story made international news, not just as a tragedy but because the Amish community—almost immediately—publicly expressed forgiveness to the killer and his family. Their actions were remarkable, inspiring even. But it didn't make the grief go away, of course. And many members of the community continued to struggle emotionally with the trauma and survivor's guilt.

Michelle did not, in fact, offer forgiveness to the killers. She had cursed Ray Bell. To his face. If finding the men gave her any sense of "closure," it was finishing the story for one part of her life. Moving on isn't the same as forgiving. The lifelong search had taken a heavy toll on her. Catching the two surviving killers ended that search. And while she knew she had caught the right guys, seeing them in court forty-three years after they'd killed her father hardly felt like justice to her. "It just hurt all over again," she told me.

I rented a car in Memphis and drove Ruby to the airport. Her grandnephew would pick her up at the airport in Dubuque. Jefferson had a couple more days left on his vacation. "I'm going to stay here and get Michelle out of jail, then find a good lawyer for her," he told me just after we got off the boat. Yolanda spent the night at Angela's house before she would head home. The three sisters had enough confidence in Jefferson's ability to arrange bail that they made plans to meet for lunch the next day.

After the cruise, Deion and I checked in with each other a couple of times a week. *Luxe Liners* nearly killed my article because of the infamy of that voyage. Ultimately, they published it with a short footnote explaining that river cruises are one of the safest ways to travel, that the risk of falling off a boat into the river was nearly zero. I didn't care. I got paid just the same.

On the other hand, the magazine *Fatal Passions* commissioned an article about murders on riverboats. I was looking forward to following up with Ted Stevens for more quotes. He may not have been part of the group that killed Isaac Green, but he was hiding something. I was eager to discover what that might be.

Author's Notes

A song. That's where my interest in this story began.

For years, I've collected songs about the Mississippi River. Hundreds of them. One song—"In the Mississippi River" by the Freedom Singers in 1964—was inspired by the horrific murders of two Black men near Vicksburg, Mississippi. In June 1964 three young civil rights activists who'd been working in Mississippi—James Chaney, Mickey Schwerner, and Andrew Goodman—had disappeared. The search for them attracted national attention and a lot of resources from the FBI because two of the missing men were white. At one point, search parties dragged the Mississippi River, where they discovered the bodies of Henry Dee and Charles Moore.

The two nineteen-year-olds had been kidnapped on May 2 by Ku Klux Klan terrorists who suspected Dee of civil rights activism (he wasn't) and wanted to teach him a lesson. Moore was just in the wrong place at the wrong time. The Klansmen took Dee and Moore into Homochitto National Forest, where they beat them severely, stuffed them into the trunk of a car, and drove them to a backwater slough that bordered Davis Island, the place where Confederate President Jefferson Davis once owned a large plantation and dozens of human beings. The Klansmen then took Dee and Moore out of the trunk and were surprised to find that they were still alive. No matter. The men tied Dee to an engine block and threw him into the river, then tied Moore to train rails and did the same. Two white men were arrested in November for that double murder, but prosecutors dropped the charges two months later.

Dee and Moore were hardly the only Black men murdered in the 1960s, nor were their murders the only ones that went unprosecuted. By the 1990s, though, momentum picked up to right as many of those historical wrongs as possible. Here are three examples: In 1994 a jury found Bryon De La Beckwith guilty for the 1963 murder of civil rights leader Medgar Evers. In 2005 Edgar Ray Killen, one of the killers of Chaney, Schwerner, and Goodman in 1964, was convicted of that crime and imprisoned. In 1999 ABC journalist Connie Chung revisited the murders of Dee and Moore for the show *20/20*, but the FBI closed the case again in 2003 without pursuing charges. Finally, in 2007, Canadian documentary filmmaker David Ridgen teamed up with Moore's surviving brother Thomas to revisit the case. Ridgen's movie, *Mississippi Cold Case*, renewed interest in that crime and ultimately resulted in a conviction that same year. The conviction was possible in large part because one man involved in the murders, Charles Marcus Edwards, testified against the ring leader, James Ford Seale. In 2011 Thomas went back to Mississippi and met with Marcus Edwards. They talked about everything that had happened and said they'd made peace with each other. Ridgen covered the story of the lives and deaths of Dee and Moore well in his podcast, *Someone Knows Something* (season 3), . I highly recommend it. (If you'd like to read a brief overview of the story of Dee and Moore, I wrote a chapter about their murders in my book *Mississippi River Mayhem: Disasters, Tragedy, and Murder on Ol' Man River* [Lanham, MD: Globe Pequot, 2022].)

It's a powerful story, and the idea that a surviving relative could reconcile with someone responsible for killing that relative is an irresistible angle. We love reconciliation and happy endings. But as much as I too love a good story of reconciliation, I don't think it's representative of the reality of losing a loved one to a vicious and hateful murder. I suspect (and have been told as much by friends) that we—white folks, in particular—are often too quick to latch on to the reconciliation angle when it involved forgiving a white killer whose victims were Black. The reality, though, is that many of the surviving family members of the victims of white terrorism don't necessarily share those feelings of relief and reconciliation when the killers finally face prosecution. Too many years of grief, too many decades of resistance and inaction from law enforcement.

The murder at the center of this story is set in Vicksburg, Mississippi, in 1974. By then the activism of the civil rights era had passed its peak, but life for Black residents in Vicksburg hadn't changed a whole lot. In 1972 a fifty-eight-year-old white guy was charged with raping a seven-year-old Black girl. The white guy was only convicted of contributing to the delinquency of a minor and fined fifty bucks. The decision outraged the Black community, so they organized a boycott of white-owned businesses. The boycott hit local businesses hard and signaled a watershed moment for the Black community. A wave of changes followed—in local politics, business, and daily life. And unlike protests in earlier decades, no one got killed.

The case of Isaac Green in this book, while rooted in historical truths, is fiction. I made it up. But Green's murder is rooted in that time and place, when centuries-old racial hierarchies were crumbling but still had tremendous influence over the lives of many folks. Tragic events reverberate through family trees, but they don't hit everyone the same. Just ask the Green sisters.

When I imagined this story, I knew I wanted to set it on a river cruise. I liked the idea of the cruise itself as a ticking clock driving the urgency to solve the crime. I'm also a big fan of Agatha Christie's *Murder on the Orient*

Express and *Death on the Nile*. Those books inspired me to re-create a similar atmosphere and story trajectory.

I've been lucky to serve as a guest lecturer on several Mississippi River cruises, and I've made good use of those experiences to take detailed notes, so I wasn't going into the writing process naive. Still, modern cruises have adopted enhanced security features that make getting away with murder much harder than in the past. I've done my best to make the events in this book plausible for a modern river cruise, but I may have pushed the boundaries here and there to serve the story. I'm sure you understand.

Dean

January 2025

ACKNOWLEDGMENTS

Just as solving a crime often requires the combined efforts of many people, so does publishing a book. *Murder on the Mississippi* would never have made it this far without the help of many folks. I'd especially like to thank my beta readers: LaBraunna and Aliya. They offered valuable feedback about the story and characters that made it all work much better. I'm also grateful to my friend Lee, who spent much of his adult life working on big rivers, including extensive stints as a pilot and captain. His comments helped steer the story back closer to reality, even if there were bits here and there where I felt the story required drifting a bit from the main channel into murkier backwaters.

I continue to be blown away by the skill and artfulness of my cover designer, Peggy Nehmen. While I used the AI tools in MidJourney and Adobe Photoshop to generate the base images, her feedback guided the process so that the image remained consistent with the other covers in this series, and she took the final image to create a memorable cover. I'm also thankful for the continuing editorial review from Allan Edmands. His attention to detail not only saves me from embarrassing mistakes, it makes my stories flow well. Every writer needs an Allan Edmands in their life.

And, as always, the continuing love and support from my husband, John, was critical. John is my first reader, and I can't imagine a better one. He's unflinching and perceptive in his feedback. And while part of me (that frag-ile writer's ego) is hoping he'll say the manuscript is great and just needs minor tinkering, that does me no good. And he knows it. It's not enough that I know what I was trying to say. John provides the reality check to let me know when I've failed to communicate those ideas in my head into words on the page. Everyone needs a John, too.

Dean
St. Louis, MO

ALSO BY DEAN KLINKENBERG

Frank Dodge Mysteries

Rock Island Lines (Frank Dodge mystery #1)

Double-Dealing in Dubuque (Frank Dodge mystery #2)

Letting Go in La Crosse (Frank Dodge mystery #3)

Murder on the Mississippi (Frank Dodge mystery #4)

Non-Fiction Books

Road Tripping the Great River Road, Volume 1: 18 Trips Along the Upper
Mississippi River

The Wild Mississippi: A State-by-State Guide to the River's Natural Wonders

Mississippi River Mayhem: Disasters, Tragedy, and Murder on Ol' Man River

About the Author

Dean Klinkenberg, the Mississippi Valley Traveler, explores the back roads and backwaters of the Mississippi River Valley, a place with an abundance of stories to tell, big characters, epic struggles, do-gooders, and evil-doers. Some of those stories inspire the Frank Dodge mysteries; others you'll find in his non-fiction books, including the Mississippi Valley Traveler guidebooks. He lives in St. Louis with his husband John and a parrot called Ra. Find out more about him and his books at the links below.

DeanKlinkenberg.com (Fiction)

MississippiValleyTraveler.com (Non-Fiction)